CEN

LANA POPOVIĆ

FIERCE LIKE A FIRESTORM

KATHERINE TEGEN BOOKS

An Imprint of HarperCollins Publishers

Katherine Tegen Books is an imprint of HarperCollins Publishers.

Fierce Like a Firestorm
Copyright © 2018 by Lana Popović
All rights reserved. Printed in the United States of America.
No part of this book may be used or reproduced in any manner
whatsoever without written permission except in the case of brief
quotations embodied in critical articles and reviews. For information
address HarperCollins Children's Books, a division of HarperCollins
Publishers, 195 Broadway, New York, NY 10007.
www.epicreads.com

Library of Congress Control Number: 2017959099
ISBN 978-0-06-243686-3

Typography by Torborg Davern
This book is set in 11pt Adobe Garamond Pro.
18 19 20 21 22   PC/LSCH   10 9 8 7 6 5 4 3 2 1
❖
First Edition

FIERCE LIKE A FIRESTORM

Also by Lana Popović

Wicked Like a Wildfire

"Behold me, lovely as no woman was or is, undying and half-divine; memory haunts me from age to age, and passion leads me by the hand—evil have I done, and with sorrow have I made acquaintance from age to age, and from age to age evil shall I do, and sorrow shall I know till my redemption comes."

—*She*, H. Rider Haggard

To my loved ones, especially the women, who held my hand and helped me through even when I didn't know I needed it. Thank you for showing me true love's many faces.

ONE

Malina

"BABY WITCH."

I couldn't remember when Dunja had come to sit next to me, our feet dangling over the empty darkness below the summit's lip. Above us, the night glared moonlit bright, stars winking like bared wolves' teeth. I could still hear their music, but just faintly, and tonight it was much sharper than usual. A violin played with a blade instead of a bow.

This sky wasn't for victors or the hopeful. It glittered cold and cutting like the wreckage of our failure strewn across the rocks, the bloodied diamonds Dunja had clawed from Mara's arms.

Despite all the light, the valley was far enough below to pool in vales of black between the even darker shards of mountains on either side. I'd been so scared to climb up here, hammering heart and palms slick with terror, metal in my mouth. And why? In case I slipped and fell and died? So stupid, when dying was so easy they sometimes called it a mercy. If I inched forward just a little, leaned into all that waiting air, I probably wouldn't even feel the landing.

And I would definitely stop feeling everything else.

"Baby witch, come," Dunja said again, more insistently this time, as if she could hear my thoughts. "We have to go."

Still, she didn't make me move. I felt a bright, high-pitched chime of love for my aunt, for letting me hurt just a little longer. Her arm lay so light over my shoulders that I hadn't even noticed when she first touched me. And her side next to mine felt just as insubstantial, as if she were made of gathered thistledown. Like a huffed-out breath would blow her apart.

How long had we even been sitting there? I wondered. I didn't realize I had said it out loud until Dunja responded. "A few hours, perhaps? Izkara wouldn't hear of leaving us be at first—that iron-cast bitch never did know when to yield a little—but sometimes our old mother *does* have the forbearance to know when to let loose the reins. The wisdom of the centuries, you could call it. Especially when there's only one way down for the horse to take, once it's ready to come," she added wryly.

Beneath the scrim of humor, her voice was desperately heavy. It sounded just like I felt. All of her sounded like I felt, wind keening over a desert so lonely that it hadn't ever dreamed of life. Fjolar might have flicked Dunja away like a burr, but when he stole Iris and disappeared with her, it still meant Dunja had lost him yet again.

And beneath that loss, I could hear the looping echo of her love. As if she stood on a mountaintop calling out his name just to hear it come whipping back to her, to land on her arm like a hunter's hawk. Sinking in its talons until she thrilled with the pain of its homecoming.

Even as much as I ached for Iris, the raw fervor of my aunt's love made my insides wilt with sympathy. Without thinking, I hummed a little to soothe her, a delicate, questing arpeggio meant to be a balm.

She flinched so violently it brought me up short. "*Stop*," she grated out. "I don't want your comfort, little niece. It hurts worse than the hurting."

"How can you stand it?" I whispered to her. "Riss is gone, but maybe—she might still come back. She's strong like that, you know? She makes it through when anyone else wouldn't know the first step to take. But him . . . he *left* you. Twice. How can you take it? How can you want him back?"

She turned to look at me, her face close enough to mine that I felt the warmth of her sigh skip across my lips. Her tears had left streaks across her cheeks, and the cool wind kept threading strands of white hair through her eyelashes and between her lips. She looked all cut into pieces and then pasted back together, a collage of pointed, perfect features and luminous skin seamed with dried salt. A darker smear trailed along on the left side of her face. When she lifted a hand to touch my cheek, it was dark too, and rough with grit from where she'd rested it on the summit's stone.

It was Mara's blood, I realized. Even dried and crusted under

Dunja's nails, it still had the faint, ancient smell of a long-lost Eden. Fully ripe fruit bending every bough, and sunlit air heavy with incense.

"Because it's what I am now," she said. Something seemed different about her wide eyes, but in the moonlight, I couldn't quite tell what it was. "I'm just a thing that loves him. I thought I could be a little bit of something else on top of that. Not quite a person, not anymore—I know what's too much to ask—but a kind of thing that loved you, too. Enough to set you and your sister free."

She believed that, I could hear it, she really did. It made my heart ache to half breaking. "But you *did* try to set us free," I argued, taking her tiny, bloody hand from my cheek and squeezing it. "You got us all this far. It's not your fault, what happened. We don't even *know* what happened."

She squeezed my hand back, so tight I nearly gasped. "Then let's make our way down, sweetness, and find out where we stand."

WITH MY CHEST an aching hollow empty of my sister's song, I couldn't find it in me to be scared of the descent. Still, Dunja picked my way down for me the same way she'd gotten me up. Pinning me to the cliffside with her body, finding me hand- and footholds for every step. So I wouldn't have to look away from the rock and face the drop even once, or feel the wind course over my back.

I didn't need her help, but I let her do it anyway. I could hear how it made her feel just a half note better to take care of me this way.

Mara and nine others waited for us at the summit's base. The first nine, I guessed, the strong ones whose gleam hadn't been bled pale by centuries of breeding for beauty and grace. They had found her a log to sit on while they waited for us. She perched on it like the burned effigy of a long-dead queen, her tattered dress draped over the wood in a ridiculously artful way. As if being the empress of her line could somehow possibly still matter.

A stone-ringed fire burned at her feet, shimmering blue as the Cattaro Bay at its base and sunrise golden in the crown of the flame. Every once in a while, Mara skimmed her fingers through it idly, like a little girl trailing her hand in water. My first thought was that it must be fake, an illusion kindled by someone's empty gleam. But even from where Dunja and I stood feet away, I could feel the waves of heat rolling off it.

It wasn't that the fire didn't burn hot. It was that she either liked the sear, or couldn't feel it at all.

It reminded me of the bowls full of fire that had surrounded her throne in the ballroom while Riss and I knelt waiting to compete against each other. The memory of it lit my belly with a different kind of flame.

"Nice of you to hang back for us," I said, flat. "But I'm not going anywhere with you, not ever. So I don't know why you'd bother to wait."

"Of course you are coming with us, fledgling." Her tripled voice thrummed in my chest like plucked bass strings. It made me want to speak back to her in the same multiplied way. As if that was our own language, special to the two of us. As if we were really family. "Nor do I know why you would think it your place to do otherwise."

I'd never considered myself a violent person. Riss killed spiders for me, and that only when the paper she slipped under the cupping glass accidentally smashed them on their way outside. And even after having seen Mama hit Riss more times than I could think of without cringing, I couldn't remember ever wanting to hit her, or anyone else.

But now the only thing that kept me from throwing myself at Mara like something turned suddenly and blindly feral was Dunja's grip on my wrist.

"You don't want to do that, baby witch," she warned, low. "Izkara—"

"Stem to stern, yeah," I said through gritted teeth. "I remember."

Izkara met my eyes, her own huge and scornful in her still-wolfish face. Even with her features warped by bones that should never have trussed human skin, the way her nose and chin pinched into an elegant snout was a weirdly pretty thing to see. Especially with the thick, waist-length tumble of her dark hair. She reminded me of maenads, the Greek maidens who served Dionysus. Women who went mad with wine and ecstatic lust, and tore men into shreds.

Under different circumstances, maybe I could have even liked her, this grandmother so many "greats" removed from me.

"You think you know what you've lost," Izkara rasped around a mouthful of too many teeth. Her incisors and canines were so long they kept her lips parted even between words. "You know less than nothing. And I wonder what your pixie princess would think, to hear you so ready to leave her behind. We have her, of course, and her brother, too; the others have already taken them home. Yet you haven't even asked of her."

Niko.

It was true. I hadn't spared a single thought for Niko, not since Iris had been taken.

And just days ago I'd finally let her have what she wanted, what had been silently hers for so long. I'd let her have *I love you*, murmured against her lips and into the hollow of her throat.

I know you love Riss, she'd said right before that. *I love Luka, too. But you can't be scared of her like this, pie. She'll think whatever she thinks, and of course she'll still love you even if you love me. And if you'll finally just* say *it to me, then maybe . . .*

Maybe what? I'd prodded gently.

Maybe I'll finally feel like I don't always come in second.

The same shame and guilt I'd felt then crescendoed inside me now. How could I have forgotten my Niko like this, so completely?

"Okay," I said, swallowing hard. "I'll come. But just for her, and for Luka. Then all of us are getting the hell away from *you*."

"Yes, you will come," Mara agreed equably. "And then you will listen to your old mother have her say. And after that, I think, you will see nothing so much as the need to stay."

The phoenix in my belly roused again, ashes raining from ruffled wings. "Why do you keep *talking* to me like you have the right—"

"Daughter," she broke in, flicking two fingers to beckon me over. "Bank that fury for a single fraction of a moment, and attend me instead."

Even without the call of her ribbons, and despite the burns, she was still herself. Gorgeously grotesque, like the scarlet hourglass on a black widow's bulbous belly. It wasn't that she compelled me to come, but more like I'd wanted to go to her to begin with and she'd just deigned to remind me of that.

She kept her gaze locked with mine as I picked my way reluctantly to her, my feet slipping over loose stones and slick grass just beginning to dew. Her squared chin tipped up, firelight flinging the ruined patches of her skin into hideous relief. I nearly shied away from it, the evidence of how horribly we'd hurt her. I would never say so to her—she couldn't deserve my sympathy—but my stomach twisted just the same.

It must have shown on my face. I'd never been able to keep myself blank like Riss. Mara flicked her free hand dismissively, her own face softening. "Do not bother with my afflictions, my tender songbird. They will heal in much less than due time. As it is, I barely feel them."

It was true. Agony had a droning pitch, a whine like the drill Natalija—*Naisha*, I reminded myself, not my plain-faced music teacher but a coven daughter centuries old—had used in her shop to engrave instruments with their owners' initials. I heard nothing like that in Mara, besides the timpani drumming of her urgency.

By the time I reached her she'd gloved both hands in amber fire, her eyes slitting like a cat's with pleasure. And somehow her burns weren't getting any worse.

"Do you see, fledgling?" she murmured in a silky braided whisper. "I feared my spell lay shattered after the three of you crashed through it, children barging into the torrents of what was once a river frozen tame at great expense. And I feel the warming within me, that I am no longer winter through and through. Yet you see— fire still fails to touch me."

My mouth filled with sawdust. "What does that mean?" I croaked.

"What it means is that the spell has been fractured, rather than entirely broken. *He* may be free again, but he is not whole, and the shackles I wrought weigh on him still. He will not be quite the monstrously powerful thing that he once was." Her face tightened, seams cinching at the corners of her eyes and lips. "At least, not yet."

A silvery note of hope sounded in my chest. So bright and sharp it nearly hurt, chimes struck with a shard of glass. "He?" I echoed breathlessly. "Do you mean that Fjolar—Death—is somehow weaker now?"

Because if he was, maybe it meant that Riss wasn't trapped where he had taken her. That maybe, somehow, we could get her back.

Mara's nostrils flared with impatience. "Of course I do not mean my death-son, fledgling." Her voice pulsed with the steady beat of truth, a baffling undercurrent of sadness lapping beneath. My neck prickled, goose bumps rippling over my skin. Those words brought back the last thing I could remember her saying, after we lost Riss.

My feckless boy—my death-son made of the flesh I lent him—is not what we should fear.

"I mean the menace, the scourge," she continued, voice forking like a snake's tongue, and then again into her tripled tones. "My greatest mistake."

I remembered the rest of it then.

It's what happens to you, and this whole unready world, she had said, *when a king of demons walks its face again.*

TWO

Iris

I WAS AN ISLAND IN A LAKE OF LIGHT.

Skeins of hair floated around me, or at least, the memory of hair. I remembered having hair, could almost still feel it with the nook of my mind tasked with keeping me solid and whole, stopping me from melting into the liquid gold. If I still had hair, then I maybe also had parted lips, gilded lashes, and wide-open eyes, reflecting an ocean's churning expanse of light. My arms and legs felt loose and boneless, the blinding glitter around me enough to keep me afloat without any movement of my own.

My contours were fuzzy, blurred and overbright. But wherever I was, I hadn't become a part of it yet.

Yet with my mouth so full of glow, I wasn't all that sure I even wanted to cling to my own form. I felt so safe here, so exalted and secure, like something tiny tucked inside a jar full of fireflies.

At the image, a memory sprang up, lancing me through with longing: Malina and me kneeling and shushing each other's giggles, combing fireflies out of midnight air with fumbling little-girl fingers, like pomegranate seeds sifted from water. Then another: my sister's twisted face when she had seen me stolen, Fjolar wresting me away from her.

Something *touched* me then, and the phantom limb of my body jerked in shock.

The light coalesced into almost shapes, and then some thing made from molten stars surged toward me. Its eyes met mine, huge and shot through with streaks of paler light, with cloverleaf pupils like crossed figure eights. The light it was poured from had a sinuous cast, and as it nudged and nosed me, I thought,

dragon?

snake?

feathers, or scales?

Now that it was here beside me, I had something to use for measure. As colossal as it was, coiling carefully around me like a leviathan that had made me its pet, set against this boundless world it might as well have been a sea monkey bobbing in a water bauble. Beyond it I caught a sense of vast citadels, buildings with columns wide around as redwoods, that would have dwarfed the mountains of my Montenegro at least a thousand times.

This world was so tremendous that I was smaller than its most minute component parts. Only this little thing could even see me with its naked eye.

Yet tiny as I was, I could feel how this realm and its sentinel creature *loved* me, and yearned for me to stay.

Daughter, it said to me, somehow both a whisper and a bellow. So loud it would have tolled in my eardrums if I'd had them, so low it sifted over me like a touch as much as sound. *Welcome, our daughter!*

But beneath my growing awareness of both bounty and magnitude, and wedged under the explosive joy of being so wanted, I could feel something else—a world fathoms below like this one's negative, a teeming, oil-slick rainbow as starving as this place was full.

There was power down there, too. It ravened and reached, for anything beyond itself.

It was so hungry. And it saw me.

Then a grip I'd completely forgotten tightened like a manacle around the memory of my hands. And with a yank so sharp it left a trailing vacuum in my wake, I left both the dark and light behind.

I HAD MY body back. Or I had something, anyway, something that could feel.

Because everything was pain.

Maybe it was a tithe for how effortless that first step had been, Fjolar tugging me through the arch of my own wisteria into that golden soak. Maybe this agony was the toll, this sense that my core filaments had been unwound and then woven carelessly back together. My bones ached as if the marrow inside them had swelled by three sizes, and my skin felt peeled back to expose glistening nerves. Compared to everything else, my throat hurt in an almost minimal way, a raw, stripped ache that I would have dismissed as barely devastating if I'd been able to make myself stop screaming.

Fjolar's voice boomed from somewhere above me, echoing in my chest. "Iris! Flower girl, what's the *matter* with you?"

With a monstrous effort, I shoved my knuckles into my mouth, bit down on them until teeth met bone, and eked one eye open. Through the film of tears, I could see the wavering outlines of his face hovering above me. As he dipped closer, the tips of a stray lock of his hair brushed my cheek.

Just that glancing touch, the slight scratch of hair over inflamed skin, was far too much to take.

"Get away!" I shrieked. "Don't touch me!"

Then I plummeted into something between sleep and unconsciousness, like a burned-out meteor thudding into soil.

IT WAS THE smell of the sand that woke me.

I opened my eyes slowly, the root of every eyelash a bright pinprick of pain. As soon as the sleep evaporated, my senses snarled to life. The cool breeze battered my exposed cheek, and where my face rested, I could feel the individual imprint of every grain.

And the smell of it . . . glass came from sand, and so I knew what it was made of, rocks and crushed shells and crumbled sea-cliff stone, swept together by wind and water. But I had never known sand to be so pungent, an acrid, mineral tang mingling with the salty kelp smell of fish and the sea.

Bile welled up in my throat, and I took shallow mouth-breaths until I felt like I could prop myself up without everything inside me rushing out. Slowly, I eased up to sitting. With every gritty blink, the blurred world around me slid into sharper focus.

By the time I'd fumbled my way onto my knees, my vision had reached the piercing clarity of a fever dream—enough to make out the nicks in the sun-bleached ribs that curved around me. They cradled me like a bone shelter from the lurid purple of the sky, so riddled with streaks of stars that I thought of it for the first time as a true celestial body. Something with its own circulatory system of glowing arteries and veins.

"Oh, *what?*" I rasped to myself, dragging a hand over my flaming face. "What the *fuck?*"

I gripped one of the ribs and shakily levered myself up. Once I was standing, the ribs came up to my thighs, and a knobbly column of vertebrae trailed many feet away from me, half buried, so long that at some point spine must have turned into tail.

Thousands of others jutted from the sand, an eroded graveyard rising from dunes frosted with mica. Shielding my eyes—that ultraviolet sky made it hard to tell what time it was, but still the light was glaringly bright—I turned in a shaky circle. Nothing but sandy crops of rock and desert spitting up chimera skeletons, flippers scattered beside bones that looked like they had once been finely articulated feet.

There was something so morbidly decadent and improbable about it, all these picked-clean pieces of lost life strewn over sparkling desert. The patterns of the remains were so precise that the gleam thrashed inside me, yearning to fractal it all. To whip this burial ground up into a hurricane of rib cage within rib cage, chained by links of interlocking tails and wreathed with gusts of speckled sand.

I could smell them too, I realized. I could smell all these bones, their petrified reek. Even after all the years it must have taken to scour them so clean, I would have sworn they still stank of blood and copper.

It brought everything flooding back: Mama on the floor of the café, wings of blood unfurling to either side, suspended in some chrysalis between death and life. Malina and me hunting Dunja through Montenegro, stripping back layers of lies. Following, hand over hand, the tangled ropes that tied us to the coven of our family, until we finally reached the central knot that was Mara.

Mara, our far-mother, who'd sold daughters to Death so she and hers would never have to die. Mara, who had let Fjolar whisk me away even as Dunja, Lina, and I broke the spell that bound us all.

That was where my logic stuttered. If the spell was truly broken, how was I even here? Because this was Fjolar's kingdom; it had to be. The haven in which he whiled away the lifetimes of his performing brides.

As if I had summoned him with the thought, I could see his shadow lengthen beside mine. It fell bulbous and too long, at an angle that made no sense without a central light source in the sky to cast it.

"Flower girl." Beneath the thin-skinned veneer of calm, I heard the simmer of excitement. He was thrilled—no, *elated* that I was here. "Are you better yet?"

I wheeled to face him, the entire world swimming giddy with the movement, as if I were the focal point of a colossal kaleidoscope. Fractals of skeleton and sand chased my vision, like the tracers I'd seen the one time I dropped acid with a group of Belgian tourists passing through Cattaro. So long ago, now, it felt like, and who knew how far away.

Lina had taken care of me that night, when I'd come crashing down from the high like a tightrope walker taken by a sudden gust. I swallowed a sob at the thought of my sister, her reedy violinist's fingers cool and gentle on my sweaty temples as she sang me into calm. Soothing and sweet as a springtime breeze.

And just as far away, while I was stuck here with *him*.

"Am I 'better yet'?" I spat at him, so flushed with fury I'd have lunged over and swung at him if just keeping my feet planted under me wasn't demanding the use of every muscle. "Oh, yes, I'm all set now, thank you. Except that you took me, you stole me from my sister and brought me here where everything hurts and everything smells, it's all too bright, and why is everything so *much*?"

"Because I thought you'd like it that way, *flower*," he shot back, and I felt a moment of precarious give inside me at the familiar challenge in his eyes—somehow even bluer here than they had been in my world, bright and variegated like delphinium crossed with fennel flower, still edged in smudged black liner. Otherwise, he looked exactly like I remembered, like he'd belong best at a rave held in a mead hall. Platinum hair tucked behind the spirals of his gauged earrings and brushing broad shoulders, the nearly neon purple light flinging the Nordic bones of his face into stark relief.

His lips the only point of softness.

"Isn't too much of everything exactly what you claimed to want?" he demanded. "Though I admit I didn't foresee the . . . side effects of bringing you here in such full blush."

"Full blush?" I echoed, my voice still warbly with rage. The edges of my vision throbbed like strobe lights, but I found if I kept my gaze locked on his face, it wasn't quite as maddening. "What's that supposed to mean?"

"I've never done it this way before. None of Mara's daughters ever came here with me in the flesh. When their souls crossed over with me, their bodies always stayed behind. But you . . ." His eyes flared with jubilance, and this time he didn't bother to feign restraint. "You're *all* the way here. Body and soul, both right here with me. I've brought you with me fully."

He paused and gave me an expectant look, one pale eyebrow lifted, as if waiting for me to discover that I was actually giddy with delight at how completely he had me trapped.

For the first time, I looked down at myself. I was still wearing the plain white tank top, jeans, and too-big pink-and-black sneakers I'd found rummaging through Dunja's sort-of-stolen van. Both the clothes and my bare arms were covered in a fine, gritty layer of silvery sand. I dusted off one forearm experimentally, and just like the rib that I'd used as a crutch, the sand felt mostly like what it was. Too keen and too gritty, but undeniably real.

But this wasn't how it was supposed to be. I remembered Dunja's dance, the way she had painted for us the sweeping, dream-spun magic of this place, the beautiful vacuum of it—just a backdrop for her performance. Nothing here had been real for her; she hadn't been able to touch, smell, taste, or hear anything but Death, in the form he'd taken to match the lover she'd most wanted.

He had been the focal point of her entire existence during the years she'd spent dancing for him.

It was nothing like that for me. For all that I wanted to slap that slick self-satisfaction off his face, looking at Fjolar felt nearly normal. Or as close as I could come to it, here where "natural" light looked like it'd been filtered through an amethyst prism.

"You sound pretty damn euphoric about that, Fjolar—Death— whatever I call you now," I said bitterly, wrapping my arms tight around myself. "Like maybe I'm supposed to thank you for stealing me so thoroughly. But it feels like poison here, all wrong. I need to leave, right now. You need to take me back."

He laced both hands behind his neck as layers of expression settled over his face, so many things at once that I didn't want to see. Smugness, radiant pleasure, and underneath it all, a bedrock base of dense defiance.

"No."

Pure despair cascaded over me. "Fjolar, please. Being here is going to kill me, I can feel it. I need to go *home*."

And I need Lina, and Luka. Luka, whose see-you-soon kisses, right before I climbed up to Bobotov Kuk with my sister and my aunt, still felt warm on my cheeks and between my eyes.

"You aren't understanding." His face turned stony. "I never had to keep a lover here against her will—and why would I do it now, with you so sullen and ungrateful? I'm not saying that I won't take you back."

"Then . . . what are you saying?"

"I'm saying that I can't."

THREE

HE HAD IMAGINED HIS FREEDOM SO CLEARLY, IN CLOSE TO countless different ways.

That was something to be said for millennia of banishment, for being buried beneath years stacked upon years. It did give one lavish time to think. And if those thoughts grew blotty and formless, wisping through the mind like squid ink through water, what of it? There wasn't a single soul anywhere nearby to hear them told.

He had never doubted it would give way eventually; nothing in this world was forever, at least nothing besides him. But how would it begin? With a hairline fracture, maybe, threading through the frozen pillar that formed his prison. Something that would spread like a slow web, fissures creeping through the column until it crackled before finally buckling beneath its own weight.

Or maybe it would dissipate in flakes, little shards shaved off by years of swirling currents. He could hear the relentless churn of the water against the ice, though he had never heard any sounds of life. The moat of magic that surrounded *her* column—the massive spear that kept him pinioned to the seafloor like a needle through a moth—warded it from anything living.

Or at least, after such long, lonely, and waterlogged silence, he thought that it must. He couldn't know for certain; her magic had never been fathomable to him. If it had, he would have begun gnawing at it when she first flung him down here.

Crunching and licking and scraping at her ice until it couldn't hope to hold him.

But he had never understood the shape and measure of her gleam. He had seen her shine with it, of course, but you could watch the sun until it scorched your eyes and still never know how its fire held dominion over the sky.

She had always been beyond his reckoning.

It was part of why he had loved her once he finally found her. Even when the hunger swelled beyond resistance or reason; even when the oily darkness in his veins rushed like a voracious tide. It was why he had been content to bask in her light, to rest his cheek on her collarbone even when the want spoke to him in its legion of whispers. *You love her, and so? Tear her to pieces, pluck her apart, flay her until all that gleam comes pooling out. Drink your fill of it, and of her, and then you will have drunk her love. She is all for you, you lord and master of this realm.*

Yours to break open, like everything else.

But he could not do it, could not bring himself to consume her. Could not douse the fire inside her, dull the luster of those clear eyes. Not when she slept curled under his chin next to their stone-ringed, flickering fire, and he could smell the warmed scalp beneath her hair.

He could not do it, not while she loved him back so well.

Except that it had been a lie. Every scent, every taste, every whisper of her skin against his skin, spun cleverly like wool to pull over his eyes. Until he was blind enough with trust to follow her to that clearing, wreathed with snowy pines beneath a star-choked winter sky.

He had known that she was something much more than simply beautiful, but he had not thought that she could possibly be so strong. Yet she had been strong enough to cast him here somehow, to sink him hissing into the water like the ember of a falling star.

On his long descent, he had seen the water's menagerie of wonders. Sleek beasts with beak-like snouts, and mammoth ones that bugled mournful songs. Turtles that spared him only half a glance, and swarms of silver, speckled fish, scattering as he plunged through them with bubbles boiling in his wake.

Then her magic had hardened around him, filling up his eyes. All he saw was darkness and the faintest sprites of light—the tiny bits of sun that augured through her pillar, to needle him with the promise of a daylit world so many leagues above.

In all this time, he'd been so severely, savagely alone, with nothing to sustain him but the memory of her face. And with little else to dwell on, he had thought he would surely feel when it began. A rending or a cleaving, the birth of some fresh rift.

Yet when the pillar vanished, it went in sublime silence.

In one moment, it crushed him as it always had.

And in the next, it was simply gone.

FOUR

Iris

"HOW LONG DO YOU PLAN TO STAY DOWN THERE?"

"What do you care?" I mumbled into the bony knots of my knees. I'd found that curling up mollusk-tight soothed me a little. The smell of my own skin, the press of my arms where they locked around my legs, the fall of my hair around me like a protective veil—they all felt like a shield. Maybe it was because the materials that made me weren't alien like everything else here.

"I said, what do you care?" I repeated flatly, when Fjolar didn't answer. He was sitting near but not quite next to me, reeking of exasperation. "You just told me you had no intention of getting me out of here. And since it hurts to move, and looking around is almost worse, why should I do either?"

"That isn't what I said," he snapped. "I told you I didn't know how to let you go, given that I've never had a flesh companion here with me before. I thought having all of you here would be spectacularly different, a *new* thing. I certainly didn't know it would be like *this*," he added petulantly. "Or I would have thought twice on bringing you, believe me."

"Can you stop saying 'flesh' like that?" I snapped back. "It's making me feel like you lugged me here like a sack of steaks."

"Why are you being this way?" He sounded so baffled and galled that I huffed an incredulous laugh into my knees. "You liked me before. Truly liked me, past the magic that bound us. You wanted me, and badly. I felt it, tasted it on you. I know you're not comfortable yet, but we're here *together*. I set you free from all that held you back, gave you everything you said you wanted—and it's still not to your taste?"

My head whipped up so fast a needle of pain zinged down my neck. "You're Death, for fuck's sake," I spat at him, galvanic with fury. "You lied to me about everything, and then you ripped me away from everyone I actually love. Yes, I liked you, when I thought you were a bad-idea boy with beautiful ink and clever hands and a mother like mine. *Of course* I liked you; that's why you came to me that way. But you're not even really human, and *here* isn't any realer than you are. So if you can't take me back, what difference does it make if I never move again?"

I heard him draw a long-suffering sigh. "Fine. Let's molder away here, then. If you want to sulk yourself to the bone under a sky that never changes, that's exactly what will happen. The many pieces of this world—they're not like yours. They don't abide by planetary rhythms, day or night, the shifting of seasons. They're only and always exactly as they are. Like living paintings."

I chanced a peek. The sky above hadn't changed a glimmer, from what I could tell. Its light still pounded over us in that same incandescent violet, and the Van Gogh whorls of supernovae and huge, bright stars twinkled as aggressively as before. They were fixed points, speared to the sky, as incapable of momentum as everything else here.

Still, they were outrageously beautiful, even eerier than the skeletal menagerie clawing through the sand around us. But as exuberant as this place looked, I could see how such a solitude of bones and stars could get kind of tiresome.

"They may be static," he continued, "but they're also wonders, stitched together in a way your world could never accommodate. There's so much to see here, if you'd bother to look. So much beauty for you to bloom for me. I molded it for you and you alone, willed it into being in the time it took for you to cross over here. I made it *with* you, like I've done for every one of Mara's daughters who's come before."

I squinted at him. "What do you mean, you made it with me?"

"We were connected by the spell, before you tried to break it open," he said. A runnel of sadness ran below the accusatory words, like an underground spring. He missed it, I could tell, the intoxicated, spellbound connection between us when I was still under the thrall that Mara's magic cast over us both.

And with a guilty start, I realized I missed it a little too. Without that sense of magnetic attraction, he was a stranger to me, volatile and hostile. Which left me even lonelier, a more desperate castaway than before. Afraid on top of angry. He'd never done anything violent in front of me, but that meant nothing now. He'd even stopped calling me *flower*.

And tall as I was, I was so little compared to him. Especially in this alien, toxic place. His place.

"I could feel the crenellations of your mind, your interests and your cravings," he continued. "I knew what would please you to see, the shapes that could tantalize you. And that's what this world is—an offering to you, made in your image." He shot me a dark, slantwise look. "Though I see I might as well not have bothered."

"You mean a *stage* made in my image, don't you?" I tossed back. "That was the idea you two had, wasn't it? To give me the perfect backdrop for my performance for you."

"You give her so little credit," he said, with such a sudden knife-edge to his voice that it startled me into looking properly at him. His azure gaze was so direct and reproachful that for a second, I actually felt the burn of shame. "It's cruel to talk about her that way. Worse than cruel, it's petty. And neither becomes you."

I barked out a half laugh. "You think I care what *becomes* me? You're calling me cruel and petty, when the both of you piled lies on top of lies? She used her own daughters to keep herself alive, and you simply used us for play. And now I'm meant to spill over with sympathy for her?"

This time I couldn't interpret the murk that crossed his eyes. "The spell she cast was colossal," he said, clipped. "And even with all the effort it took—with everything it cost her—she didn't want you to suffer. This world I built for you *is* meant to make the most of your gleam, but it's also meant to bring you joy."

"How do you build anything, anyway?" I snapped. "You're Death. You're a negator, not a creator."

He lifted a pale eyebrow. "And who do you think crafts what comes next, for every sentient thing that dies?"

I felt a sharp nick of surprise at that, like a paper cut before the blood welled up. It was so easy to forget, having touched all the parts of him that were warm and so convincingly human, who I was really talking to. Regardless of what he looked, sounded, and tasted like, he wasn't just a demanding, self-indulgent boy. The piece of him by my side was only a fraction of a force that I couldn't begin to understand.

The culler of every living thing.

It hadn't even occurred to me that I could die of being with him, at any moment. The others before me had, yes, but it had been by performing until they burned themselves out. But now, I was a person like any other. He could snuff me out like a midge smeared carelessly between two fingers, because that was who he was. That was what he was for.

Maybe I needed to be so much more careful with him than I was being.

"Ah . . ." I opened my mouth and closed it. "So that's what happens after we die? What about reincarnation? Shouldn't—wouldn't God have created whatever comes next? Or gods, whatever there is."

He gave a rugged half shrug, like a wolf twitching its hide. "The right isn't mine to share those kinds of truths with you. And

I didn't bring you here to debate theology. We're here to be happy together, so that our bliss . . ." He trailed off, his face shuttering.

"So that our bliss what?" There was something else going on here, then. I could practically feel him holding back from me. But why? "Are you telling me there's some purpose to you crafting this world for me, and me making things beautiful for you? Something beyond letting Mara live forever, I mean?"

He stood abruptly, dusting silvery sand off his black-trousered thighs. "Of course there's a purpose. She's never been one to do things on a whim. I won't deny how much advantage I've taken of the pleasures on my end, but everything in her life has always had a price."

His admiration of Mara hung palpable between us, and I abruptly remembered the fondness with which she had gazed up at Death during the ritual banquet before Malina's and my contest. Callous as he was with me, clearly real respect lived between them, somehow.

"Well, what is it?" I asked, tilting my face up to meet his gaze. Anger would only drive him further from me, and with the pit of desolation gaping inside me at every thought of Lina left behind, I needed to try something different. I needed to make him want to talk to me. "What are we meant to be doing together? How am I even here to begin with, if the spell is broken?"

I could see him teetering on the precipice of telling me, wanting us to share something again. "It's damaged, not broken," he finally conceded. "I can still feel the shreds of it, clinging to the magic's original shape. If I hadn't claimed you when I did, sealing my end of the bargain, it would have broken fully. But there was still enough of her will left for me to salvage some of her spell."

I remembered the network of black roses that had imposed Mara's will in infinite scope—I had overwhelmed it in the last mad rush of battle, throttled her blossoms with the surging wisteria of my own will. Had I somehow missed a part of that tremendous web? "So if you had left me there, would Dunja and Lina and I have broken the spell entirely?"

"It would have shattered if I hadn't stepped in, and I couldn't let that happen. Not when . . ." Then he shook his head in a single bitter, brittle snap. "No. You hate it here. You hate being with me. What this place *should* be doesn't matter anymore."

Steeling myself for nausea, I rocked forward onto my heels, one hand on the tooth-grindingly gritty sand to help me ease to my feet. Once the world stopped swimming around me, I looked up at Fjolar, trying to blink the dizziness away.

"But it does matter," I said softly, forcing my tone gentle. This wasn't something I could wrest from him with rage. Anything I stole from him would have to be much subtler than his theft of me had been. "It matters to me. If something about this kingdom isn't what Dunja told us—if it's more than just a pleasure dome for you—then maybe . . ."

Maybe knowing how it works will help me figure out how to get loose from here, I wanted to say. *Maybe if I can understand its shape, I can teach myself how to crack it open and crawl out.*

He wanted me to want to be here with him, and for once, maybe I could be more like my sister and take the subtle path. Be a kiss instead of a fist. And if he wouldn't tell me whatever he was hiding now, I could hold on until he would. For Lina and Luka—for Dunja and Mama, if she was even still alive—I would fake whatever it took.

"Maybe you can start by showing me how it's supposed to be, then," I finished. "The way it was before, for you and Dunja. You and the others. Like you said, none of them were here with you the way that I am, were they? So it might just take more time for me to get used to it."

His face stayed walled off. "But look at you. You can barely stand. And worse, you don't even really want to find your footing here."

"Remember what you told me, though," I persisted. "About my name. A flower that grows in rocks and deserts, refuses to die, clings to just about anything? You say you made this world for me; there must be something here for me to cling to, then. And besides . . ."

I dropped my eyes slowly, let my lashes fan out lush over the hollows beneath them. I might not have been trained like my sister was by Naisha all those years, like all the mothers and grandmothers before me, but I could imagine how I looked to him. Glossy hair, the dark and dainty swipes of brow and lash, the diamond hollow between my nose and cut-glass lips. All painted in the watercolor wash of that uncanny violet light.

I might not have been raised into seduction, but right now, it was the only tool I had.

I reached up carefully, as if I was uncertain, until my fingers just barely skimmed his shoulder. "Besides, I have you to cling to, don't I?"

He crossed his muscle-corded arms over his chest, but he didn't move away from my glancing touch. "And why would you be willing to cling to a thieving bastard like me? You've made your feelings for me—and for this gift of a world—more than clear."

I opened my mouth to spool out more lies like silky thread, but another wave of dizziness crashed abruptly over me. The ground seemed to almost tilt under my feet, as if we stood on a ship's deck. With a little choke of a gasp, I stumbled forward, pressing both hands against Fjolar's chest to catch myself—almost exactly like I'd done on the Cattaro beach our first real night together, when being around him still felt like the best kind of drunk—and he reflexively reached out to steady me.

As soon as his hands wrapped around my arms, the world went still.

With Fjolar touching me, all of it settled. I could still smell the desert, its cold and salt; the bones around us still glowed beneath the purpled sky. But now the beauty, and the swarming potential behind it, felt gentled. Like an invitation instead of an assault.

"What?" Fjolar demanded, giving me a little shake where he held me. His many rings and the arrowhead bracelet he always wore were cool against my arms, but now their cold gave me a tingly chill, nothing like the bitter agony it would have been before we touched. "What is it?"

"I'm starting to see it, I think," I replied, half laughing. "Maybe because you're touching me. Like you're the place we can meet in the middle, me and your world, the connective tissue between here and where I come from. The tendons or sinew, or—"

"A minute ago you were up in arms at being talked about like meat," he said dryly. "I'm starting to think I should be entitled to the same courtesy."

"You're not entitled to anything," I said archly, cocking my head to the side. "You brought me here without asking, and this time I didn't even owe you a single kiss. But since I *am* here, could I at least get a tour?"

He watched me warily, but I could see the seed of interest sparking in the depths of his cool blue gaze. Neither of us had moved, and despite myself I took a deep breath of him. He still smelled deliciously like I remembered from my world, earth notes of peaty whiskey, chocolate, and fresh tobacco. "And what would you offer me in return?" he finally said.

I held his eyes, watched them flicker to my mouth when I licked my lips as if they were dry. A warm bloom of triumph unfurled in my belly. I could do this. I could sway him. "I'm sure I can manage something."

Before I touched him, the world had been far too much to fractal. But now that it had stilled into some semblance of peace, I could work all that intricacy into a filigree of my own making.

With the familiar sense of letting some internal river loose from its dam, I unleashed the gleam and fractured the landscape around us into a revolving starburst of a world. I began with the neon sky, with its Van Gogh whorls and blinding spill of coruscating galaxies—graphing it out into squares of varying dimensions, like a three-dimensional Soma puzzle with its cubes being shuffled.

Leaving the sky to throb above us, shifting in and out like a geometric mosaic with a heartbeat somehow attached, I turned my attention to the swath of sand riven with skeletal remains. Whipping them up, and up, and up, I trapped us in a woven bone prison like a basket or a loom, alternating rib cage and spine to weave the warp, and looping the tails and limbs through to thread the weft. The skulls I left for last, multiplying and impaling them on each rod of the fractal structure, pinning them like finials.

"I think a very old skull might be staring at you," I whispered coyly up at him. "In triplicate. Does that get me anywhere?"

Despite himself, he smiled, not-quite-straight teeth flashing tiger bright as he gazed up at the sky. "Oh, I think it might, flower girl. I think it just might."

FIVE

Malina

MARA LED US HOME IN TATTERS, A GROUP OF SPECTERS SLIP-ping through the dark spears of the pine trees. Like a ghostly wedding caravan that had somehow lost its bride.

Even Mara was faltering. Roots snagged at her feet and she stumbled, leaning hard against the two who gripped her forearms to support her. I could hear her from where Dunja and I brought up the back, the rusty groan of her fatigue like an old organ-grinder. Eventually, Izkara stepped forward. Silently, she flowed through a series of fluid, complicated steps that reminded me of the kata Niko'd practiced during her few earnest years of karate. Her limbs lengthened, joints locking outward and back. At her sides, her fingers splayed wide before curving into claws.

I cringed at each new angle, steeling myself for the sound of her pain, the howling mangle of werewolf movies. But there were no wet pops or crunches. Nothing more than the grace of a ribbon being swirled through the air, one thing unfurling easily into another. And she sounded so exultant as she changed, an ecstatic, swelling crescendo like an orchestral movement reaching its peak.

Finally her hair cascaded into a sleek wave of shining black fur. It swept down and around her body until she eventually fell forward silently onto all fours—an inky, amber-eyed panther, much bigger than any real wildcat. Her tail swished at Mara in almost playful invitation.

Dunja gently tipped my slack jaw closed with a finger under my chin.

"She can just—she can *do* that?" I managed.

"That," she confirmed grimly, "and a great deal more."

Mara set her teeth as the panther padded toward her, nudging her calves with its glossy, rounded head. "While I appreciate the gesture, my warrior-heart, I am perfectly capable of—"

The wildcat yowled at an earsplitting decibel, then delicately locked her jaw around Mara's ankle.

"Stars and gods," Mara muttered sourly, burying her hand into the charred twists of her hair and giving them a disgruntled tug. "*Fine.* But just this once."

And that was how we made our way back to the coven's clearing. With Mara riding a panther as if this was a thing that happened every day, swaying with the rolling rhythm of Izkara's gait. One of the other daughters lit our way like a living flame, the same blue-and-amber fire she had set for Mara curled in licking loops around her body. Even her auburn hair burned harmlessly with its light.

My throat tightened as the forest in front of us parted to reveal the chalet, massive and blazing against the mountainside. Like the hull of one of the glittering ocean liners that knifed into the Cattaro Bay at night, the warped, distant burble of their musicians and milling guests filtering over miles of water like a haunting.

Now that I was so close to seeing Niko again, yearning for her began sprouting spines in my belly. I missed her that way so often, even if we'd seen each other only hours before. It used to make me curl up tightly in bed, my back to Riss, knees stuffed against my chest to stifle the rawness of the ache.

And then as if I'd dreamed her up, I saw her petite silhouette press against the ballroom's floor-to-ceiling windows. Sweet, small fists clenched against the glass, fogged with the ghostly bloom of her exhale.

Even though I couldn't see her face with all the light behind her, I still felt the exact moment that she saw me. All that tension fled her body, like a tightly wound coil finally sprung free. A moment later she burst into the clearing with Luka close at her heels. I only caught the briefest glance of her little, lovely face—her eyes so big, and shining in the dark with captive tears—before she was in my arms.

"Oh, *Lina*," she whispered into my collarbone through a bit-back sob, and I half melted at the contralto rasp of her voice. The tumult of her love and relief sang out in my mind, sunlit and pure. She sounded like an entire choir of church bells ringing in a holy day. "You came back, you're here. Thank God, pie, thank *God*, I thought—"

"I'm here, princess," I soothed, sliding one hand into her silky nape and the other down her back. My fingertips followed the fragile, staccato ridge of her spine. Beneath the thin top, she was almost feverish-warm, like she always was. "I didn't have that much choice about it, you know? It was either make it through, or think about all the horror movies my poor revenant would have to watch after you learned necromancy just to make me sorry for dying."

She sputtered with laughter, then whiplashed to concern. Niko's emotions were like that, quicksilver ripples. "Riss," she said, searching my face. "Is she . . . ?"

Luka appeared from behind her. "Where is she, Lina? Where's Iris?"

The sound of him was so dire and overwhelming I took a reflexive step back, expanding the bubble I sometimes used to shield myself when all the hearing got to be too much. I'd imagine a birdcage building itself around me, wrought-iron bars falling into place as a heavy cloth pulled over it and drowned out the world beyond. Locking me into my own little bubble of night and quiet. A silly thing, but it helped a little.

"I'm sorry, I didn't mean . . ." He took a ragged breath, dragging a hand down over his face. "I'm so glad to see you, Linka, of course I am. I just—I have to know. Please. Where's Riss? I don't see her here, so I thought maybe she was hurt, lagged a little bit behind . . ."

I bit my lip, my eyes stinging with the salty well of tears. "We lost her, Luka," I whispered, and not even the thought of all my sister's steel could keep my voice from trembling. "I'm so sorry. Death took her. It was Fjolar, it was always him. We half broke the spell, I think—at least, we did *something*—but he took her with him at the end."

It hurt so much to see his face collapse as the last of the hope burned out. A twist of paper blackening at the point of a flame, before curling into ash. Even with my bubble in place, I could hear the mountainside avalanche of his loss. The great crack and grind of boulders so loud I thought they might bury him like a cairn.

"What does that mean, then?" he said, his voice breaking. His face twisted as he clenched his teeth, trying to wrestle himself under control. "Is she dead?"

"I . . . I'm not sure?" Flimsy as eggshells, barely even a whisper. "I can't hear her, but that could be because she's too far away. If she were dead, I hope . . . I think I'd know."

"Lisarah is not dead," Mara proclaimed from behind me. I wheeled to face her, my heart leaping so high I actually balled a hand up against my chest. "She reached the kingdom safely. I can feel it spinning, still, as the last of the spell stutters along—we have some time yet before it fully fades. Perhaps time enough, if we stand beneath auspicious stars, to prepare for his advent."

I stole a glimpse at Luka, who held a clenched fist against his mouth, his eyelids trembling with emotion. The relief pounding from him harmonized with my own.

"If she's alive, how do we get her back?" I pressed frantically. "And who *exactly* is this 'he' you keep dangling in front of us?"

"He is a monster," she said simply. "And my beloved, once."

While I stood reeling, she tipped her head to the chalet. "Let us all take some rest before we delve into so much past. You sway where you stand, fledgling, and I will need some mending first, before I find the strength to talk of him. And even my Amrisa does not wield her miracles in moments."

"There's something else, Lina," Niko broke in, stepping to my side and lacing our fingers together with a tight squeeze. "You should be ready for it, before you go in. If it's even possible to prepare for . . . something like that."

My insides dropped like an anvil, and I felt suddenly so exhausted and put-upon. Everything was too much. It wasn't *fair*. "Ready for what? What's inside?"

She pressed her lips together and gave me a solemn, sloe-eyed look. "It's your mom, pie. Jasmina's awake."

"FAISALI, AWAKE," MARA murmured to herself in the stunned silence that followed. "That might well be the heart of it."

Faisali, awake, my mind echoed dumbly, over and over. Like the cry of seagulls above the bay.

Faisali awake, awake, awake.

Last I'd seen Mama, she'd been bloodless as marble on Mara's chamber floor, drowning in black roses. It'd been part of Mara's symphony of lies, the idea that she was keeping our mother from waking to a deathless agony—the last victim of our line's invented "curse." Every once in a while, I remembered, Mama had made a gasping sound like the living sick. But I could hear the grim tolling behind it. I hadn't told Riss it was over, but I'd known then. No one came back from sounding like that.

But now Mama was awake, and awake meant alive.

Our mother was *alive*.

While I stood quivering and dumbstruck with hope, Dunja rounded on Mara. Before any of the rest of us could so much as twitch, she charged over and gripped Mara by the throat, driving her to the ground until they were nearly nose to nose. With her snowy blaze of hair and dainty doll's profile, she looked like the afterimage of Mara's black sun. Like her negative.

"I saw her," Dunja hissed through her teeth. "I saw what you did to my sister, to entice my nieces to you. To wring even more out of us. You crushed her *heart*, and then you wouldn't let her die. How could she rise from that? *How could you allow it?*"

"Unhand her, Anais," Izkara half growled from behind her. She'd mostly shifted back to human, but the hand on Dunja's shoulder had stayed wicked with claws. I could see them digging into my aunt's skin like tiny scythes, leaving taut divots in their wake. If Izkara put even a fraction of force into it, she'd shred Dunja to the bone. "Can you not see how weakened our *sorai* is? Show compassion for her, at least, if you can't muster respect."

"Sorai," I repeated under my breath. It was the false name Mara had given us for herself, but it also meant something to the coven. It was her honorific, the designation of "highest."

"Daughter, please," Mara added, sounding so bone-weary and unlike her imperious self that Dunja's grip faltered just a fraction with surprise. "Faisali's rising is not my doing, I swear it. And I *am* a touch ill-used to be dragged about in the dirt. Once Amrisa sees to me—and after you hear the full truth of my shame, not the bits and scraps you have mistaken for the whole—you can judge me as you will."

Hairline cracks of uncertainty threaded through Dunja's porcelain face. "What do you mean, bits and scraps, old witch?" she demanded scathingly. "Truth is *truth*."

Mara closed her eyes for a long moment, and when she opened them again, they glittered with very human tears. "What a relief it will be just to speak of it, after all these many years. To lay the burden of so much deceit and silence down. If even then you wish to dredge me in a bog and drown me in salt water, your efforts will be welcome."

"If she's still inclined to drown you whenever 'then' is," a cool, toneless voice interjected, sending chills skittering down my spine, "I hope she'll let me do the honors. Or at least consider sharing."

I *knew* that voice. It sounded like sleet, and was even more wrong in inflection—but I'd been hearing some version of it for seventeen years, and I couldn't help the chime of joy that rang in me at the sound.

I pried my eyes from Dunja and Mara and turned slowly to the chalet—to where Mama stood in front of the threshold, haloed in the light flooding from the doorway.

Enmeshed in a living web of black roses that had grown into her skin.

She was maybe naked underneath them, I thought. But they grew so clustered thick she didn't need any clothes. Pitch-black from stem to leaf, petal to thorn, they wound around her legs and torso all the way up her neck. As if she were a human trellis. Two of them crept up so high they'd sunk into her left cheekbone and right temple, the trailing leaves half embedded in her flesh on either side. Framing her face in twin crescent shapes.

And her hair hung so thick and heavy with them it looked like a chestnut briar. Against the nest of her curls, the captive petals shone glossy-bright with the honey light spilling from inside the chalet.

Everyone had gone breathless, staring at her. If Niko and Luka had seen her before I got here, many of the other coven daughters must have too. It didn't matter. No amount of looking could chip away at so much horror entwined with beauty, skew it even close to normal.

Her gaze skipped from left to right, cold and light as snow-flakes carried on a gale. I could almost feel when it finally landed on me, an icicle lodging in my chest. It reminded me of a story Riss had read to me many years ago, of a little boy who'd crossed a snow queen's path and wound up with shards of ice in his eyes and heart. Seeing her had tainted his vision, turned him into something else.

This new version of Mama felt like she might have the same potential to transform. And not for the better.

"Lina," Mama finally said, and there it was. The tiniest thawing in her voice, a high note of pure human relief in her familiar alto. Enough to remind me that this uncanny stranger was still really my mother, even if she did look carved from a fairy tale's heart. "You're here, my cherry daughter. She didn't steal you from me after all."

She made her way to me, graceful even in her eagerness. Cutting an easy swath through Mara's nine, and the other coven daughters who had come surging out of the chalet to watch her. She stopped right in front of me, so near I could see the petals fanned over her chest fluttering with her breath. So she still had to breathe. That was good to know. And from this close, I could see where the flower roots branched into her flesh, fading to ink blue as they tunneled under the layers of skin. It made her look like she had sprouted a fresh, new network of veins.

And maybe that was it. Maybe she *had*. Whatever was fueling her now, it wasn't blood—at least not the kind that ran through me. I knew, because I'd seen exactly where all of hers had been spilled.

That last red memory of her sprawled on the café floor pricked the bubble I'd blown around myself. I could feel the tears start, rolling fat and hot down my face, and then *everything* came pouring in. All of everyone's sound.

The maelstrom of shock that whooshed around me, coalescing from the crowd.

The relentless tolling of Mara's ancient bell, a basal hum of lovestruck allure.

Luka's grief and loneliness, the baying of an abandoned dog lost and far from home.

Niko's concern, delicate yet vehement as a moth's wings brushing against a windowpane.

And in front of me, my mother's love. A distant, eerie fluting that rose and fell without a steady cadence. As if snatches of it were constantly being stolen by the jaws of some starving wind. Mama had sounded like an army once, broad and aggressive and sometimes jubilant. But now, only these frail trills were left.

There was something else, too, beneath that. Something I could barely hear. A dark, dry, hungry sound like the rustle of something reptilian and ancient stalking through the ferns of a primordial forest.

As I balked, overwhelmed and tingling with fear, Mama spread her arms and simply waited.

That was what convinced me. Whatever she'd become, she knew how she looked to me, and she was letting me decide.

But she was my *mother*. Like there was even a choice.

I stepped into her embrace, and let myself be small. Her grip was even stronger than I remembered, sturdy as oak branches. Like being wrapped in a dryad's arms. And she was tall enough that I could rest my head against her chest just like when I'd been a little girl.

Just like that, anyway, if I could make myself ignore the velveteen stir of the flowers under my cheek. They were unnervingly warm and alive, moving in a way that had nothing to do with the breeze. It reminded me of how they had filled the room the first time Iris and I had come face-to-face with Mara-as-Sorai, nosing and nudging us like animals.

Because they weren't flowers, not real ones. They didn't smell like true roses—not like anything, really—but they had a buzzy, thrumming sound. Together they rang in canon, a miniature melody echoing Mara's behemoth bell.

I couldn't help shying away from them. Mama made a dismayed little sound, sliding a palm flat between my shoulder blades.

Her hand was so cold I could feel it leaching through the fabric of my shirt. "Please don't go yet," she whispered in that unnerving toneless way, as if each word weighed exactly the same. All identical pebbles dropped into water one by one. "Let me hold you just a little longer, now that I have you back."

"I . . . ," I began haltingly, sneaking a desperate glance at Niko. She gave me a reassuring nod. *She's your mother*, she mouthed, with an eloquent shrug that I guessed was meant to acknowledge the overarching weirdness of the situation, and her suggestion that I roll with it.

Reluctantly, I let myself relax against Mama until my breathing smoothed from its ragged rhythm, and I realized that the strand tickling my nose was just that. Not a tendril of unnatural roses, but simply her hair. My mother's hair, somehow still smelling as familiar and complicated as I remembered, of lavender and cedar, rising yeast and confectioner's sugar.

No matter what she had done to me and Riss—to Riss, especially—through all those years, it had always been from love. And even when I hadn't known it, I'd loved her anyway. She was my mother, my anchor, my cornerstone. I had lost her for what should have been forever, and now I somehow had her back. And not just back, but holding me tight, clinging like someone starving for warmth.

The kernel part of me that I'd managed to harden against her over the years cracked helplessly open, tender to rawness.

I curled my fingers around her bare shoulders. "Thank you for coming back, Mama," I whispered to her, my voice tremolo with tears. "Thank you for being here."

"You're welcome," she murmured, stroking my hair. "My cherry girl, so sweet and warm. But where . . . ?" She drew back a little, alabaster brow creasing. One of the rose tendrils curled against her temple like a fiddlehead, as if it wanted to comfort her. "Where is your sister? Why isn't my hibiscus daughter here?"

I couldn't help it. My face crumpled, and I shook my head, wordless.

When she started to cry too, her tears dripped onto my nape and trickled down my back. Cold as winter rain.

SIX

AIR.

Sun.

Sand.

He needed none of those things to live, of course. Air was simply an indulgence, a tasty trifle like food or drink. Or like the glorious beating of the sun on the skin of his back, stretched tight with dried, caked salt when he finally clawed his way to shore. He sank his fingers into the crumbly grit of wet sand, sighing with pleasure at the feel. The pure luxury of touch and texture, after all these years of numbness and ice. This, too, was something in which to wallow.

He might not even have needed his soul in order to live—he could feel the gaping lack of it, like a hole where a tooth had been;

he could even feel how far it was, impossibly beyond his reach—but he could still enjoy these gifts easily enough.

Eventually he propped himself up on his forearms and lifted his head, to see where he had washed up. A blissfully warm breeze stirred the strands plastered to his face; he scraped a hand over salt-crusted hair to sweep it back, squinting at the wonder of the sky. So many years with his back pinned to the silty dregs of the seafloor, too far down for any proper light or color to reach, yet he'd never forgotten the exact azure of a high summer sky. Blazing with the ferocity of the sun's fiery eye.

He matched it for long moments, gaze to gaze, grinning like a wolf. It would never burn his own eyes to cinders, no matter how it tried. Nothing in this world could best him, neither with brute strength nor cunning.

Besides *her*, of course. She who would never have the chance to entrap him twice.

Blinking away the golden haze of sun, he levered himself onto his knees and surveyed his surroundings with hooded eyes. He'd chanced upon a sheltered little cove, slanting up into a grove of evergreens. He sniffed at the air, nostrils flaring, testing the astringent bite of pine and the clean sweetness of its sap. He might gather handfuls of those needles when he chose to stand, and rub their spice all over his skin to set it tingling. Just as he had done to *her*, once, by the pearly light of dawn. He might—

Then the storm of Lightless whispers crashed over him like a shipwreck, and the black oil in his veins began to churn and writhe.

LOOK WHAT IT IS, it chanted at him, both low and shrill,

a cacophony of velvet pierced with rusted spikes. *LOOK WHAT IT IS LOOK WHAT COMES TO US FOR SUPPING LOOK AT HOW IT HOW IT GLOWS SO INVITING—*

The "it" was in fact a "she," he noted, and the marrow in his bones began to pulse with hunger. A solitary mortal female emerging from the shade-dappled copse beyond the beach. She looked perhaps eighteen or nineteen turns; a woman grown, muscled elegantly through the shoulders like a well-bred mare. Her chestnut hair looped over one shoulder in a wrist-thick braid. Her clothing was so bright it both fascinated and repelled him, in its garishness and how little of her it covered. A marigold yellow scrap clung straining to her torso, dipping low over full breasts and barely skimming her navel, leaving bare strong arms and a sturdy neck. A pair of something like tiny white breeches cut high above her knees, revealing legs as trim and robust as the rest of her.

The cluster of bracelets around her wrist chimed as she lifted her arm to shift the satchel slung by its crook. He could smell her from where he stood, scented with the imitation of some sweet fruit he didn't recognize, cloying in its artifice. And other things too: the yeasty warmth of bread, savory cured meats, and the tang of ripened cheese.

His stomach stirred in response. She had come here to eat, then. To be alone, to enjoy her repast in the sun.

That much they had in common.

A woman of his time would never have done anything half as foolish, to stray so far from the safety of huddled clan. But this was a different time. The Lightless snaking through his veins had whispered sagas of the passing eras while he endured beneath the fathoms, showed him each century's sights even as he lay encased in ice. This new world fairly boiled with its masses. Its denizens soared through the clouds in giant artificial birds, and other similar contraptions ferried them over the dirt at speeds unlike anything he could have conceived of on his own. They spoke to each other across unimaginable distances, words hurtling through air and somehow arriving safely on the other side. And their dwellings stabbed ruthlessly at the sky, sharp and brilliant as stalagmites.

There would be so much to claim here. So much over which to lay dominion. So much on which to sup.

It would be very good to start with this girl.

He was on his feet and halfway to her before she even saw him.

The moment the danger struck her was even sweeter than expected. It crossed her face like a shadow, a bank of clouds rolling in to mask the sun. He could imagine what she saw as her wide eyes flickered over him. His corded hair, matted and tangled to the small of his back. His body, birth-bare and powerful as the day that he'd been cast under—the Lightless that sustained him would tolerate no weakening of their vessel's flesh—with thick black circles tattooed around his arms, from wrists to shoulders. Rings of ink, shot through with branching lines like lightning strikes, and stippled with a flurry of starbursts and dots.

The inked language that had opened him to the Lightless like a portal, and bound his spirit, soul, and form to them for eternity and beyond.

Whatever this girl made of him, he doubted it filled her with comfort.

She could have fled; she had time to at least stage an attempt. He would have run her to ground if she had, of course, but futility rarely prevented prey from at least attempting flight.

Instead, uncertainty and fear chased each other back and forth over her face, across features that were bright and pleasing if not precisely pretty. By then he'd drawn close enough to trace the faint freckles on her nose, a smattering like pollen between clear and clever brown eyes. Yet still she stood waiting for him, though he could see a slight shifting in her stance. Hips dipping as she shifted her weight to one leg, leaving the other light and limber, hands curling into loose fists at her sides.

Amusement rilled through him, alien after its long absence, more welcome than chilled wine. Perhaps this little doe fancied herself a horned buck. Perhaps she styled herself after the warriors of her clan.

And then she tilted her head and spoke to him, lifting a hand in question.

The words were garbled nonsense, no language he'd ever heard—at least before they filtered through the viscous lens of the Lightless in his mind. His constant companions fell upon the words like carrion birds, gnawing away the useless flesh of sound and leaving only the clean skeleton of meaning behind.

"Are you hurt?" she was saying to him. "Do you need help?"

If the rest were anything like her, this new world was much

softer than it had any right to be.

Smiling, he advanced on her.

"I need no help, little sweetling," he replied in his own tongue, and he could see her fear finally catch a proper hold, like brushfire breathing oily smoke. "But a powerful many years have passed over me since my last sup. And I do need all that light you hold."

She couldn't have understood him, but whatever she heard in his voice must have been warning enough. She whirled on one fleet foot, preparing to launch herself back into the trees.

But she was just a girl, and he the living dark.

He caught her easily by that thick, healthy braid—marveling at its density as it slid silky through his fist—and with a brutal yank whipped her back against his chest. Her bracelets flashed silver as she flung up a hand to fend him off. Through his eyes, the moment stretched languorously long, and he had ample time to count the little dangling charms. A kitten, a ribbon folded into a loop, and round, twin somethings the Lightless called *boxing gloves*.

Then he snaked an arm around her to pin down her own flailing arms, leaving her time for one shrill shriek before he clamped his other hand over her mouth. For a moment he simply held her as she strained to break free, her panting breaths damp against his palm, her skin sun-warmed from her walk. She felt so sweetly female, curves and softness merged with muscle. With his cheek pressed against her hair, he could finally smell true skin and sweat beneath the miasma of perfume.

It reminded him of Mara, and for a savagely bitter moment he wondered if he would ever shed the memory of her scent.

"Shh," he murmured to the struggling girl. "It won't hurt like anything you fear."

Brushing her earlobe with his lips, he exhaled a long, slow breath. Borne along it, black tendrils of smoke extended like inky tentacles, quivering with hunger as they quested the air.

Then they plunged into the whorl of her ear, and the Lightless began their gnashing feast on this woman's assorted joys.

She loved to dance, he saw; she loved to spar. Those *boxing gloves* that swung in miniature around her wrist were made to protect the fine bones of her fists, as she jabbed and struck with fierce abandon. She brought stray cats home whenever she found them, made them her own or found them other homes. And at night and in the early morning, when the water was the coolest, he tasted how much she loved to swim.

She was no saint, this girl, as no one was. Searching deeper, he found a baser kind of love, for rumors she invented and then fanned gleefully to life.

In the meantime, the Lightless had ramped up their all-consuming clamor, until his head felt full of hordes of bats shrieking for more, and yet more still. But he was them, and they were him; to nourish them was what he wanted, just as much as they demanded it. He tipped the girl's slack head back, unresisting, until he could angle his mouth over hers. Parting her lips into something like a kiss to let the Lightless surge madly down her throat.

Then the culmination of the feast began.

The faces of her beloveds were eaten, one by one. The joy she took in anything, from cool drinks to flushed, impassioned couplings, was chewed and crunched and swallowed whole. He and his companions cracked her soul open wide, and like the jellied marrow from a bone, sucked out all its light.

And with that, she was wholly snuffed.

The Lightless left her in a snaking rush, coiling back into his mouth and settling, sated, into his blood. Full to nearly swooning, he released the girl, turned her around to face him. She swayed on her feet but didn't fall, though her jaw hung slack and her eyes drooped heavy-lidded. Her braid had unraveled into wisps and waves, and her face gleamed slick with the first wash of tears she'd cried, while she'd still been capable of shedding tears.

In body, she remained alive and hale—as much so as any other mindless, starving thing. But there was no soul left where she had been.

He tipped her chin up until her blank gaze met his, only because the angle demanded it. Dark blots swam across her eyes, jetting from one to the other like black jellyfish.

"It was just as I said, was it not, my sweet and salty Vera?" She'd loved her own name, too—it meant *faith*—and so now it belonged to him along with everything else. "What's lost is lost. And if I lied about the hurting, at least you won't suffer the burden of the memory." He patted her cheek, fitting his thumb to where her favorite dimple showed when she smiled. She would not smile anymore, but that was as it should be. He remembered exactly where it had been. "Now let's see if you'll break some of that bread with me, and share a nibble of your fine meat and cheese."

SEVEN

Iris

"SO WHAT DO YOU CALL ALL THIS?" I SWEPT MY FREE HAND out to indicate the sandstone cliffs and buttes that hunched over the shimmering boneyard around us. My other hand was knit loosely through Fjolar's. I'd found that as long as I maintained skin-to-skin contact with him, I could walk his world comfortably without being overcome by it.

Fjolar didn't like it, and that was a savage little satisfaction in itself. On the one hand, it galled him to have to tend to my frail mortal self when I wasn't even properly filling the role he'd brought me here to perform. I might have given him the single gift of those bloomed bones, but even that had drained me quickly. I'd lost his bright smile almost as soon as I won it, once the bloom withered away.

On the other hand, he still enjoyed touching me. Every once in a while, he'd slip up, forget himself, and lightly sweep his thumb over my knuckles as we walked, before remembering what a dull disappointment I was turning out to be and nearly dropping my hand in a snit.

What was worse, even with the full knowledge of all that was wrong here, and despite my forcefully banked fury at him, I couldn't thwart the slight surging in my belly toward his touch.

But that was all right, I told myself, quelling jabs of guilt. Whatever I betrayed while I was here wouldn't count if it meant he kept talking to me, even if grudgingly, showing me the true workings of this world until I could find my own way out.

I had to do this. I *had* to be the courtesan I would have been anyway, to find a way to free myself. Luka would understand. He would.

"It's called Wadi El Hitan," Fjolar replied, startling me out of my thoughts. "The Valley of the Whales. And *I* didn't call it that; that's its proper name. Where you come from, it's in Egypt, a hundred miles or so south of Cairo. It's where whales lost their legs, where they turned from creatures that walked the dust to ocean-dwellers, eons ago."

I scoffed. "There's no way a place on earth looks like this. Everyone would know."

His mouth quirked a bit, eyes glinting cobalt. "Well, I took some artistic license, of course. I picked the best of it for this replica, and chose what kind of sky I thought you'd like best above it. Was I somehow wrong, yet again?"

"No," I murmured. "You weren't. Bones that don't make sense—but do now that you've explained it—and under a sky as impossible as this? It's perfect."

It was. I couldn't have asked for a better kind of morbid.

"I thought you might think so. Do you remember the bone nest?"

I hadn't thought about the nest for years, but as soon as he mentioned it, the memory sprang so vivid it might have been made yesterday. Lina and I had been fourteen or fifteen, maybe, roaming around the little bayside park across the street from our house. That day, we had been foraging for ferns, leaves, and early spring buds. Before I took them to the studio to diagram the fractals they would become in glass, we liked arranging the plants together based on ikebana designs we found online. It was always a stealth operation between us; Mama interpreted any striving toward Japan as a frantic squirming away from her.

I was picking through a still-frosted viburnum shrub, my cheeks glowing with cold—that winter had been unusually chilly and lingering for Cattaro, hanging over the city like a misty hand—when I found it. A nest had tumbled down from one of the surrounding trees, dislodged by a gust, and had tangled with the base of the shrub. Gingerly, I picked it out. It was brittle to snapping from cold, and would have dusted apart like dried flowers from anything but the lightest touch.

Somehow, the speckled eggs inside hadn't shattered in the fall. And twined through the bramble of grasses, twigs, and caked mud, tiny bones held the structure together like a truss. Some were sharp and slender as toothpicks, and others had the rounded edges of what might once have been minute, hollow skulls lined with little teeth. I couldn't tell what small animal they had come from. But seeing them there, part of the nest's essential fabric, chased away the chill. Even as I acknowledged how morbid it was—and kind of cheesy, even—to be so happy to hold the dead nest in my numbed hands, I couldn't help my joy.

Lina had come to lean over my shoulder then. "Ooh, Riss," she breathed. "Do you think the eggs are still alive? We could take them home. We could wrap them—"

"No," I broke in. "I shouldn't have disturbed it. Let's leave it all right here."

Lina had squinted at me, skeptical; I'd never been the one to let scruples get in the way of bringing something scavenged home. But I didn't want to find out if the eggs were alive. Because they almost certainly weren't, and knowing for sure would have burst the moment's fragile magic. It was the potential of it that gripped me, the beauty of new life cupped inside a cradle knit from death.

"How do you know about that?" I whispered to Fjolar, my throat thick with swallowed tears for that moment, for my missing sister. "I never told you that."

For just a heartbeat, his eyes lingered over my features in that heated way I remembered from when we'd met. "I know many things about you that you never had to say out loud. More than anyone else could know."

"So does that mean"—my cheeks flared—"does that mean you could read my mind before? When we were connected?" An even worse thought occurred. "Can you *still* do it?"

His face iced over in an instant. "Not since you fractured the spell. And even then, it wasn't like I had some script of you. But I could see you, like a collage, or a mosaic of the images that had shaped your mind over the years. There was so much more in there, of course, but I sifted for what I needed to help me build the perfect world for you." He snorted scornfully. "For all the good it's done either of us."

So much more in there, of course. It made me want to unwind my fingers from his—the idea of him roving through my mind like a child with grubby fingers, as if he had the right to be there. Like an invader, or a colonizer.

"And what about Malina?" I asked, trying to keep my voice even, as if the question stemmed from simple curiosity rather than revulsion. "Did you do the same to her?" Somehow, the idea of him rummaging through my sister's thoughts offended me even more, knowing how she had felt about him from the start.

He shook his head, and I relaxed a fraction. "She was the one who caught my notice first, when she fell in love," he said. "But when I came to find you both, she was already spoken for. I could have had her anyway—if I had chosen her, the spell would have ousted her earlier love—but I wanted you from the start. Since that silly party, when you tasted like trash brandy and offered to make the Christmas lights into a galaxy for me." He cast me a barbed glance through pale lashes. "Formalities needed to be observed, but you were always the one I planned to choose."

I couldn't help softening slightly at that—until I remembered the cleaving between me and Malina, when we believed the choice of which of us would be sacrificed was truly ours to make. The pounding exhilaration and driving terror of the contest Mara had put us through when we couldn't decide. The look on my sister's face the morning she'd found me on the beach, spent and shivering from having given Fjolar too much of what he'd asked for.

And the unselfish way Luka had offered himself to me, the mutual claiming of each other that night in the forest. I'd only started learning what it felt like to love Luka before Fjolar tore me from him. But if I wanted to see him again—to have him back, and my sister by my side—I needed to muffle the rising mutiny inside me.

I forced my shoulders to relax, smoothed my face into earnest openness. "I might not like the way all this was set up, that's true. But I *do* like knowing you would have picked me regardless, and spun all this glory up for me. And I . . . I know I'm being a burden, but I'm getting better, I think. And I'd love to see more. Will you show me?"

The fawning, he liked. His eyes lit like candles sparked to life in a dark room, reined-in excitement spreading over the devilishly stark, handsome lines of his features. So that was what it took to wield him. Lies, half lies, and the heart note of a pure truth.

The same things he had done to me, I realized with a start. Well, I could do it too, if it meant he'd trust me enough to tell me whatever he was holding back about this place.

But he didn't trust me, not yet. He turned away, swallowing, wiping at his mouth with the back of his free hand. "Let's go, then.

We'll have to walk to the boundary that leads to the next piece of the realm. If you were here only in soul, I could whisk you along with me with just a thought." His mouth twisted ruefully. "But with you as you are, it'll have to be a trudge."

"Sounds about right, doesn't it?" I teased. "A marathon of trudging: the Iris experience."

Yet despite his casual disdain, I thought I felt his hand tighten slightly around mine.

WITHOUT THE INDICATORS of reliable shadows, clocks, or a mutable sky, it was almost impossible to keep time as we walked through the bone desert. Every moment blurred into the next in smeary succession.

Then the black gates reared up from the sand as if they had every right to be there.

The strangest part was that until the gates leaped out at us, I hadn't seen them in the distance. They should have started out as a speck on the horizon, growing larger as we neared. Instead, they simply hadn't been there at all, right up until they were—wrought-iron both linear and ornate, worked into a gridded framework like a maze, and twined through with ivy vines, elaborate padlocks, and snakes with flicking tongues.

"'These plants can kill,'" I read from the two signs inlaid into each gate, the stark lettering arranged around a leering skull and crossbones. "Fjolar, what is this?"

"A poison garden." I heard the hint of a smile in his voice. He was particularly pleased with himself over this one; I'd have to remember that, I thought sourly. Ply him with compliments on his special poison ivy. "Full of the most unruly, tricky plants—ones that burn and maim and prick, that still the heart and steal the breath. All while looking like such pretty things."

"Oh, I *love* gardens," I breathed. "The deadlier, the better. I hope this one has flowers."

He tipped a wink at me in the daredevil way that still had an effect, deep in the pit of my belly. "Of course it does. Even ones that like to bite, like you."

I don't know what I had been expecting as he swung the gate open—a rusty squeal, maybe, or an ominous creak lifted from one of Niko's favorite horror movies—but instead there was an absolute absence of sound that felt somehow even more unnerving. As if whatever noise the gate should have made had been swallowed by some gaping void.

And over his shoulder, through the opening, I could see the spreading expanse of sparkling sand and jutting bones, a streak of ultraviolet sky pinwheeled with stars. Looking at the mirrored desert beyond the gate made me queasy in a deep-down way, like my mind had been carved up into puzzle pieces and shuffled just slightly out of alignment.

Frowning, I turned to him. "But that's just more of the same."

"Only because we haven't passed through yet. We're still in this piece of the world, not the neighboring one, and on this side of the seam, this piece is all that exists. Ready to see something else?"

"Ready, sir." I snapped off a crisp salute. "Lead the way to the bitey flowers, sir."

He rolled his eyes, fighting a smile. "The mouth on you," he muttered as he stepped through the gate, tugging me behind him. "Almost enough to make me miss the old days."

What old days would those be, I wanted to snap, *the ones where your brides were too force-fed with love to even think of talking back?*

Instead, I swallowed the venom and took a step to follow.

And lost everything with it.

There was no sight, or touch, or smell, or sound. I couldn't even taste the inside of my own mouth. And now that I couldn't feel it in a chest I no longer had, or hear it rushing in ears that were long gone, I knew that I'd always kept the fondest company with the beating of my heart. I had to be *somewhere*, because there was still an "I" to think so in the first place. But beyond the fact that I existed, there was simply nothing else.

I had never imagined such a loneliness.

When Fjolar finally pulled me through—it might have been seconds or lifetimes, or the cascading rush of near-infinite eons later—I was sobbing so hard I thought my heart would burst, and my throat was raw from screams stolen by that void.

For a moment, he watched me guardedly, something close to panic flickering across his face. And I realized, through the tears, that for all the lives he'd culled since the birth of time, he'd likely never seen a living girl cry like this in front of him.

Because of him.

He reached for me cautiously, then when I didn't shy away, drew me up against him until my face tucked into the space between his neck and shoulder. I burrowed into him, far past caring who I took comfort from. I locked my arms around his waist and keened against his chest, gulping in the smell of him. Terrified of lapsing back into nothingness, that awful abyss of total deprivation.

"I didn't think it would be so terrible for you," he said quietly, stubbled cheek pressed to my forehead. "But of course it would. You're not made of what I'm made."

"What . . . was . . . that?" I whimpered. "Where . . . ?"

"Some call it the veil, or space between worlds. Though of course it isn't really a veil, or true space," he said. "I call it the Quiet. It's what I use as thread every time I remake this patchwork kingdom. Without it, the component pieces would slide apart, dissipate. Evanesce back into the ether from which I conjured them."

"So why didn't I feel it when I first came here?" I murmured into his chest. "There was all that light, and that hungry dark somewhere below it, but nothing like that—like that *nothingness*."

"It's because on the way here, I led you through existing fissures in the Quiet." He wasn't going so far as to stroke my back, but his hands were very warm where they rested. And his voice sounded like an apology. "Like wormholes between your world and this one. Here, the Quiet is fine as spider silk, threaded *through* the fabrics of this world—between its distinct pieces, stitching them together. There are no openings in the seams here. No other way to cross it except by plunging through."

"And being in it doesn't make you want to die of being alone?" I whispered, before I thought of how silly that would sound.

He huffed a laugh through his nose. "It just feels like quiet to me. Hence the name. It feels like the closest I ever come to home."

If that felt like home to him, I wondered with an icy shudder, what must it be like inside his head? The roaring silence of a black hole that had eaten every last speck of light? No one ever grieved for black holes, but what would it feel like to crave light so badly, when it was the deepest of your nature to inhale it into nothing whenever it ventured too close? No wonder he had made that deal with Mara. No wonder he had wanted us.

And no wonder Dunja had loved him so hard, even as she scrabbled tooth and nail to keep her nieces from ever taking her place.

He finally ran a hand down my back, and I flinched at his touch in surprise. Mistaking the shock for recoil, he let me go, stepping away so abruptly I nearly stumbled. The delicate bubble of rapport between us burst. "Take my hand if you need to," he offered coolly. "I don't want you falling over. Especially not here."

Nodding jerkily, I laced my fingers through his. A damp breeze like seaside summer lifted my hair, and I liked it so much I tipped my head back and let my eyes slide closed.

Then I opened them, and lost my breath to the sky.

EIGHT

Malina

INSIDE THE ENTRYWAY, MAMA CLUNG TO ME LIKE SOME chilly, overgrown child, refusing to leave my side until Dunja gently peeled her away. "Amrisa wants to see you, Jas, after she examines Mara," she'd said softly, running her fingers through Mama's hair as if the writhing roses didn't faze her. "To see what can be done for you." Mama had glanced at me in that distant, glassy way, both vulnerable and cool, as if asking for permission.

I'd shifted uncomfortably, awkward in this new role. "You should go, Mama. I'll be here if you need me."

They'd drifted off together in a weird sort of symmetry, like opposing chess pieces. Dark and light heads bent together, the black queen and the white.

After that, Izkara herded Niko, Luka, and me back to the room

I'd slept in the one night Riss and I had spent apart before the contest. Niko and I crawled onto the massive four-poster bed and she fell into a fretful doze beside me, curled up under a fur throw. Luka sprawled over the window seat across from us, silently brooding at the dawning sky. The nonstop grind of his worry and longing wore away at me, like a pestle churning a mortar's insides. The sound of it set my teeth on edge enough that I couldn't even graze the edge of sleep.

Not that I would have anyway. I'd gotten so used to always hearing Riss, the shifting rains of her moods. She sounded gentlest at night, right before she fell asleep herself. A soft, lulling patter like a light summer rain. I kept catching myself straining, listening for her. Without her, the song of the whole world sounded off, an orchestra ruined by the twang of a badly stringed violin.

Eventually I got up and wandered to the ornate vanity mirror, a heavy oval held up by two haughty lamias, their serpentine coils supporting the glass. I'd meant to look at the fine detail of the carvings, but I glanced at my own reflection first out of habit. My hair was a storm of curls, and I'd scraped my cheek, maybe during the climb down from Bobotov Kuk. And my eyes—

My *eyes*.

I leaned so close to the mirror that my breath spilled over the glass, heart kicking hard in my chest. One was still almost like it had always been, wintry gray circled by a nearly charcoal line. But the other . . . beneath the familiar, lacy fringe of my dark lashes, it was a deep brown, distinguishable from black only by its contrast with my hair. A color so totally, jarringly alien, it felt as if someone else's eye had been grafted onto my face.

And even the gray eye now held a narrow slice of that same dark brown.

Leaden with dread, I wondered what this new strangeness could possibly mean.

I was still staring queasily into the mirror when a resounding knock came at the door. Niko sprang awake at the sound the way she always did—semi-insane, with all the poise of a baby bird falling out of its nest. "What?" she demanded, unfocused eyes darting between me and Luka, her fine hair mussed across her face. "Who?"

I went to shush her back down, picking caught strands out from between her lips. "Easy, princess. Someone's at the door. You wake up all the way, and I'll go see."

A petite, dark-skinned brunette stood outside, dark ringlets falling over her eyes. I recognized her as Ylessia, Riss's tutor from before the contest. The sprightly aerialist who painted her silk backdrops with exploding skies.

"Azareen. I wanted . . . ," she began, then bit down hard on the words, running her tongue along the inside of her cheek.

"You wanted what?" Luka snapped from his perch. Waiting for Mara to summon us was preying on all our nerves, but he was fraying especially fast. "Either spit it out or get out, will you? If you're going to stick us in here for hours without bothering to tell us anything, at least have the decency to let us be."

Her bowed mouth tightened, eyes narrowing, and my heart juddered as I realized that her irises were mismatched like mine. One was still wolf-gray, but the other had become a warm, amber-shot brown, like sherry. And like my own, the gray eye seemed to be slowly turning amber too.

Whatever this was, maybe it was happening to all of us. I abruptly remembered that Dunja's eyes, too, had seemed somehow different, even back in the star-pricked dark of the mountaintop. With everything else swirling so chaotic around me, maybe I just hadn't noticed the transformation.

"I wasn't speaking to you, you boorish boy-child, was I?" Ylessia retorted. "And if we haven't told you much, it's because most of us know as little as you. Perhaps you might take this gift of time to learn manners in addressing your elders."

"I don't care who you were speaking to, and you're not *my* anything." He turned back to the window. "We wouldn't even be here if it wasn't for you. And Iris wouldn't be—"

"Luka, would you stop?" Niko broke in, now fully awake. Her voice was even raspier than usual with fatigue. "We all know you're ready to rip everything up by the roots to find Riss. So are we, okay? But it's not that one's fault that Riss isn't here. Or not hers specifically, anyway. You're just extra pissed because she dragged you back here from the summit with, like, one of her arms, as if you were half her size instead of the other way around."

I winced at the high, sharp-edged new note of Luka's hurt. Niko could be like that under pressure, sometimes, shooting off words like poison-tipped arrows without caring where they struck. *Stone-cold bitch mode*, Riss had called it, totally oblivious to the irony. It was part of the reason their friendship had always been half a step away from throwing punches.

The regret had reached her face by the time I squeezed her knee in belated warning. But Luka had already launched himself up, heading for the door.

"God, Nikoleta, how can you stand being such a fucking scalpel all the time?" he fumed. "You're old enough to grow a little range."

"Luka, wait—" I reached out to him as he swept by. "She didn't mean—"

He squeezed my hand in passing and spared me a tight half smile, then shoved past Ylessia. "Must be so easy to spit up whatever venom you want," he tossed over his shoulder to Niko as he swung the heavy door open. "Since *Lina's* still here to smooth everything out for you, once you're done."

The door slammed shut behind him like a rifle shot. Niko and I flinched, and even Ylessia's muscular shoulders bunched in response.

"I wanted to apologize to you," she said eventually, once the ringing aftermath of the slam had settled into silence. "To you, Azareen—"

"Malina," I corrected. "I don't want to be called by her name for me."

"Malina, then. I wasn't very kind to your sister, before. It seemed"—she cleared her throat—"it seemed very unfair to me that the two of you should have had what none of us ever had. So much power. Such free rein. And even after being given all that strength and freedom you had to be cajoled, wheedled into the sacrifice by deceit when the rest of us had done it willingly for centuries. As if you were so different, special enough to require such coddling."

I exchanged a wry look with Niko. "I'm not sure where you're going with this apology," I said to Ylessia, "but you've maybe gotten kind of derailed?"

She pursed her pert lips. "It does still smart," she admitted, "to feel so very weak and little next to my own granddaughters so far removed. Everything feels different now, unruled by Mara's love. What seemed to me like self-indulgence in you and your sister appears more like true devotion to each other. And whatever hunts us in this new world—whatever it is she's been keeping from us all this time—I would like to think I can stand with my youngest kin against it."

Looking at her, it was almost impossible to imagine that any comparison to me could ever make her feel little or weak. She might have been a head shorter, but every part of her looked so compactly powerful and poised. And beneath the riot of her hair, her heart-shaped face shone bright with resolve.

Yet I could hear it, the wrenchingly sweet, harp-string pluck of exactly how vulnerable she felt.

"I don't hate you." I couldn't have even if I'd wanted to. "Riss didn't either, I'm sure. It's just . . ."

She shook her head briskly, shining curls springing wildly around her face. "I don't wish to tell you how to feel, either. I simply want you to know that this time around"—her level eyes met mine, amber and gray—"you'll find me by your side."

ONCE YLESSIA WAS gone, Niko made us a pillow nest. I sat between her slim brown knees, leaning back against the softness of her chest. The swooping, dusk-blue swaths of the gossamer canopy above dipped so low they nearly brushed the tops of our heads.

"How are you feeling, pie?" she murmured to me, lifting the heavy upper layer of my curls out of the way so she could start another tiny braid beneath. I loved it when she did that. The deft twist of her fingers and the pull against my scalp calmed me like nothing else. "I don't want to upset you if you don't want to talk. But I can't hear you like you do me. So just tell me what you need."

"I don't even know where to start," I whispered, sinking into her touch. "Nothing sounds right. We know Riss is alive, but I can't stop thinking about where she is, so far away and stuck with *him*. It makes me want to die inside. Then my eyes suddenly turn wrong, and Mama's alive, but . . ."

"Is also a rosebush," Niko finished for me. "I agree that part is problematic."

Despite everything, I burst into hiccupy giggles. "Ah, princess. I love you so much. Have I told you recently?"

"No, and it took you *forever* to say it the first time." She dropped a delicate kiss on my ear. "So feel free to overcompensate."

"Love you, love you, love you," I singsonged, tilting my head back against her shoulder and nuzzling into her silky neck. She shivered a little at my exhale against her skin. She was so ticklish there, in the best way. Beneath the familiar melody of her, the feathery brush of many wings beating together—Niko always sounded like flight—I could hear the slow, drumming stir of her rousing to my touch. It was such a comfort to recognize the sound of her, unchanged, when everything else was coming unstrung so fast. "How's that, for starters?"

"Atonement really suits you, pie. Keep going, if you want."

"Speaking of atonement . . ." I sat up a little. "Should we go find Luka? You were hard on him, princess. He's hurting so much, almost as bad as me. I know you can't hear it, but he used to sound so solid. Like knocking on wood for good luck, if that makes sense. Now he's gone so hollow I can practically hear his heart rattling around like a peach pit. You could be gentler with him, or at least try? He'll crack if you don't."

She sighed so deeply that I lifted along with the rise of her chest. "I know. I'm sorry. I just can't take how angry he is," she mumbled. "He doesn't get to be so pissed that you came back and Iris didn't."

"And how would you have felt?" I asked her softly, twisting around on my knees to face her. Running my knuckles down the nectarine curve of her cheek. "If it had been me who didn't come back to you?"

With a wordless sound of protest, she clambered onto my lap to straddle my thighs. Her hands plunged into my hair, twisting tight, her forehead tilting against mine. She gave me a soft, lingering kiss, grazing my top lip with her bottom, then canted to the other side for the next one. And another, and another, changing the angle each time until my head swam with her scent and nearness. The plush give of her mouth.

I could hear the purring bass thrum of her rising lust, and the piercingly pure, higher notes of her love ringing above it. And I couldn't help but hum it back to her, against her lips.

"You would *never*," she whispered fiercely, dark eyes locked on mine. "You wouldn't *ever* leave me that way. No matter what happened. No matter who tried to take you. Tell me you wouldn't."

"Of course I wouldn't." I wrapped my arms around her sparrow waist and flipped us, taking her with me. Her hair fell around us like a warm curtain drawing closed. "And I can show you exactly why."

She smiled at me, close-lipped and so sweet. "Let's see you try. And for the record, I think your eyes are gorgeous this way too."

Then the knocker fell against the door again, in three sharp raps.

AMRISA'S CHAMBERS WEREN'T what I expected. While the rest of the chalet was shamelessly opulent, her rooms were nearly spartan. Airy and sparse, everything in white, or steel, or glass. All tastefulness and restraint, flooded with the light of the bright day outside.

Despite the exasperation zinging off her like an ungrounded current, Amrisa herself was stunning—full-gleamed first tier, Mara's actual daughter. I'd noticed her before, but she'd kept to herself more than the others. She had the darkest skin I'd ever seen, a deep inky black with almost purple undertones. Like night still clinging to the violet tide of dusk. It glowed against her one-shouldered lavender dress, as if it gave off its own deeper spectrum of light. Her shifted eye was nearly as black, and her hair was piled into a heavy, complicated coil on the top of her head. It balanced the impossible delicacy of her profile—plum cheekbones, pillowed lips, a pointed chin like—

"Could you stop staring at your great-grandma like that, pie?" Niko said tartly, under her breath. The song of her beating wings veered toward ruffled, in warning. "You look like you're composing odes in her name. *Someone* might get the wrong idea."

I looked away from Amrisa, chagrined. She really had almost been enough to distract me from Mama, who sat on a cushioned examination table with her glazed eyes fastened on me. Though the roses never stopped their crawling, her form beneath them seemed unnaturally still.

Dunja leaned against a corner of the room, slim arms crossed over her chest and one dainty ankle over the other. Her glossy, snowy hair draped over one shoulder like a pelt. Even that casual pose seemed on the brink of movement, vibrating with pent energy. And now that I knew to look for it, I saw her eyes *had* changed, just like mine. One had turned a bold sapphire blue, and a dazzling thread of the new color had already spread to her gray eye.

"I tried my best with her, baby witch," she said to me, as if Mama wasn't even in the room, her delicate jaw set tight. "But she wouldn't let Amrisa touch her unless you were here too."

So that explained Amrisa's annoyance. She clearly wasn't used to being thwarted.

I also caught an odd, faint jangle of something like hurt from Dunja. Hurt and . . . jealousy? Ah, that was it. Her twin needed something, badly. And she wasn't it.

"Lina," Mama said, and my eyes flew to her. It was beyond disconcerting—not only how little she sounded like her former self, but how such a toneless voice could be so forlorn. "Will you come sit with me? Amrisa would poke and prod me, and I—I feel so strange. Everything feels so strange." She broke off into a shuddering gasp. "Except you, my cherry girl. My most beloved thing. If I can't have you and your sister both, will you please come, at least, and hold my hand?"

My insides twisted with helpless sympathy. Maybe she hadn't always been the best mother, or even a very good one. But she was mine, and she needed the best of me now.

I let go of Niko's hand and went to sit with Mama, scooting myself up onto the table next to her without quite touching her. From this close, I could see that her uncanny stillness was an illusion created by the most minute trembling. She was shivering so hard and constantly that it actually blurred her outlines and made her seem too still.

Gingerly, her hand crept onto my leg, and I nearly hissed with cold where she grazed my skin beneath my borrowed skirt. Then I caught her hand, turned it over, and tucked it between both of mine.

Amrisa approached us, her face schooled back to kind briskness. "May I dowse you now, Faisali?" she asked.

Mama gave a single, tight nod, and her fingers curled through mine.

Amrisa closed her eyes and lifted her hands, holding her palms an inch apart as if she were about to pray. That wasn't it, though, I didn't think. I'd never seen any of them pray, for one, and the way she felt sounded more like a calibrating hum. Whatever her instrument was, she was tuning it.

Eyes still shut, she cupped both hands around Mama's face, not quite touching, lifted a hair's-breadth from her skin. As she slowly traced my mother's outlines, something like a silvery sheet of water sprang to life, following her almost-touch. I heard the familiar catch of Niko's breath, and I nearly gasped myself. I'd never seen anything like this. The living water flowed and flickered over my mother in strange patterns—whorling in eddies around the roses' heads, braiding into tangled, transparent ropes that looped over and under each other.

All leading to Mama's chest.

"What are you doing?" I asked in a rapt near-whisper, afraid to break her concentration.

"Dowsing, of a sort," Amrisa replied absently, hands moving like a sculptor's. "Energy is life, and all life energy. I'm looking for your mother's meridians, the flows that sustain her. I can see them this way, and manipulate them for healing. And—"

She broke off, eyes rolling from side to side beneath her lids. "Oh," she breathed, "oh, so *that's* it . . ."

"What is it, daughter?" Mara's tripled burr came from over my shoulder. I hadn't even heard her enter, but now I could sense her behind me. The insistent drumbeat beckon of love. "Tell me what you see."

"She lives off your will, Mother," Amrisa whispered, awestruck, her curled lashes fluttering. "When you wounded her but didn't let her die as she should have, you bound her life to your will. And when the spell was damaged, the force that caused the fracture— the sheer torrent of Lisarah's own will, her infinite bloom—seized

Faisali and hauled her back from the brink."

So it had been Riss who brought Mama back, I thought, astonishment clanging through me. Her magic like electric paddles during cardiac arrest. Except our mother no longer even had a real heart.

"The portion of your will that sheared off and cleaved to Faisali now sustains her," Amrisa continued in the same hushed tones. "A cutting of your mighty will, serving as her heart, her lungs, her blood. While you live, Mother, so will she live. When you die, so will she die too."

The roses. I'd known they were manifestations of Mara's will, just as the wisteria were Iris's. But Mama wasn't the trellis for them to cling to—they were *her* trellis. And I'd been right to think of them as her new veins. They were her new everything, keeping her alive—or something like alive.

No wonder she'd gone so strange. Weird as Dunja, in a wildly different way. Like the glass in Riss's furnace, their humanity had been tempered. Nothing could skim so close to death like they both had and step away unchanged.

And now they were both something else altogether.

"And deeper still . . . ," Amrisa continued, then broke off with a ragged gasp. Her eyes flew open, and she actually staggered back, clapping a trembling, long-fingered hand over her mouth. "I cannot do it, Mother," she whispered. "I cannot touch it. I don't know what it is, and it is too cold to dowse. I have never felt anything like it."

"It is cold," Mama agreed, and I ached at the hollow desolation beneath that bland tone. "And it hurts inside me. It *hurts*."

The emphasis on the last word was almost inaudibly slight. But compared to the flat line of the rest of her timbre, it might as well have been a shriek.

Dunja materialized on Mama's other side in a spectral blur, a pale, small hand landing on her sister's shoulder. Petals thrust up through the gaps between her fingers. "What is it? What's wrong with her?" she demanded, speaking to Mara, who'd moved to stand in front of us. Barefoot but wrapped in layers of cashmere, soft suede, and fur, she looked not just better but completely restored. All her visible skin shone smooth and burnished bronze, like it had never known a single burn. And her hair was thick and sleek, just like it'd been before.

Mara shook her head, confusion skating across the broad, glacial planes of her face. Her eyes had shifted so that one was black as obsidian. "It cannot be," she murmured, as if to herself.

"*What* can't?" Dunja pressed.

"It should be inside me, not Faisali," Mara continued, as if Dunja hadn't said anything. "If it is not, why have I not warmed entirely?"

Neither of them was even talking to me.

Sick to death of being swept to the side, as if explanations didn't involve me even when I was sitting next to my own mother, I turned to Mama and listened hard. I knew what she sounded like. If something was inside her, I would hear it.

She looked back at me, wide-eyed. The mournful, fluting trills that sang of Jasmina, the broken remnants of who she was, floated toward her surface. But I could still hear that roaring wind beneath it, snatching at them. And the longer I listened to it, the louder it grew. Whistling and whining, keening like wolves in winter, their cries muffled by wild flurries of tumbling snow.

I knew what that was. Seasons had a sound, a melodic motif to them. The way people smelled the changing of the seasons in the air—the tang of springtime green or the must of dying leaves—I heard them before they came.

And I knew which one was inside my mother.

"It's winter," I broke in, my voice faint and upturned with shock. "Isn't it? It's *winter* inside Mama. How is that *possible?*"

Mara's ancient eyes turned to rest on me. Like always, I could actually feel the weight of her regard. "It must have come from me," she said simply. "Before the spell fractured, I held an immensity of it inside me. The true essence of winter, as much as I could stand. When my death-son took your sister, he held up his end of the bargain—perhaps just enough to salvage a piece of the spell, to retain a slice of winter. And when the spell began to fracture, it must have traveled along the easiest conduit there was"—her eyes shifted to Mama—"the cords of will connecting me to you, Faisali. And there, in you, it lodged. Because we are bound together, I can still feel its remnant, but what is left of it is in you now."

Moving by instinct, I turned toward Mama and pulled her closer. Drawing her tight into a hug as I hummed the toasty contentment of palms out over a beachside bonfire. Her dark feathery eyelashes fluttered with the relief of that brief memory of heat.

"Get it out of her," Dunja ground out, danger gathering in her face like a thunderstorm on the horizon. She might have become mostly a thing that loved Death, but she was also a thing prone to fury, I thought. It reminded me of Riss, the quick wick of her temper. Maybe she'd inherited it from our aunt, before dancing for Death had burned out everything but Dunja's extremes. "Call it back, melt it, snuff it out. I don't care how you do it, old mother, but I won't let you torment her any further."

"Please, sorai," I forced out between the notes of my warming song. I'd call her that, if she fixed my mother. I'd call her anything she wanted. "Just chase it out of her, please?"

"I cannot do that for you, fledgling, or for her," Mara said, and all three of her voices were gentle at different registers. "She might not survive it. And even if she did, we need the winter left inside her. It must be why *he* is not upon us already. That wintry vestige continues to weigh on him like chains. And you can see it in your own spell-struck eyes, can you not? One has thawed already. And the other does too, but slowly. It is so with all of us."

I raised a trembling hand to my own eye, as if I could touch the altered color. So that was what it meant.

Our eyes were an hourglass of ice instead of sand, counting down the moment that Mara's monster would come home to roost.

I listened closely to her for the telltale discord of a lie, but everything she said rang sibilant with truth. And I remembered the legends we'd read about Mara's many names, what the myths had made of her over the millennia. Goddess of nightmares, of death—and of winter. No wonder we'd only been able to scorch her surface with our makeshift spell, the one we'd cast with Dunja on the bank of the Black Lake.

What was a lit match against a winter gale?

And as Mama shuddered next to me, I wondered—if this was only a slice of what had been in Mara, how had *she* ever borne it? And why?

"Why?" I asked out loud. "Why would you do something like that? Agree to so much cold, for so long?"

"I did not merely agree to it," she said, lifting her chin to an imperious height. "I willed it so. It was needed to right the wrong that I had caused." As if she could hear the rest of my litany of questions, she turned toward the door. "Come now," she commanded, inclining her head. "The time has come to tell."

I slid off the table to follow her, reaching back for Mama's cold hand. Dread weighed inside me at her touch, heavy as swallowed lead. Because I hadn't heard just winter, either. Even deeper down than that, and much more distant, there had been something else— an echo of what I'd heard the first time I'd seen Mama newly risen. That rasping, hissing darkness, something hungry and venomous.

The sound of whatever Mama's winter was working to suppress. The noise of the thing slithering toward us all.

NINE

Iris

IT WAS NIGHT IN THIS DIFFERENT SECTION OF THE KINGDOM too, but stripped of stars and the boneyard's unnatural purple light. Instead, we stood beneath a million moons: waxing, waning, and dark; full and nearly full. Some were streaked with ghostly swipes of clouds, others circled by moonbow halos. The tinge of the sky around each was subtly different, as if all these had been culled from separate nights before being threaded together to dangle above us like a child's lunar-phases mobile.

Like the kind Lina and I had slept under in our shared cradle, another handmade gift to Mama from Čiča Jovan when my sister and I were still so little.

"Is this because of the mobile?" I asked Fjolar, and even I could hear the wonder in my voice, limned over the dense ache of missing my sister.

"It is, flower." His tone was the warmest I'd heard from him since I landed here, I noted with a stab of satisfaction. It was doing its work, the nymph version of myself that I was painting for him. Bit by tiny bit, he was thawing for me. "And also because I wanted you to be able to see this garden as it should be seen, moonlit and under cover of the night."

I managed to peel my gaze from the orb-and-crescent splendor of the sky, enough to take in the bower around us. We stood on a pebbled, winding path, hemmed in and overhung by plants left to grow largely unfettered. At the center of the garden, if you could call it that, a massive, ornate sundial loomed—its gnomon a caduceus with a serpent wound around it, striping the base with twisted shadows from the crisscrossed light of the many moons. Glossy leaves and blossoms stirred in the warm, summery breeze, and the entire garden hummed with that rush of air running like fingers through swaying, rooted living things. The air smelled both sweet and astringent, from layer draped over layer of poison-laden scent.

And the flowers grew everywhere in a tangled profusion, dripping down the walls and weighing down the shrubbery, creeping up Roman columns that didn't seem to lead to anywhere, crawling into long-abandoned, crumbling birdbaths and dry fountain beds. The blossoms were all a slightly muted rainbow of color, but the bright flood of moonlight made their shades much more vibrant than they should have been at night.

"It reminds me a little of our garden back home," I said through a sudden well of tears. "The one behind Mama's house, where we used to sit when she still let us eat the moon with her." What had happened to her, with the half breaking of the spell? Had she died fully, without either me or Lina by her side? I bit the inside of my cheek at the thought. I couldn't mourn her, too, not now. It was just too much.

"I know. Though the closest you would have come to what grows here would have been your oleander tree."

"'These plants can kill,'" I repeated. "Is this place real too, then? Like the bone desert?"

"Again, it's my own take of something real—but tweaked for your pleasure," he said with an acerbic twist and a flick of a glance in my direction, in case I'd forgotten all the trouble he'd gone to for me. "There's a garden like this one at Alnwick Castle in Northumberland, planted by a very twisty duchess. It's full to brimming with poisonous plants, over a hundred different kinds. Laurel, hellebore, datura, nicandra. Most are poisonous from root to berry, flower to stem."

"Are all those here?"

"Some, and many others, too. I chose the prettiest for you. And the real poison garden is much more manicured than this. Can't have its keepers keeling over from stray tendrils." He gave my hand a tug, waiting for me to step closer to him. "But you'll be fine, as long as you don't try to sniff things and we keep to the path. And as long as you stay by me."

"Do I detect ulterior motives at work?"

That startled a low scrape of a laugh out of him. "It wasn't *foremost* on my mind, no."

"Oh, if you say so." I slid my hand free of his and took his elbow instead. "Why don't you show me some of your favorite ones?"

We wandered together down the path, pausing every few feet so Fjolar could introduce me to a new specimen. He touched things heedlessly to show me what they were, unfurling curled-up leaves and splaying petals that could have melted his skin like tallow. Even when the giant hogweed in his hand—frilly umbrellas of white flowers like Queen Anne's lace, above hairy, purple-splotched stems—should have given him blisters, blinded him, and scarred him. Even when the blue clusters of monkshood perched like butterflies on their green spears had roots so poisonous they could kill an entire village if steeped in its drinking well.

But he wasn't human. None of them could leave their mark on him.

"I saw a man eat six naked-lady bulbs once, on a dare," he said, fanning out the blossom's delicate pink petals, shaped a little like a stargazer lily. "His 'mates' thought the name was just hilarious raunch, had no idea what flower it was. It's beautiful and common enough, easy to grow and easy on the eyes, but it's one of the nightshades, amaryllis belladonna. Lays waste to the heart when eaten." He flicked both eyebrows up, gave me a roguish twist of a smile. "A lot like any lady's love, naked or otherwise. He collapsed ten minutes later, twitching, foaming at the mouth. They thought he was playing with them, until he died."

He led me past foxglove, hemlock, and bloodroot, telling me

how each could heal or kill—though mostly kill—and it struck me that he knew because he had seen every single instance of death brought about by these pretty poison vessels. This garden was full to bursting of his instruments.

And it was clear how much he loved them.

"Do you enjoy it?" I said to Fjolar, tugging us both to an abrupt stop so I could turn and look up into his face. "When people die? Or animals, or anything, I guess? Does it feel good to you somehow?"

All expression slid from his face in an instant, leaving his features stark and stunning, empty of emotion. I thought to myself, *his death mask*, before it occurred to me that he was always so much more startlingly handsome when he was keeping some part of himself hidden from my reach. The opposite of how I felt whenever I looked at Luka's open, tender face. I had always been able to see him feeling, watch thoughts drifting over his face like clouds streaking across a clear sky.

And yet. That sense of the buried unknown that followed Fjolar like a shadow, the slippery, delicious danger of it. Even when the spell took hold and bound me to him, I wouldn't have put it past myself to like something like him for its own sake, too.

"And I know you can't tell me details, no 'great truths,'" I went on. "I'm just curious what it *feels* like, to be you."

The breeze riffled through his pale eyelashes, and his eyes narrowed like a wolf's. For a moment, the focus of his gaze seemed to fall infinitely far away. Unimaginably distant from me. "It feels like being everywhere at once," he said. "Perched on the shoulder of every dying thing. Living in the lungs of every creature drawing its final breath. No one's asked me that before, you know. None of her daughters."

"Well, they wouldn't, would they? It doesn't seem to me like much talking ever happened here." This was broaching risky territory; if I ventured too far, I might blunder into the quicksand of his irritation and suffocate in it. But I had to pry him open further, enough that he'd be willing to tell me things that mattered. "Not enough time for it, what with the wedding contest, all the honeymoon years, and then the obligatory dying of the bride to make room for the next one."

He grimaced at that, baring those bright teeth. "You make it sound so . . . shallow. When it was the opposite of that."

I shrugged. "It was what it was: lots of long and very beautiful one-night stands. But I don't think it was ever more than that for you before my aunt, and even Dunja was willing to dance herself dead for you. Then all of a sudden, you've got me. The nuisance of my body, all these questions I have for you . . ." I gave him a wicked, impish smile—and realized with a shock that I couldn't be sure it wasn't at least partly real. "It's almost like we're getting to be *friends.*"

He chuckled through his nose, lifting my hand to press a kiss to my knuckles without breaking our gaze. His lips grazed the sensitive skin between my fingers, and a tingle spiraled through me like a whirlybird seed. It was the first time he'd touched me in such a purposeful, romantic way since I'd come here, and somehow, even with everything I was playing at, it made me catch my breath.

"It is taking some getting used to," he admitted. "I'd gotten very comfortable having everything just so, exactly as I liked it. Easy, you could call it. But I like that you ask me things." His blue gaze was so unwavering I could feel that initial tingle flare into an ember in the pit of my stomach. As if he sensed my response, he dropped his head and angled his lips to mine, close enough to feel the sweep of his breath without sealing it into a kiss. His pale hair brushed my cheek—whiskey and smoke—and my insides swam, giddy. "Maybe I want a friend like you."

"Do you really?" I murmured back.

"I said 'maybe,'" he retorted with a wry twist. "And I wouldn't call your body a nuisance, flower girl."

I pulled back with a laugh and tipped my chin up at the sky. "Oh, that's half nice of you. Now, take a look."

His eyes followed mine, the tendons in his neck cording in a very appealing way. Above us, I had drawn down the moons into a carousel of waxing and waning, fingernail crescents, full and gibbous. Circle within circle, a sky full of moon-shaped fairy lights. I set them rocking up and down like carnival horses, and between them I flung up fountaining explosions of the rosy mountain laurel and snowy veratrum that spilled over the garden's walls.

Under my fireworks, his face glowing vivid with delight, he slid one hand into my hair and dipped down to kiss me.

I shouldn't have let it happen; this was far too much to give him. He was a thief, a lovely liar, an unrepentant user of my kin.

But I found I couldn't help the fervor with which I wanted it. I caught my breath against his mouth; he tasted like I remembered from home, but even better and so much *more*, shocking sweetness and heat along with the softness of his tongue. His lips were gentle and yielding against mine, but I could feel the force of his grip around my waist and at my nape, and I curled into him like ivy creeping over slabs of stone.

I didn't understand how I could want him at all, after everything he'd done to me. It shouldn't have been possible to reconcile so much rage with so much wanting. All the flirting wasn't *me*; it was a role I had chosen for myself so I could find my way home. I knew that.

But he felt so goddamned undeniably *good*.

His hands slid down my sides and over my backside, and I could feel him cup my thighs in readiness to pick me up. Anticipating the lift, I tightened my arms around his neck—and then abruptly remembered the last time someone had held me that way.

With my back scraping roughly against a pine trunk and my legs locked around a leaner pair of hips, as Luka whispered in my ear how much he wanted me.

I unwound myself from him as if he had caught fire, stumbling back. "I'm sorry. I can't. It's, it's too soon, and—"

Something brushed lightly against my back, and I whirled around in surprise. Massive, trumpeted yellow blossoms yawned at me, glowing faintly in the dark and exhaling scent into my face. I could feel Fjolar's hand grip my shoulder, pulling me away, but it was too late.

In my shock, I'd already gasped.

And drawn a deep, prickling breath of poison directly into my lungs.

I had a moment to consider that this poison smelled rich and sweet, with pinpricks of lemon rind—before my pupils dilated so hard I could actually feel them blow my irises into oblivion. Nausea tore through me, dropped me to my knees onto sharp pebbles. My thoughts scattered wildly, like a flock of birds startled into sudden, shrieking flight. I couldn't hold on to anything for more than a moment—my name, where I was, what even was happening to me. Nothing but the sense of a terrible, impending doom cresting over me like a gargantuan wave, shimmering black and near-invisible against the deeper darkness of the night.

It was going to pull me under. It was going to drown me.

I had never been so terrified in my entire life.

And if I was going to die, I wanted nothing more than my sister.

LINA, I screamed, either aloud or in my mind. I couldn't tell if I could really speak. My mouth and tongue felt lockjaw stiff. For the first time since I had been reeled here, drawn through worlds like a fish dragged by the line, I was terrified and desperate enough to reach for my wisteria.

Before, it had always been because my sister needed me, badly enough that I would split myself open to let the gleam grow out from my center.

Now I was the one who needed her.

The roots of the wisteria were still threaded where I had left them, coiled into a tight ball at my very center. Maybe they always lived there now, my core their sustaining loam. Through blackness and bright bursts of terror, I reached into the wisteria of my will and flung it frantically outward.

Before, my gleam—the infinite bloom, as Mara called it, the imposition of my will over space and time—had always rushed away from me so that I could see it spreading, slender branches forking away and bisecting each other, dripping whorls of pastel blossoms like the most delicate floral monsoon. This time, what I wanted most was to go with them, to be borne along with the rapid budding of their growth. Even as I drew and threw them out and out, I continued clinging to them, feeling the bark imprinting into my palms, the satiny give of the petals I pulped with my grip.

Take me with you take me with you take me with you
Take me to her take me take me to her

And then, there she was.

My sister knelt in an herb garden, her back to an ornate bird-bath and moonlight crowning the spill of her hair. Two silver candles burned on either side of her, and a goblet of dark wine sat in front of her knees. Her mournful face was tilted up at a sky hooked by a crescent moon. I startled at that; the moon had been nearly full when Fjolar took me, I remembered from the nighttime battle with Mara on Bobotov Kuk. And this one had waned down to nearly new.

While what felt like barely a day had passed for me, I was seeing my sister weeks into her future.

It wasn't even the strangeness of it that doused me with icy shock. It was that I'd lost so much time with her already.

Her hands were lifted with palms up; I could see her so clearly that I could trace their familiar lines. She wore a loose, white lacy dress that could have been a nightgown, and looked just like the woodland nymph she'd once sung herself to be for Death. A speared wrought-iron fence circled the garden behind her, and a dense, dim forest loomed above it from behind.

I called to her, or tried to call. It emerged warbling and strange, words suspended in bubbles, like talking underwater. I had the disjointed feeling of being trapped in a lucid dream, as though only part of myself was here. My consciousness, or at least a sliver of it—while the rest of me huddled miserably on the poison garden's floor, curled like a fist around a full-body muscle spasm with pebbles digging into my side.

Her hands dropped and she frowned a little, tensing, as if she heard something in the distance. Then she looked up, and her eyes went wide with surprise. She stumbled to her feet with none of her usual grace.

"Riss!" Her gaze kept flickering to the left and right of my face, as if it couldn't find a solid place to land. I went to take a step closer to her—or merely thought about it, there didn't seem to be a difference—and suddenly she coalesced right in front of me like a ghost.

Judging by her expression, it was more likely me who'd been the ghost.

I tried to touch her shoulder; my hand drifted right through it. She let out a clipped little half scream, her eyes never quite settling on my face. Finally she closed them, hissing through her teeth, her own face clenching with frustration.

"You're everywhere, Riss, in a thousand different broken places. It's so hard to look at you. I can't tell which one you really are."

A thousand different broken places. Whatever part of me the wisteria had brought here looked multiplied to her, and mute. A silent fractal of myself.

I couldn't hug her, and she could barely see me, but I let myself steal just a moment for us both, tipping my forehead right to where it would have met hers if I was really there.

"I miss you so much," she whispered. A film of tears lined her lashes, glinting in the starlit night. "You need to find his soul. Please find it, *please*, there's still time, find it and bring it back—"

Then a horror cascaded over me, a spiked, encroaching dark calling out to me in a ravenous roar. I recognized it instantly, knew it as the black hunger that lived beneath that golden world I'd swum through to reach Fjolar's kingdom. But this time it was so much stronger—this time it felt so dreadfully close. It tugged at me in its familiarity, like some sickening beacon. Like the forgotten memory of a nightmare, the primal terror of terrors, resurrected.

I could feel its thrashing hunger. Not for me—where my body was, I was safe from it—but for my sister. And for Dunja, Mara, and all my coven kin.

And as if the direction of my thoughts determined where I should be, Malina vanished, along with the garden and its birdbath and tidy rows of herbs. I didn't feel any sense of movement; it was as if I stood still, and the world around me shifted. When it rushed to a halt, I found myself in the unbroken dark of a mountainside forest, deeper than the moon could reach. I'd never have been able to see anything with my real eyes, but the part of me that was here saw perfectly.

Between the pines, a man straddled a mossed boulder as if it were a throne, his hair long and loose and wild around bare shoulders. He was striking in a rough-hewn way, with brazen bones that made me think of ages long gone. The dark around him writhed like vipers, striking at the air, and thick, crude tattoos ringed his powerful arms.

A throng of people surrounded him, some on the ground, others crouching like animals in the trees, and even hanging from the branches. There was something worse than wrong about the way they held themselves.

If I'd brought my body here with me, my skin would have crawled right off it at the sight of them.

And behind them, even deeper in the trees, enormous things darker than the fabric of the night flailed too many limbs and shrieked.

The man smiled wide at the sound, his face lighting like a fond father's. "Gather, sweetlings," he called out. "Gather, pets. Gather closely round! The time for storming almost comes."

One of the dark things bugled so eagerly, I tried to clap a phantom hand over my mouth before remembering that I wasn't really here.

The man laughed with both pride and glee, and lifted a finger. "Not yet, not yet, but very soon. Later tonight. We are on the cusp of supping, and this time we are strong—the little spy-witch has broken our last shackles. There will be such meats, and so much light to spill. Enough bright, shining witches to sate us, enough that we may sup our fill."

I shouldn't have understood him—the words I heard weren't the ones he spoke—but I knew what he meant. What spy-witch was he talking about? I thought frantically. Who—

He froze abruptly, cocking his head like a bird of prey. His eyes roved over the forest, and fell unerringly on me, narrowing, then glinting with something like lust turned inside out. And if I had thought I'd been afraid before, in the poison-garden flower's thrall, I'd never even dreamed what it meant to be truly afraid.

And then, like a rubber band stretched far past its limit, the wisteria of my will snapped me back.

TEN

Malina

"THERE ARE MANY OTHER REALMS THAN THIS," MARA SAID. "I suppose that is a good place as any to begin."

We were all gathered in the ballroom, or what they called the Great Hall. Mara's two hundred or so coven daughters, and the three of us. Niko sat beside me, with Luka to her left, still half glowering. She'd apologized to him before we went in, but contrition wasn't really my princess's strongest suit. And "I shouldn't have said that to you, I know. I'm sorry Riss's gone, I really am. But could you stop being an asshole now?" wasn't prime apology material even in the best of times.

Normally Luka knew how she was and took it in stride. But we were so far past "normal" that it sounded like a nonsense word, something that had shed its meaning after you said it to yourself too many times.

If I had any doubts about that, all I had to do was look behind me and meet my mother's green-and-gray eyes through her rose canopy. Dunja sat next to her, watchful, her milk-and-porcelain face a jarring contrast. Every once in a while Mama trailed her fingers down my back, as if to reassure herself that I was still there. And each time, the ice of her touch made me jump.

It was midmorning, but the skylights had been shuttered and all the curtains drawn, blocking out the sun and any prying eyes. The glass and metal ceiling fixtures spiraling down from the eaves were lit again by someone's projected gleam. Last time we were both here, Riss had fractaled them into a domed and spired city from the sky. It had been spectacular, even compared to the passion song I'd sung for Death. A tiny part of me had actually been jealous of how beautiful she'd been. I'd always had the prettier gleam before, but how could my music compare to that brutal splendor?

I'd actually had that thought, while she was saving me. The memory of my own pettiness toward my sister stirred the ache inside my chest to a ferocious pain, an anthill poked with a stick.

This time, the glass encasements above us held a darker tinge. The onion bulbs cupped burgundy orbs so dim that the light they shed was nearly black. And the delicate spheres and storm lanterns swarmed with moths and bloated gray butterflies with heavy, furled antennae. Sooty designs were etched onto their wings.

Despite the hall's airy height, all that dark made it feel shrunk down to the size of some firelit prehistoric cave. Mara presided over the room's center, swathed in leathers and furs, on the black marble dais shot through with amethyst veins. Candles surrounded her like wax supplicants. Pillars and votives, tapers and tea lights, mismatched candelabra dripping tallow. As if she wanted to pull light around herself, a dome against the dark. Wherever it touched her, the candlelight softened the striking edges of her face into the rounded blush of youth and gleamed in almost liquid rivulets along the black flow of her hair.

"Like spokes on a wheel, some are above us and others below," she continued. "For whatever the mortal notions of 'up' and 'down' are worth, in a cosmos unbound by such narrow strictures."

She skimmed her fingers over the candle flames clustered closest around her. They rose up to meet her touch and fused into a fiery arc, a circle of flame spinning around her.

"There are boundaries like this between them," she said, her face beautifully sinister in the revolving light. Cheekbones like spades, and ancient, dark-rimmed eyes beneath heavy brows. A jungle cat that had prowled too close to a campfire. "Meant to remain uncrossed by those on either side. 'The veil,' the mortals sometimes call it, though it is nothing so sheer and flimsy as the word implies. But strong as it is, it remains fallible, forked through with fissures and passages. Which can become conduits when in the presence of a powerful will."

She beckoned the circling fire to her. It rushed eagerly into her hand and curled into a molten sphere above her palm, flicking out licks like lizard tongues. From there she drew it out like taffy, then whirled it into a cat's cradle around her fingers—before condensing and dancing it over her knuckles like a magician's coin.

"A will like mine," she said, the fiery coin reflecting in her eyes. "A will that *gleams*. Because it came from a creature born from light and raised in it. One curious enough to find their way to this dim shadow of a place. And tender enough to fall in love with it and thus give rise to our line."

"I'm not saying this is an exact translation," Niko whispered into my ear. "But I think what your great-grandma's trying to tell you is that one of your ancestors probably boned an alien."

I dug my nails in where they rested on her thigh. "Hush, you degenerate," I whispered back, fighting a smile. She always knew when I needed a little light myself. "She'll hear you."

"Yes, *she* will," Mara rang out, that resounding voice laced with tartness. She gave the ball of flame a pointed flick in our direction before twitching it back to her like a feather on a string. "Our Azareen's lover Nikoleta is not entirely wrong. Whoever begat us so long ago would have been lovely beyond reckoning, far past the grasp of human wit. But when names were needed, as they always are, words were made to fit. So when it came to naming something beautiful, bright, and winged—something so clearly *not* from here—a word already existed as if handcrafted for it."

The murmur raced around the room. A single word whispered behind hands and breathed into mothers' and daughters' ears. Looking around at this gathering of women, uniform in their practiced grace, it wasn't even very hard to believe. Shining hair, pure skin, and fine-boned hands folded in laps. Every shape and shade of beauty, their scents mingling into an intoxicating, heady perfume.

Maybe something so like perfection really had been painted from a palette of heavenly design.

But then I thought about Riss and me growing up in Cattaro with Mama. Early mornings of work at the café, sleep still gathered in the corners of our eyes. Days on pebbled beaches so scorching hot we wound up with peeling soles. Years of scabby knees and hangnails, calluses and split ends. Yes, we were beautiful—that much I'd always known, even if Riss hadn't let herself see it. But I couldn't bring myself to believe we were anything other than human at our core.

Mara's eyes landed on me as if she could hear me coming to conclusions. "Of course, it was only a name as good as any other false one. What is the sense in styling something an 'angel' or a 'god,' if it hails from a place where all are gods compared to us? But it was useful in one respect. Where there are things one might call angels, one can expect things like devils, too."

She paused for a moment, tracing a fingernail over the creases of her full lower lip. Despite the thousands of years between them, Mama did the exact same thing when she lost herself in thought. I glanced over my shoulder to find her already watching me, her eyes glittering in the dim. Not the way eyes usually glistened, but closer to crystalline, like something with facets.

On second thought, after everything I'd seen, what did I know about what we were? Or about what being human even meant?

"He did not look like a devil when he came," Mara murmured pensively, dragging my attention back to her. "But then I suppose they never do, to start. We had been hearing the strangest things for months, brought by survivors fleeing their lowland villages. We took them in but thought them ignorant foreigners, and dismissed their tales as outlandish fears. The Greeks may have called us all *Illyrioi*, as if we were one people, but we were far from one; many clans scattered over the lands, with different customs, different tongues."

It shouldn't have been such a revelation, but it was. I'd read about the Illyrians in schoolbooks, the collection of Indo-European tribes that lived in the ancient Balkans. And somehow that name made Mara's age shockingly real in a way nothing else had. I'd known she was over four thousand years old, that two hundred generations separated me from her. But for the first time I fully felt the depth of the chasm of all those years between us.

"My people were the Ansannae," she went on. "My line—*our* line, from mother to mother—had ruled them for centuries. When it came my turn, no other clan we knew of boasted a leader of my ilk. We had our gods, but the times we called upon them were few and far between. Why do so except in obeisance, when there was no true need? My people wanted for nothing while they had me."

She sounded like a mother when she talked about these people. Her first family, so long dead even their burial mounds must have turned to dust. She would've been a thing apart from the people she led, with so much magic twisting through her blood. But I didn't hear even a hint of aggression or conquering, just that desire to nurture and protect.

Listening to her made me think of Romulus and Remus curled against their wolf mother's belly, sharing her warmth and milk.

"The stories were all the same," she continued. "Villages stormed by a demon king who commanded legions, battalions of black-eyed devils on horseback whose steeds bore the same black eyes. This army withstood hacking, flaying, fire. None of it saved any of the attacked; no defense they mounted did any good. And instead of murdering their victims, the horde somehow consumed their spirits, turning the fallen into their own.

"The few who fled from the scourge made their way to the mountains. To me." She gave a labored sigh, as if remembering weighed on her down to the lungs. "I offered them succor, but they never stayed. They felt our doubt; even then such claims as theirs were not easy to believe. Yet they still dreamed of him, they said. They dreamed that he was *coming*, so they moved, they ran, as if having me at their back might shield them. Perhaps it all would have been different if even one of them had stayed."

Her eyes were so bleak, I could almost see the strata of millennia bearing down on her. Like she might collapse into a buried fossil before she could finish her tale.

"Then a man came in early spring, alone, on a blue roan mare. It had only just turned warm enough for wider foraging. I had two daughters by then, and both Amrana and Amrisa were gone that day, gathering the sweet cattail reeds that grew by the glacier lake. It was some small blessing, perhaps, that he saw me first rather than them. I was past thirty myself, at least ten years his elder. Any other woman of the tribe would have waded well into old age by then. But the other-blood that runs through our line had kept me hale and beautiful.

"He sought an audience with me, offered himself into my service as a cunning man. He was the last of his tribe, he said, from a settlement not so far from us, down in what is now the rich, green Zeta Plain. The rest of his people had fallen to demons and then risen again to join their ranks, and he had been left to wander, grief-struck and alone."

She let her head drop low, her chin nearly tucking into her chest. Her shining hair rushed forward to hide her face. "And in my abysmal weakness, I *believed* him," she said, softly, bitterly. "I believed every last word, may the gods and stars curse what is left of my soul. I swallowed the story whole, like a bird a poisoned worm. And it was not just his face that swayed me, though he was a pleasure to look upon. Such strong shoulders and capable hands, eyes green as forest fern. He told me his name was Herron, and the way he smiled at me . . . not as a man bending knee to his new queen, but as one lover at another. As if it were already certain I would take him into my heart."

My insides aching preemptively for whatever was coming next, I reached for Niko's hand. Even from here, I could hear the thundering of Mara's dread. And I remembered what she'd told me when I first asked her who he was.

A monster, she'd said.

And my beloved, once.

"Before him I had known whichever man I pleased, for a night or a moon or a turn. But I had never known one quite like he was. He was a cunning man, just as he had said. He knew how to heal with herbs, with various kinds of earth. That was not extraordinary in itself; we had wise ones among my people too."

She flung the hair back from her face, then swept her eyes over us all. Like she was drawing strength from the sight of us, all her children together. A side of her mouth peaked up in a rueful quirk.

"But there were things he showed me that not even *I* could do. Sometimes, when we were alone, he took hold of time like clay between his hands. He drew moments out into whole days, slowed down the world to honey dripping. He caught birds for me mid-flight, showed me a bear cub frozen between blinks, its mother rearing up like a clawed statue next to it. I remember putting my hand against her chest, over the mat of coarse and reeking fur. To feel how long it took for each great strike of her mallet heart to hit.

"When I asked how such things were possible, he told me that the oldest gods of all spoke to him. That in his grief for all he had lost, he had offered himself to them in body and soul—such that they now lived inside him and fed him power, bound by the ink in his skin."

She shook her head in disbelief. "I took it to mean that he had become something like a priest. And in my foolishness, I questioned him no further. His loss was still so raw, I thought, writ large in the hungry way he looked at me. And it was such a heady, rich relief, respite from a loneliness I had not even known I felt, to have my strength entwined with his strength. Like dragons wound around each other, or the harmony of some tremendous song. It did not occur to me to think," she added with a rueful chuckle, "that those ravenous eyes might hold a very different kind of hunger.

"I still cannot guess why he held off for so long, but that some part of him must have truly loved me. Yet the *things* inside him would not let him rest easy by my side. So that autumn, the horses went."

She rubbed her temples, digging deep. In the candlelight, the tattoos down her arms stood out stark. The diamonds plucked out by Dunja were gone, but they hadn't left the pucker of scars behind. The lines of the constellations ran smooth and unblemished.

"My people were terror-struck," she continued. "None of us had ever seen such abomination. Our herd was still alive, if life simply meant an absence of death. They didn't feed; they could be dragged ploddingly to water, but once there, they wouldn't drink. Their eyes had turned a tainted black, and they behaved as if they had forgotten what being alive even meant."

Her jaw set hard. "They had also become unnaturally strong. None of us could stand to let them live as they were—but when threatened, they fought back like true demons. Faster than the eye, and so vicious, kicking and biting and rolling over like horseflesh boulders. It took me, Amrisa, and Amrana to restrain them all. The things we had to do to them before they finally succumbed . . ."

Her face twisted, and a single tear slid down her cheek like a glass bead. It was the first time I had ever seen her cry.

"I do not like to think of what it took to bring them peace," she finished in a hitching whisper. "And still, I never thought to blame *him*. Because by then, I loved him. By then, I had borne his child. Amsherra, my third daughter, named for both me and him."

My breath caught. I remembered the dream I'd shared with Iris, the first we'd ever seen of Mara. The spell she cast in the snow-cloaked clearing, shapes carved into the crust of ice. Dried flowers and ground powders spread out all around her. The pervading sense of some terrible, soul-deep sacrifice.

I shook my head against the thought. It was too terrible even to consider.

"After that taste, the thirst must have grown too much for him to further contain himself. Only a few weeks passed before he shook me awake before the dawn. He was so glutted with stolen strength that I could feel it, like serpent tongues flicking against my skin. The tattoos around his arms writhed like things alive, and his green eyes had turned to night.

"'Mara, my sun,' he said to me. 'Rise now, and come. There is something you must see.'

"I knew enough to veil my fear, though my skin crept away from his touch. Then he led me through the settlement, and I saw what he had done. All my people stood gathered outside beneath the spreading fire of the dawn, stiff like pillars outside their homes. Just like the horses; blank, black eyes, all living yet lifeless. From the youngest children to the death's-door old.

"'Oh, no, please, no,' I whispered, though I did not know whom I beseeched. I felt as if my body might bury itself into the ground. All these people—now flesh-clad ghosts—had trusted me and loved me, placed themselves into my hands. And I had let myself be beguiled by a man's honeycombed lies.

"'I beg forgiveness for paining you, my sun,' Herron said to me, cradling my face. 'But it was more than time. The Lightless gods demand their tithe of souls. But I would not take you as I took your people, nor would I take your daughters and ours—not without permission. I've searched for you since I felt your glow, from so many leagues away. Now I would have you with me, my tigress and my queen, to live forever by my side. The Lightless will sustain you as they do me, and will never let us die. Together we will storm and sack this world, twist it into dripping halves and suck out all its pulp.'

"Under the madness of his gaze, all I could think was of my children. Amrisa. Amrana. And little Amsherra, not even weaned. I brought this on them and now I would save them, however I must. By stars and gods, I would. I *would*.

"'What would you have me do?' I asked him, searching for false sweetness to give him, finding only gall. 'What—what must I do to take my place by your side?'

"'I will show you,' he whispered, kissing my hands. 'I will ink you with the gateway patterns, and I will teach you the words. Once it has been both inscribed and spoken, they will claim you as their vessel. All you need do is let me show you how to let them in.'"

With that, Mara stood so abruptly that I jerked against Niko, who gripped my hand hard. I could hear the shallow flutter of her breathing beside me. We had both been spellbound by the sound of Mara's voice, just like the mass of coven daughters. I could hear the rumbling avalanche of their reaction, all this unwelcome revelation. This wasn't a story most of them had heard before—though I could see by Izkara's stony eyes that a few of them *had* known.

Mara's first daughter certainly would have.

I scoured the crowd until I found Amrisa's face, dark and

impossibly lovely. Her eyes were closed, her tear-slick features sculpted into an expression of agony so keen it looked almost like epiphany.

Everything in me shied away from hearing how this story ended.

As Mara rose with blazing eyes, the furs and shawls fell away. Under them she wore a black rib-cage corset that laced up the back, above a black leather skirt with ragged hems. With her clenched fists and wide-legged warrior's stance, even the dancer's clothes seemed cut for battle.

"I told him I needed three days to myself," she said, her eyes still burning. "To purify and to prepare. And as he was only too eager to grant me whatever I wanted—so he could finally have all that *he* wanted—he left me to my work."

I'd almost forgotten that she was what Dunja came from, until she began the dance.

We weren't going to hear the ending, then.

We were going to see it.

ELEVEN

Iris

I CAME BACK TO MYSELF WITH A SUDDEN, SHEARING BREATH.
Terror still rolled through me like waves, in sharp dips and crests.

That man's face. His *eyes*. That hideous, serpentine dark squirming around him.

He had seen me, and now he wanted to eat me. And not just me, but Lina, and all the rest of our coven kin.

I thought my ribs might crack from the force of my hammering heart.

"He's coming!" I half shrieked, flailing feebly. *"He's coming!"*

"Flower, hush," Fjolar soothed from above. My head was pillowed in his lap, and his coarse palms cupped my burning face. The cool chain of his arrowhead bracelet felt like bliss against my skin. "Easy, now. You're all right."

I pawed at him like a frightened child, and he caught my fingers easily with one hand. "I saw Lina, I *saw* her, and she told me—she said to find his soul." His grip stilled over mine for a moment, tightening hard. If I hadn't been so crazed, I would have yelped with it. "And the man, the man, with tattoos and black eyes and all the dark," I gabbled. "He's going to hurt Lina, and he's going to . . . to storm and sack . . ."

His hold relaxed, and he ran warm lips over my knuckles. "Just bad dreams, flower girl. From the poison you inhaled, and that's wearing off. Angel's trumpet is a strong hallucinogenic. Nasty stuff, notorious for nightmares. I've never—I've never seen you so afraid. Not even the Quiet shook you like this. I should have been more careful to keep you to the path."

He swept his thumbs over my cheekbones in a remorseful caress. I barely recognized him, the new tenderness with which he cupped my head.

He was actually taking care of me, without even begrudging it.

Little by little, I calmed, my breathing steadying. Could that really have been a hallucination, a poisoned dream? Lina had looked so real, and that blight of a man . . .

My head still pounded like a beaten anvil, and I felt feverish and jittery. I turned my head and moaned against his palm. "Can . . . ?" My voice died into a rasp. I worked up a pitiful amount of spit and swallowed it, so thirsty my tongue clicked in parting from my palate. "Can we go? The air . . . there are too many smells here, and it's too hot. I think it's making me worse. I'm sorry, I—"

He nodded briskly. "Don't be sorry. It's not your fault. Sit up a little, flower. I'll take you somewhere with clearer air."

He shifted us in a single fluid motion, propping me up and turning me so he could slip an arm behind my back and knees. I let my head droop against the solid bulk of his shoulder as he picked me up, cradling me against his chest. Through gritty, slitted eyes, I watched him carry me to a simpler, less imposing set of wrought-iron gates.

"I'll have to put you down for the passage through the Quiet," he said, brushing his lips over the top of my head. The gentleness of the touch made me want to cling to him even harder, fold myself into his heft when I still felt so weak and small. "So I can lead the way. Do you think you can stand?"

Everything inside me wilted at the thought of submerging myself inside the Quiet again. The loss of my senses. The loss of my self. I'd forgotten that we'd have to wade through it on our way out as well as in.

But we couldn't stay here, not when every breath made me want to swoon.

"Mm-hmm," I grunted vaguely. "I can try."

He set me down gingerly. I swayed a little but stood, clinging to his hand. Once I was stable enough to take most of my own weight, he propped a foot up on the gate's iron bars and booted them open.

As soon as they swung outward, I began to quake. I didn't want to do it, didn't want to, would have done anything to evade another foray into the Quiet. It had been such a misery last time, and this time I was weak. What if I forgot how to keep myself knit together?

What if I unraveled like a ball of yarn before I reached the other side?

"You'll be fine, flower, I promise," Fjolar said, drawing me to his side and pressing a light kiss of encouragement into my temple. "It won't be pleasant, but you'll pass through just as you did before. I won't let you go."

I nodded slowly, tearfully. The care in these new kisses, and in his touch—I was beginning to almost believe in them.

He tugged us both forward, and stepped through the gates. All that fresh trust in him lasted until the exact instant the void of the Quiet sealed around me, closing over me like water across a drowning girl's face.

The thrash of fear was so great that for a moment it sustained me on its own, expanding to fill me until it brought up short against the very edges of my silhouette. And then, rising to meet the direness of my need, my wisteria rushed up to take the panic's place. My infinite bloom had been hovering near my surface—whatever I'd done in reaction to the angel's trumpet poison, it clearly *had* summoned the bloom somehow—and now its flowered branches burst out of me again, weaving themselves around me to shelter me from the Quiet. I could firmly feel the borders of my body where latticed wood and petal pressed against me, keeping me enclosed.

Cupped like a yolk inside the confines of my own will, I wouldn't dissolve or lose myself.

My own gleam took care of me, until Fjolar pulled me through.

෯

WE STEPPED OUT together into bracing cold. I stumbled a little, squinting; the sky was blindingly blue, and whirled with white. Not just snowflake flurries, but also strings of thousands of white flowers suspended by nothing from above. Lilies, orchids, and daisies, peonies and magnolia, hundreds of others I knew by sight if not by name. Their petals looked soft and living, despite the shimmer of snow dusted like powdered sugar over them. The air was sunlit, in a diffuse, consistent way that somehow came from everywhere at once, though I didn't actually see a sun.

A snowflake struck me squarely in the eye, burning with cold. As if to match, the rest of me immediately broke into tooth-chattering chills. My bones felt like they'd been swapped out for blown-glass substitutes.

"Ah, damn it." Fjolar turned to peer into my face, his hair blown back by the wind. Captive crystals winked in its white-blond threads, his narrowed eyes a blue more electric than the sky. Even bare-armed, in the same black tank and charcoal trousers he'd been wearing since I got here, he looked perfectly at home set against all the snow. "Now you're *freezing*. You were so feverish before. I thought for sure you'd like a little more chill."

I couldn't help a weak chuckle at the sheer consternation sweeping across his face. "Sorry to be so tricky with my meat. This is a little more chill than I needed, I think. I don't suppose you'd have something warm for me to wear?"

His features clouded, then cleared just as abruptly. "As a matter of fact, I do. Wait here a minute, flower."

He strode away from me, leaving me to look around, blinking

against the snow. Sky flowers aside, we were in the oddest little glade I'd ever seen. The trees and shrubs around us, traced with a crisp, slim edging of white, seemed like they'd been crafted to upend expectations of how plants were meant to look. Some of the trees grew from slim trunks into a stiff, bushy inverted canopy, like umbrellas blown inside out. Others had fat trunks, lumpy and gray, like disembodied elephant legs growing from the ground. At their tips, they split into incongruously delicate branches riotous with bright pink blossoms.

"Those, he *had* to have made up," I mumbled to myself.

"He did not, in fact," Fjolar informed me, appearing from behind to drape a cloak around my shoulders. I burrowed into it, burying my fingers in it to the knuckle. It was lined with some luxuriant tawny fur, sliding heavenly soft over my bare arms. "Those are dragonblood trees, and the gray flowering ones are desert roses. They're all from Socotra, one of your world's weird little treasures; almost everything that grows on the island doesn't grow anywhere else. And you'll recognize the flowers in the sky. Those are especially for you."

I did. They were a dazzling, larger-than-life mimicry of Rebecca Louise Law's work. She was an artist who worked with flowers, which she turned into first living and then dried sculptures as they aged according to her precise design. Her pieces were some of my favorites; I'd wondered when I was younger if she saw flowers like I did, in fractals she could capture.

The fact that this was another mosaic tile of my mind he'd stolen from me and repurposed—like a magpie lining his nest with the contents of my brain—might have stoked the smoldering ember of my anger if I hadn't been both starving and so thirsty. Manifesting the infinite bloom took strength, and this time I'd used it while poison-struck. If I didn't get something to eat or drink, I felt like I might keel over and freeze on my way to the ground.

When I said so to Fjolar, he closed his eyes for a long moment, pinching the bridge of his nose. "Of course you need food and drink," he muttered. "Of course you do."

Realization dawned. "And you don't have any here. None of the others needed anything like that."

He shot me a genuinely rueful smile. "I never had to build a world for a real girl before. But I'll find you something. You stay put and rest."

He left me sitting beneath a limestone overhang to shelter from the snow while he went foraging. I tucked the furs snug around me and leaned back woozily against the rock, letting my eyes slide closed. Beneath all the physical discomfort, I ached for my sister. Instead of slaking the feeling of missing, that brief fever dream of her had churned all the pain back up like fresh-turned earth.

Fjolar returned to offer me a strip of cactus, peeled smooth from spines so I could suck out its tangy water. He'd also found some half-frozen fruit that looked enough like stunted pomegranate to risk tasting.

"Remember the time you brought me skyr cake?" I said wistfully, nibbling on the cold, pithy flesh clinging to the seeds and yearning for real food, something doughy and rich to chew. "I want another time like that."

"That was in *your* world, and it was a gift for wooing. A patisserie for you wasn't in the kingdom's original plans."

I picked a seed out from my mouth, and started in on the rind. At least I wouldn't be short on fiber, I thought dourly. "But why can't you bring me something else from home? You brought this fur earlier."

He shook his head. "I never left. The furs were already here, part of this piece of the kingdom."

I paused mid chew. "Why? If I'd come in soul like the others, I wouldn't have needed any warmth. I wouldn't even have felt the cold here."

"You weren't going to be wearing that cape for warmth, flower girl," he replied, and when he met my eyes again his had deepened to such a stormy blue that it drew heat to my cheeks. "It was meant to lie between your back and the floor."

"Oh," I said faintly, as the thought sprang into vivid life. Him and me on that plush fur. Me beneath him under the swirling, flower-strewn sky. His own back so warm and broad that I would barely feel the sting of falling snow. None of it would reach me, and even if it did, maybe I'd even like little pinprick kisses of ice against the insides of my thighs.

With significant effort, I stamped the image down. These flares of desire disturbed me deeply, when everything else that I felt—the expanse of my fatigue, the longing for home—should have opposed them, canceled them out.

I cleared my throat and broke our shared gaze. "Why couldn't you bring me something else, anyway?" I asked. "You're not stuck here just because I am, are you?"

"No, I'm not." All the heat subsided from his eyes. "I could leave if I wanted, but the existence of this realm demands our presence to sustain it. Both of us, together. If I left it would collapse, with you still in it. You wouldn't survive it."

The cold fruit mush went sour in my mouth. "But you left Dunja to come look for me. And she didn't die."

"No. When I left, she simply woke back in your world. But that's because she was here the way she was meant to be, only in soul."

"But then both of you would have been gone. So how did this place carry on after that?"

His voice took on a slight cautious note. "Because you were there to pick up the mantle, once I chose you. Between each choosing, the kingdom continues to exist in a sort of stasis. Waiting for me to mold it for the next chosen. And while the original spell is mostly broken, you and I arrived here just in time. And as long as we're still here to stoke it, together, my domain will continue to exist."

I went rigid, a murky suspicion wisping through me. "And with what, exactly, do we *stoke* it?"

His face turned wary at the measured danger in my voice. Expressions flitted across his features, almost too many to parse, but I thought I caught the moment in which he decided it was better not to lie to me.

This time.

"This kingdom is meant to be our haven," he said carefully.

"Love between us is its mandate. Just being here draws you to me. It lures us back into well-worn grooves, the rhythms of the dance. And that's what keeps sustaining this place—the energy generated by the courtship and the performance. Like a positive feedback loop."

Or like the kingdom was a symbiotic parasite.

It all fell into place. My punch-drunk desire for him, the burgeoning closeness between us, the singsong cadences I sometimes used when speaking with him. Flaring up intermittently at first, and then growing stronger and more consistent the longer I stayed here.

Like something externally imposed. A wanting not my own.

"So that's why I feel the way I do about you?" Wrath rose in me, buoying me up. "Because being here is *making* me want you?"

"It can only amplify what's already there." His eyebrows peaked. "You liked me just fine to begin with, flower. There's no denying that."

"And you didn't think this *amplification* was worth telling me about?"

"If I had told you, you'd just have fought it harder instead of leaning into it," he said bluntly. "And besides, I like it that you want me. This way is better for both of us."

The selfishness took my breath away, the cold, inhuman logic of it. While I thought I'd been playing the courtesan for him— something I chose on my own—the kingdom had been twisting me toward him all along. Forcing my artifice into reality with every breath I drew here.

I felt like such a fool. A child playing grown-up's games, when no move was hers to start.

"You unbelievable, self-centered bastard." I breathed. "You *still* haven't stopped lying to me. And you honestly think it's justified."

"It wasn't a *lie*," he protested, a splotched flush rising up his fair skin. "I simply didn't tell you. And you can't leave here, anyway, even if you can snatch glimpses of your sister somehow, so why would I ruin it by telling—"

He clamped down on the rest of the words, realizing what he had already let slip.

"I thought you said that was a dream," I said slowly. My cheeks ached from strain, and I realized that I'd peeled my lips back from my teeth like a cat. "Talking to Lina, seeing that hideous thing that's stalking her. Just a poisoned little girl's bad dream."

He blinked at me deliberately, implacable, his face shuttering to guard the lie. "It *was* a dream. I misspoke. I meant—"

I exploded up from the ledge, stalking away only to wheel back on him.

"You knew," I snarled, abruptly remembering how his hand had tightened on mine while I babbled to him what the infinite bloom had shown me. "*You knew* something back home was hunting my sister. Have you known this whole time and just didn't tell me, so it wouldn't ruin the possibility of fun? I wasn't going to be much good to you terrified for Lina, was I? *How dare you lie to me when it comes to her?*"

His jaw tightened, but he wouldn't speak. It infuriated me so intensely that I actually wound up and kicked a flurry of snow at him. He didn't even tense, just sat like a stone while it struck him in the face.

All this time I'd been behaving like some helpless, cornered thing, relying on charm and pretty guile while this foul, lovely place wrung emotions from me. But I could do it differently. I could lie the way he did, just as brutally.

And I could threaten.

Now all I needed to do was make him believe.

"You think you can keep doing this," I ground out, my voice ragged with rage. "Hiding from me what this world is really for, refusing to tell me what you know about what's happening in my home, pretending all that omission isn't a lie. And I've played the doll for you so far, because it felt fake-good and I thought I had no other choice. But I was wrong about that. There *is* one other thing I could choose to do."

He looked up at me, hollow-cheeked, his eyes both stark and guarded. "And what's that, Iris?"

"I can just stop," I said, letting the furs drop from my shoulders. The cold struck in an instant, savage way, like something that had been lying in wait, and my skin burst into goose bumps. "I can stop everything, lie down and die. It wouldn't even be so hard. You might have chipped bits from my mind to make this kingdom, but we both know this realm isn't meant for me. Eventually I'll probably starve, but I could stop bothering to keep living long before then."

"Iris—"

"*No*," I forced through clicking teeth. "You might own

everything here, including me, but you can't own this. If I sit down somewhere and just let it snow on me—or leap off a cliff you put there for the sake of scenery—you won't be able to stop it. You're *death*, for fuck's sake, that's the best part. You can't keep me from letting myself die."

"You wouldn't . . ." His voice was weaker than I'd ever heard it. "You wouldn't do that to me, Iris. Or even if you would, there's still your sister to consider. And that boy."

Hope flared bright in me. He was using my name. He understood the gravity here, believed what was at stake. I just needed to persist.

"If you won't tell me whatever it is you know, what good will I ever be to them?" I snapped. "And the way things are looking, I won't even be seeing them again."

As I said it, I realized that I believed it too, and I nearly collapsed with the abrupt sense of cleaving, of such comprehensive heartbreak. My heart had been so waylaid—first shunted to the side in my struggle to survive, and then falsely tangled up in Fjolar—that I hadn't fully let myself know it. But I was going to lose them all; I really, truly was. Not just Luka and Malina, but everyone else, too: Čiča Jovan, Nev, Niko. Mama, if she was somehow still alive. And Dunja, the aunt I had just found, along with all the other coven daughters who might have crossed over to our side.

"So either swear to me now that you'll tell me what it is," I finished, crying silently but hard, the tears frosty on my cheeks, "or get ready to say good-bye to your pleasure palace. Because this world ends with me, doesn't it? There's no one else for you to choose. So

I'll be free and *you'll* be all alone without any toys—for the first time in how many thousands of years? How will that sit with you, you overgrown spoiled brat?"

He watched me impassively for long moments with his chin propped on a clenched fist, gauging me, his eyes such a piercing blue I could nearly feel the blade of their regard. I stood my ground as best I could, though without his touch the world felt like a bucking winter beast under my feet.

Then he shook his head, just once.

"Bullshit," he said mildly.

I was so astonished I forgot my tears. "Excuse me?"

"You forget that I know you, Iris, to your core. This was a well-crafted attempt, I'll give you that." He gave a mocking, slow clap. "You might even have believed you meant it. But you would never go through with it—not if there's any chance one of your own might need you alive. I may be selfish, but *you* aren't. Like Mara never was. Nowhere near selfish enough to die for no better reason than spite for me."

He knew.

Damn him—damn *everything*—he knew better than to believe it. He knew *me*, and he was right. I would never have done it. How had I even thought I'd fool him? He was the biggest lie that humans told themselves—that he would never come for them.

But with the deluge of helplessness came an equal flood of driving need.

I turned away from him, ignoring the fall of his footsteps as he stood to follow me. "Please," I whispered to myself, clenching my hands into fists until my nails bit in.

The last two times, my wisteria had burgeoned in response to blind, primal need. This time I was lucid and aware, all this cold having blown the fever from me. But my need was no less forceful, battering through my veins. I had to know what Fjolar was keeping from me—what was threatening my sister. Especially now that I knew the monstrosity was real, and that some spy-witch was helping him; maybe even someone on our side.

I needed the truth so badly, more than anything.

Please.

Slowly at first, and then in a headlong profusion, the flowers flung themselves out of me, twisting and weaving into a grand column that grew around me as if I stood in the heart of a cylindrical trellis. I let myself surge up with them just as I had before, clinging to the outward onslaught of their growth—and then I found myself fractaled down to one of the atrium balconies above Mara's Great Hall.

TWELVE

Mara's Dance

THE FIRST DAY SHE SPENT THINKING, AND GRIEVING.

On the second day, she rose.

If these accursed gods of Herron's could deal with death, then she would find a way to do the same.

She felt the potential of an answer humming in her blood, the gleam lighting her way like lanterns as it often did. The only hope she could muster. If she wished to bargain with a force larger than life, she needed to be able to speak with it. And to call Death to her, and fashion it something like a body, she first needed many things to kill.

On the third day, she hunted with abandon, blessing the generous creatures that crossed her path and let her fell them. She needed their blood; she needed their bones. With every creature she killed and distilled to its most essential parts, she sounded a call to Death, like blowing breath through a spiraled hunting horn.

And as she moved from deer and mink and foxes to birds and snakes and slugs, she came to see that their lives would never be enough. Some things demanded more than was one's right to give, an offering carved from the heart's own blood.

And when she heard Amsherra's squalling milk-cry—little Amsherra, with her father's fern-green eyes—her womb contracting at the plaintive sound, she knew what must be done.

SHE HAD ASKED Herron to meet her in the clearing that had seen some of their sweetest stolen moments, at the darkest hour of the third night. By then she would be ready, she claimed, to renounce her former life. She would be ready to welcome his gods into herself, to take in all the darkness that she could stand to hold.

If there wasn't so much else at stake, she might even have sunk so low as to succumb. Two of her daughters might still have been living, but Amsherra's loss had turned her heart to a bramble in her chest. With every thought of the child she had given unto Death, the tender lining of her lungs felt like it tore anew to bleed again.

She had stolen her youngest daughter's life for this. And neither all the gods there ever were nor all the stars that pierced the sky could bring it back to her or flush her of that guilt.

When the time came, she went early to the clearing, while twilight's waxen peel fell away to reveal the darker pith of night. As she built a sacred circle of powders, dried flowers, and cutting stones, the winter winds wrapped around her like icy cloth, sinking into the deep fount of her warmth.

When her own blood dripped onto the powders and clotted into streaked whorls on her belly, breasts, and cheeks—when the beings that had died by her hand coated her skin from limb to limb—she felt the abrupt shift of pressure that heralded an arrival. A feral, ancient darkening, tunneling down around her body and expanding in her head. She fought the urge to scrabble away from it; to flee from the essence of endings, the aching solitude, the sense of terminal descent.

But as Death bore down on her, she dug deep and found the strength to first whisper fretfully to it, and then to sing. Wooing it with all the love in her blood, molding it a shape with her glowing hands.

"I call on you, I summon you, master of night, and change, and all that ends!" she bellowed at the ground below her feet, the air around her, the snow-feathered sky above, flinging out her arms. "My first name is Mara, and I entreat you for your help. Something brutal and grotesque has slunk into this mortal realm, an evil that I would lay to rest!"

Death had taken a shadow of a shape by then, a dark column of air in the vague outline of a man. She could sense nascent curiosity, the slow, precise unfurling of an akin-to-human mind. One that attended to her and wished to know more, to deal with her in kind.

What would you ask of me, Witch Mara, sorceress who walks in her own shed light? She felt the words more than she heard them, an echo in her breastbone. *You are not fully of this realm yourself, with your blood that smells of fruits and sacred herbs, your heart like a swallowed sun. Why would you need my help?*

"This evil is like a death that walks," she said. "And makes more of itself. It is beyond even me to quench."

She could feel Death's intrigue rise, the oppression of its dark regard. *Go on*, it almost-said.

"He will not *die*," she replied, gritting her teeth. "He lives in death, for all that no one deserves life less than he. What sustains him is stronger than anything in this realm; he evades your touch, even when dealt mortal blows by mortal hands. So I would ask you to kill him for me yourself—for what could wreak a greater death than Death?"

So you would use me as your assassin, lady of the light? Wry amusement colored the not-quite-voice. *A lofty demand. And what would you offer me in return?*

Of course, she thought bitterly. Nothing but love was ever free, and often not even that.

"What would you have from me?" she asked.

I am alone, and lonely, it mused. *As I have always been. My nature is of solitude, and yet, why does it have to be? Perhaps one such as you could withstand being by my side. You could come away with me and see such things, Witch Mara. Become my sunlit bride.*

She stirred in surprise at that. She would not have thought that even Death itself balked against its fated lot.

"I . . ." She steeled herself, railing silently at whatever cruel hand had shaped her and this place. Why could she never guard herself, or her own, from the demands and whims of men? "Yes, I will do it, then. If you kill him for me, I will leave my life behind to stand by your side."

He—for now he felt distinctly male—fell into contemplation. *Perhaps this would suffice*, he mused. *But only perhaps.*

Desperation hatched and crawled inside her like spiders. "If you do not see the need for it yet, I bid you to wait and see him for yourself. You will know him for what he is, something that should never have come here. A thing passed beyond redemption."

As if she had summoned him, Herron emerged from the snow-shrouded pines. Wisps of black trailed him like floating serpents, darker than tree trunk or night, the same oily iridescence teeming in his eyes. Even after everything, a sliver of her still leaped with foolish joy at the sight of him. Plumes of breath streamed from between his fine-cut lips, and his long, dark braid and muscled shoulders sparkled with melting snow. Because he was as warm as she was, warm enough to melt the frostbit night.

The slice of his smile flashed white against the dark. Though Death hovered so close to her that she could feel its withering presence with every inch of skin, Herron did not sense it—maybe could not, girded as he was by tainted black. He still thought she was doing what he asked.

He thought that she was his.

She had loved him so much, so ardently. And he had taken everything, and would never cease to take.

"My savage sun," he called out to her, hands lifted in beckoning.

"My midnight queen. Come to me, close the distance between us. Let us begin."

Death rose in subdued outrage behind her, a rustling like old bones shifting against each other. *A living death, just as you said. A former mortal who dares thieve from me. You have the right of it, Witch Mara; he cannot be permitted to abide. I accept your terms as they bind us to each other. Consider the pact between us sealed, and proceed as you will.*

"Thank you," she said under her breath. "For attending to me, and for your help." Even if the help came at the steepest price a mother could have paid. One daughter dead, the others lost to her.

But at least they would be safe.

She made her way to Herron, moving like a lover shedding veil after veil. The gleam roared inside her, building into something truly like a fire, until she burned the snow beneath her feet with each slow, deliberate step.

Then she began focusing her power, drawing a cloak of love around her, calling on the strength of her many names. Mara was the first, her given cradle-name, but there were others already. And in years to come, when she became legend, there would be many others still. Already she could hear them, whispered by the voices of the ages caught in the wind.

"Mara," she crooned as she advanced on Herron. He waited for her, trusting, eager and open-armed. Unsuspecting, even as Death followed in her footsteps, dogging at her heels.

Once she reached Herron, she gave him one last, sweet smile, the kind that she had woken him with every morning by the dawn.

"Marzanna. More. Moréna," she whispered, almost against his lips. She laid her fingertips on his cheeks, lightly, but still he hissed in a breath at their heat. Then she undid his plait and wound her fingers through his hair, stroking the strands from root to tip. Gentling him with the full force of her love, until she knew all he wanted was to chain himself to her, to drown willingly in the pool of her perfume.

That was when the moment came.

She let herself fall back and plunge wholly into Death, such that it both enveloped and leached fully into her. It felt wrong, so wrong, and far beyond terrible, to make herself into its shell. It thrashed and bucked like tigers trapped within her, alien past all reckoning. Nothing that should ever have been allowed to share her skin.

But she needed it inside her, to do what must be done. To allow Death to do her killing in her stead.

She caught Herron's face between hands grown heavy as mountains, and the fear that finally breached the surface chased the black out of his eyes. For a few moments they were fern-green and bright, just as they had been when she first loved them and him.

"Mara," he gasped, straining against the vise of her grasp, finding nowhere to escape. "What are you—"

"I am *Maržena*," she hissed through gritted teeth, "and Morana, and Mora, and MARMORA!"

And with the last invocation of her own name, she plunged the hand she shared with Death into Herron's chest, the howling wind that rose around them almost drowning out his shriek.

The thing that she drew out from between his ribs was not quite his heart. It wound like silvery filament around her bloody hand, pulsing like a dying star. The last dregs of his human soul.

The part with which he had loved her.

And even that was tainted by darkness. With the hands she shared with Death, she lifted it up to their shared eyes. Black threads wisped through it, the silver honeycombed with coal. It brought sick bubbling up her throat.

Stripping Herron of it had brought him wailing to his knees. He knelt hunched around his chest, but the gaping wound had already begun to seal itself. He gazed up at her, swaying, eyes blazing with pitch-black hatred that ran down his cheeks in inky rivulets. Even stripped of his soul, he would not die. He was weakened—she could see him struggle to gain his feet, only to collapse back down each time—but still very much alive.

"Do it," she choked out, speaking to Death inside her. "Snuff him fully. *Kill his soul.*"

That lies beyond even my domain, sorceress, Death whispered back to her, bristling with outrage. *I snuff bodies, but cannot snuff a soul. Such is not my mandate. If ripping out his blighted soul does not kill him, then even I will not be his death.*

Helpless fury threatened to choke her. She couldn't fail, not now. Not after everything she'd already given up to right her wrongs.

"Then build a prison for the soul instead," she pleaded. "A lockbox world set between the worlds to hold it captive, while I imprison the rest of him here. And pass me by when you come to cull. Avert your eyes from me and from the remnants of my line, so that we may keep watch over him."

That is not what we agreed on, Witch Mara. She could feel Death begin to withdraw from her, and relief though it was, she clung harder to him. She couldn't let him leave her, not now. Not yet. *You* swore *that you would be my bride. I have upheld my end as best I could—why should I do anything further, if you will not come be mine?*

"You cannot have me, for I will be needed here, as a living anchor for this spell." She took a deep, shuddering breath, through lungs compressed by his presence inside her. "But in my stead, I would offer you the daughters of my line. Gleaming beauties of your choosing to hold you by the hand, to serve as your consorts and your brides. To line the lockbox world with beauty, make it more than just a jail."

She could feel his excitement as if it were her own. Not just one bride, but many. All bright and lovely as she was.

Yes, he murmured, a susurrus of dead leaves scraping over each other. *Yes, I accept. I will dance with your daughters in your stead.*

The relief that swept through her was rivaled only by the deeper loss.

"Then take it, and go quickly," she ordered Death, stifling a scream as he wrenched loose and shucked off her body, the silvery tangle cupped carefully between the shadowed outlines of his hands. "Build the lockbox we agreed on. The rest of him, I will seal away."

She felt a surprising, momentary flare of something before

Death left with Herron's soul, a warmth like a shoulder-clasp of respect. *I know what you are doing, Witch Mara, and I know all it cost you*, he rasped in parting. *And I will always know it, even if no one else understands how much you gave of yourself.*

With that, he and the soul were gone.

She looked back down at Herron, still writhing on the ground and watching her with murderous eyes. "How dare you do this to me, you faithless, envious bitch?" he spat at her. "I know how you loathe weakness in all things, and what is this treachery but weak? You may have left me soul-gutted, but I will rise again and hunt you, I will *hound* you, I will never let you steal even a measure of peace—"

"I do not need peace, if it means setting you free," she broke in softly, laying a hand atop his head. "And whether I deserve it or not, I will surely know none after this."

Then she began spooling in Winter itself as if it were icy wool, and wrapping it around the bright spindle of her core. Just as she had needed Death to do what must be done, she would need Winter's spirit for what was to come.

If anything, this was worse than hosting Death had been; the spike of Winter that would dwell inside her like a pillar wouldn't melt an inch over the centuries. The only way she would survive it was through the sustenance of the gleam, coursing through her with its loving mimicry of warmth.

When she'd gathered enough inside herself, she lifted Herron up with Winter's own hands, like a whirlwind of chains forged from links of snow and ice. As he hung splayed and suspended, his scream stolen by the frozen bridle caught between his teeth, she began to weave the web of roses that would knit them all together.

Herron and Mara, Death and Winter, bound by an infinite tapestry woven into the fabric of the world. Her own will-knotted pattern of petals, stems, and thorns.

But it was Herron who would be trapped most of all, flung into the sea that sat just beyond her mountain's feet. Plunged into its dark depths, pinned down by a pylon of will-forged ice. Winter itself would staunch him with its colossal weight, for as long as her spell maintained. As long as her daughters danced with Death, and the line of her blood remained.

And when it was fully wrought, her knotwork of ice prisons and black roses, she finally allowed herself to sink into despair for all that she had lost.

Even as her eyes lost their own dark luster and frosted over into gray.

THIRTEEN

Malina

MARA FINALLY SANK BACK DOWN, SWEAT POURING FROM her hairline and pooling in the hollow above her heaving chest. About half the candles had actually gone out, from the force of the air swept over them by her movement.

Then the Great Hall erupted into sound. Though no one moved even to let out a long-held breath, their feelings were a grating din, all rusted tin and broken glass.

And Mara's guilt was worst of all. It boomed from her, the huge, raucous cacophony of it. Even with all the amends she'd tried to make, I could hear how she held herself accountable for a thousand sins. For not recognizing Herron sooner for what he was, or finding a way to stop him before he stole her people. For Amsherra's death—her murder—and for saddling her line with the constant curse of loss to keep Herron imprisoned.

And even for letting Mama go. For giving in just enough to let me and Riss taste freedom, thinking it wouldn't bring everything tumbling down so hard.

How could she even stand upright, I wondered, with all that weight on her shoulders? No wonder she kept her spine stiff like a steel rod. Even the slightest bit of give would break her back.

I couldn't bear to hear another second of it. Leaning on Niko's shoulder, I stumbled up.

"Lina, where are you going?" she whispered, doe eyes wide. Even her concern, loving as it was, sawed painfully at me.

"I have to get out of here," I forced out. "It's—it's so loud. My head's going to explode."

She tucked her legs under her, getting ready to rise. "I'll come with—"

"*No*," I snapped. Her face went wounded, and her flight song tucked tight in hurt, like wings folding around her. I sucked in air, breathing in and out steady as a bellows, like Naisha had once taught me to do when the music of the world swelled out of my control. Even my bubble couldn't help me here, not with everything so horribly loud. "I just need to be alone for a bit, princess, okay?" I finished, more gently. "I'll come back and find you once things settle down."

My neck prickled as I turned to leave. Beyond the tumult, I thought I heard something faint but familiar—the crashing of rain on sea that I'd only ever heard from my sister. The sound she made when something took her by surprise.

Wheeling around, I caught a flicker of light high up on the third balcony. And for a split second I thought I *saw* Riss, the air broken up into a herringbone pattern, each of the diamonds holding a flash of her face.

Then it vanished into the nothing it must have already been. Just a trick of the light. My heart lurched with loss, and I fled outside, where at least I hopefully wouldn't see any ghosts.

I THRASHED MY way through the forest that slanted up behind the chalet, until I came across a sweet spot between a boulder and a rill. Just enough space between for me to tuck myself in, and dabble my fingers in the trickle of freezing mountain water. Under my back the ground had the perfect give to it, thick with a crisscrossed mat of pine needles and sod. The dapple of the sun that filtered through the pine boughs striped my face with warmth.

Here, all I heard were ruffling feathers and trills of birdsong high above me, and the rustle of little things in the brush, chirping bugs somewhere below. The air smelled sharp and green, a little metallic from the clean water wending over rocks. I couldn't think about everything, or even anything. It was all too much, without Riss to split the burden with me.

I'd been drifting for nearly an hour when a shadow fell over me. I resolutely tamped down my gleam, but a snatch of familiar, fluting melody stubbornly wove its way through the chinks. And now I could hear the vast gale of cold behind it, like wind pounding against wooden shutters bolted tight.

I scrunched my eyes shut tighter. "Not now, Mama. Please."

"I'd just like to sit with you for a bit, if you'll let me, my cherry girl. And I brought you something."

I opened my eyes reluctantly. Mama loomed above me like a giantess bound by a rope of flowers. In broad daylight, her skin was even paler than it had been before she died-but-didn't-die. The veins that ran beneath the delicate angles of her chin were threads of sapphire blue and emerald green, like rivers in winter.

I sat up and scooted away from her, my back pressed against the boulder. In the gauzy light of the forest, she seemed even more like something that could have grown naturally from the ground. A bowl cradled in her hands, she crouched easily in front of me, bringing us eye to eye. A simple, natural curl of chestnut hair sprang above her two-tone irises.

Looking closely, I could see that nearly a quarter of her gray eye had shifted to spring green. My heart turned over at the size of the slice. We still had time, like Mara had said. But it was running out. Winter was receding.

And when it was gone, he would come for us.

"May I sit with you?" she said again, tipping her head to the side. Even her lips were pale, like a marble madonna's.

I slid even farther back and to the side, making room for her against the boulder. Moving gingerly, but without shedding that stuttering grace, she slipped in next to me.

"I wanted to make something with cherries for you, but I couldn't find any," she said, lips pursing with disappointment like a little girl's. "So I took some strawberries instead. They're just chilled, topped with sugar and some simple cream I whipped. Will you try them?"

I took the bowl from her, cupping its cold bottom. The strawberries were perfectly sliced, fanned around a smooth dollop of cream swirled to a flawless peak. I spooned a bite into my mouth while she watched me avidly.

"What does it taste like?" she said, a faint tremor of hope in her voice.

Cool and creamy sweetness melted onto my tongue, citric with fruit. The sugar granules crunched heartily between my teeth. It tasted exactly right, for what it was. But nothing more than that.

"It's good," I answered, swallowing. "But it doesn't . . . there's nothing to see."

She sighed once, deep. "I didn't think so. What happened to me stole the gleam, along with almost everything else. But I thought, maybe—remember when you were small, you and your sister? And I brought you to the beach in swimsuits with little strawberries to match mine? Since we were all there, I thought, even without the gleam . . ." She trailed off, dropping her gaze to her hands.

She'd lost so much, I thought, aching for her. Not just the gleam, but the force of the woman that she'd been. Her way with customers at the café, gorgeous wide smiles and neck arched back, laughter ringing at even the lamer jokes. She'd sometimes let herself be stunning even when I could see.

Once, our mother had been bright as the northern star.

And now, she was this. A sculpture of ice subsisting on roses instead of blood.

"I do remember that, Mama," I said softly, my insides tender with pain. "I don't have to see it to remember."

And I didn't. It was the exact memory Riss and I had shared when we thought Mama was lost to us forever.

I nearly flinched when her arm brushed against mine. "Do you think maybe you need to put something else on? On top of all the briars?"

"It doesn't help. And I'm finding I mind it less and less. It's like a punishment, crafted for me."

I stole a glance at her bold, falcon's profile. "What do you mean? A punishment for what?"

"For what Dunja and I did," she said with an air of obviousness. "To Mara. We may have acted out of ignorance and not malice, but the outcome is the same. She sacrificed all she had to keep everything safe from him. And we tore it down. I see what I should regret so much more clearly now that I barely feel it." She huffed a pale laugh. "At least I still know irony."

"But you didn't *know*," I argued. "You and Dunja thought you were doing it for each other. For your freedom. Why wouldn't Mara have just told you all this? She didn't have to manipulate and lie, practically enslave her whole line with all that forced love to make us willing to sacrifice."

"She answered as much, after you had already gone," Mama replied. "True names have power in a witch's mouth, as does truth itself—I used to tell you so, when you were little, remember? That pillar of winter she built barely kept Herron contained. Mara couldn't risk lending him any strength by letting her daughters know of his existence or his name." Her voice softened just a touch. "And I think she was ashamed, too, to have us know how deeply she'd failed us, or thought she had. As if the guilt was solely hers to bear."

I frowned. "What do you mean?"

"What could have been more selfish than what I did?" She gave a measured shake of her head, as if she were trying to remember how to be rueful. "Especially when I couldn't keep myself from having you. And then the way I had to twist you and your sister, to keep you quelled and tied to me. I was so cold to you, so frozen through, long before I felt this way."

I hugged my knees to my chest. "Why didn't you just tell us? Why didn't you even try something other than lies?"

"It's hard to remember now," she answered carefully. I was getting used to the monotonous cadence of her voice, the slight upticks of emotion to it if I listened hard. "My reasons all seem so flimsy, flat. I think I was afraid of what you would do. My hibiscus girl especially, always so eager for Japan. For the whole world. I could see her hatching plans for escape every time she looked at me. What if she knew what kind of life the coven could have given her? How could I have known one or even both of you wouldn't have been willing to sacrifice, if only so the other could have such luxury?"

Fury lit in an instant, a gas flame flicked to life. It wasn't like me, to leap to anger like this. But just having her back, this cold yet needy shadow of her, wasn't enough to erase the sense of betrayal that hadn't fully left me. "You could have trusted us, for one. And maybe Riss wouldn't have always been trying to escape if you'd been willing to tell us anything real about our father, like you weren't hiding him from us. I mean, his name, birth city, favorite food? That was really the best you had?"

"What I told you was even more than I had, sweet," she said, something close to bitterness stirring under the surface of her voice. "I knew him for a single night. I never even asked his name. It wasn't something that the spell demanded."

"But you said it was Naoki," I protested. "You said he came from a port city in Japan, that he liked—"

"Naoki comes from *nao*, the kanji for 'sincere,'" she interrupted. "And *ki* means tree. I was trying to give you two a gift, if a lie can ever be any kind of gift. The least I could do was name you an honest father, unlike your liar of a mother—you grew up never even knowing my own true name. And I meant the tree for Iris, for the one I knew she loved. That wisteria she painted everywhere."

I swallowed back the bitter swell of tears. For once I understood Riss's constant, simmering discontent. We'd had so much less than we even thought we had. "So, Shimoda then too? And the sea-urchin sushi you said he liked to eat?"

She twitched her shoulders in a shrug. "Shimoda is a port city, with the look of Cattaro. I thought it might quench the curiosity a bit, to find so much similarity when you researched it like I knew you would. Make you feel like you weren't missing out on the whole world. The sushi, well . . ." Another shrug. "I stepped on an urchin while I was pregnant with you. The memory lingered. And I'd always heard their meat was delicious."

"So you thought, what?" I bit back. "The scraps you fed us, you might as well make a joke of them?"

She ran her knuckles down my arm, leaving goose bumps in their wake, and this time I didn't even try to fight the flinch. "Try to understand, my cherry girl," she murmured. "I was so young, lost in a foreign world. Alone save for Jovan's kindness, and he wanted the kind of love I couldn't give him, so I could never lean on him too much. Sometimes levity was all I had. That"—she traced my jawline with a tender fingertip—"and the two of you. You're the only thing I feel now, you know. How much I love you. Maybe it's because you're made of me—the only part of me left unfrozen, still warm and alive. All I want is to be near you, and to have your sister back with us."

I couldn't keep the anger stoked, not with her like this. So vulnerable, in a way I'd never seen. And the mournful melody of her love, beseeching trills snatched away like scraps by hungry seagulls. She reminded me of Dunja, sisters in opposites. Where Death had blackened my aunt down to nothing but fiery wrath and single-minded love, winter and resurrection had left Mama even more bereft.

I leaned my head against her shoulder, shuddering as my cheek met her skin. I was so lost too, and desperately afraid. Whatever we were—half goddesses or angels, monsters made of light—I couldn't make myself believe it would be enough. Not after what Mara had shown us.

"How are we going to get Riss back?" I whispered. "I'm so scared we won't. And I'm so scared of him."

"I know, my sweet," she whispered back. "I know. But if anyone can draw her back down, it's you. And until then, I'll put myself between you and anything that comes."

"How?" I dropped my forehead onto my knees. "What could you do when he comes? What could *any* of us do? Only Mara can use the gleam to fight—her, and the first nine, I guess. But the rest of them, useless. None of them are even as strong as me, and what good am I, even?"

"We were never meant to be strong like you are, or like Mara is," she said softly. "We were meant to be lovely. Our gleams molded into beauty by the training."

"Training," I murmured. Something occurred to me, just the outline of an idea. The shadow of a notion. "How exactly *were* you all trained?"

"Learning and repetition, for years and years. Perfecting our gleams by practicing, using the instruments or accessories that showcased our beauty best. And Mara was always urging us into beauty, singing us toward the loveliest incarnation of our gleams."

"Singing to you," I murmured. My heart began to pound, straining with the sudden surge of hope. I'd used my own songs for encouragement too. Except I'd used them for more than just prettiness or peace.

I nearly slipped over myself, scrambling to my feet on the slick grass. "Mama, let's go. I need to talk to Mara. There might be something I can do to help."

"YOU TRULY THINK you can sing them into being able to fight, fledgling?" Mara said. She stood next to me in the Great Hall, in one of her full-body sheaths, burnt-cherry suede that clung to her like butter. Her hair was pulled back into a complicated loop of shining braids, the first time I'd ever seen it up. "Turn my daughters into soldiers?"

I had underestimated the depths of Mara's desperation. She'd latched so eagerly onto my suggestion that I finally realized what I was hearing from her—not just guilt, but resignation laced with hopelessness.

She thought that after the millennia she'd spent trying to protect them, all her daughters were going to die anyway. To save them, she'd try anything.

Including vesting her hopes in me, the youngest of her line.

"I have no idea if I can do it for them," I answered. "But I do know I've done it before for Riss. When we needed to free Dunja from the ice you trapped her in—I sang Riss into shattering it with her bloom. And that was just the first time I helped her. I sang to break your spell, too."

"Why risk the others when we have me, sorai?" Izkara muttered in her husky half growl, from where she prowled the room's perimeter behind us. She never quite seemed to leave being an animal behind, even when she took on full human form. I'd seen her sniff the air and flick her ears like a fox listening for prey. And sometimes she leaned far out of open windows like a dog in a speeding car. I'd been half hoping to see her loll out her tongue when she did it, but no luck yet. "And Amaya, and Terasai—"

"I know, my warrior-heart," Mara crooned. "I am well aware of who could hold their own in combat. But where we are few, and untrained, he can simply make as many soldiers as he needs. Even his mindless could mow any number of us down, and they are far from the worst of what he commands. The remnant of winter is a quarter gone already; you can see it in your own eye. He will have begun to muster his forces as he regains strength, and we need more of our own to stand against him. Do *you* know a better way to make more full-gleamed soldiers, my warrior-heart?"

Izkara's lips tightened, and she spun on her heel to stalk back to the window in sullen silence.

I swept my hand out at the women clustered in front of us, hands clasped behind their backs. Not all two hundred were here. I'd asked Mara for only the eight or nine with the most dramatic gleams. The ones that could be readily bent to battle. "You sang them into beauty in the first place," I said to Mara. "Can you help me with this? To strengthen their gleam?"

"I will help, of course, for now. But if this works, you cannot rely on me." Her face went feral. "When the time comes to fight, everything I bring to bear must be notched like an arrow at him, if we are to have any chance at all. I will have nothing left over to help you with."

"You keep talking about him. But what about her? What about *Riss*?" Urgency crackled my voice. "I know we need to fight him— I'll do whatever it takes to help, you see that—but how are we going to get her back?"

Her face softened at that, and she ran her knuckles under my chin. "You worry for your sister," she said in her low, velvety triptych of a murmur. "Of course you do. But when the last of the winter fades, the spell will break all the way through. The kingdom will collapse and release Lisarah; she will come tumbling out, back to us. And if we live to see it—if he does not best us—I will be there to catch her with my own net of roses. I swear it to you, Azareen. Malina."

It sounded true, a pure crystalline chime. Her oath was the best assurance I had—and even it wouldn't matter if we couldn't stand against him. If I couldn't do my part.

Twisting my hands together, I turned back to the coven daughters on display. Some of them I knew both by gleam and name, so I thought I might as well start with one of those.

My gaze landed on Oriell, with the wine-dark lips and the teal bramble of hair pinned up with glittering treasures. She had clockwork beetles strung in it today, brass and pewter and colored glass. I remembered her gleam from the showcase on the day Riss and I first arrived—she could project illusions, as long as they were directly behind her own body. An extension of herself.

Maybe it was the tattoos of wild water and blooming vines that sleeved her arms, or the anticipatory sparkle in her densely lined eyes when she met mine and took a step forward. But I thought maybe I could coax out some spirit there.

"Okay," I began, fighting down a wave of shyness. I could practically feel the expectant weight of all those eyes on me— and hear the bright, electric hum of newborn hope. This had been my idea. What if I couldn't do it at all?

I glanced back over my shoulder at Niko, who sat with Luka on tasseled velvet cushions next to one of the floor-to-ceiling windows. They'd finally smoothed things out between them. Niko scrunched her face into a pixie grimace of encouragement. Next to her, Luka jostled her shoulder and tipped me a big-brother wink.

Fighting back a smile, I turned to Oriell. "Could you show me some of your wings?"

She dipped her head, stirring the miniature carnival of her hair. "Of course, Az—Malina. How about these?"

Without any warning, she flung out a massive pair of cobalt wings, the brilliant plumage trimmed with white and black and rakishly flared at the tips. I took a startled step back as she fluttered them in my direction. But there was no feather-brush or gust of air as they flapped at me before folding back behind her. Just like the rest of what they all called up with their gleam, her illusions were empty.

What kind of song did I even need to flesh them out, make them real enough to lift her? I wondered. Something that felt like rising, like flight.

Like Niko felt to me.

The memory that fizzed up was from a couple years ago, when Niko and I had snuck off by ourselves and taken a ferry to Ostrvo Cvijeća, the Island of Flowers. It had been a riot of foliage in bloom, sandy beaches strung smooth like canvas. I would've been happy to spend the day wandering hand in hand, or finding nooks to curl up into together, in a tangle of limbs, coconut lotion, and salty, air-dried hair.

But Niko found an overlook jutting twelve feet above the water, the sea spread under it like a sheet of ruched blue silk. She'd have jumped it by herself, if I'd stuck with my initial no. She liked to push me beyond my own boundaries, but only ever with gentle prodding—never a bully, not with me. And any kind of leap was irresistible to her.

But she'd wanted me with her so badly, I could hear her ringing with it like a tuning fork. And there were so few things I let us do together out in the open, where anyone could see us. At least I could give her this much, even if it scared me past reason.

I'd never forgotten the force of that run, the pounding of our feet over the sharp rocks and to the edge. Niko's tiny hand clutching mine so hard, as if the grip could keep me from changing my mind before we leaped. I was so terrified I kept my eyes open so she'd be the last thing I saw, in case she was wrong and we wound up splatter-dead.

And when we jumped, there was this *moment*, right before the drop. Shimmering suspension, as if the air around us had turned just a little closer to honey. Just for long enough to let me watch her watching me, her pretty eyes squinched against the sun. Her mouth open wide and round into the fullest laugh, as if she could gulp down all the joy of being with me in the air.

Then we fell, obviously, but that wasn't the point.

Aloft. That was the word I wanted. That feeling both of freedom and of not being alone.

Aloft was what we'd had that day, what Niko always meant to me.

I hadn't even realized that I had started to sing, but in front of me Oriell stood with her plumage fluttering as if caught in a cross breeze. Dark mascara tears streamed down her face.

"I think . . ." She clenched her hands into fists by her sides, and I could see her venom-green nails sink deep into her palms. "I think I can feel them, and I want it, I want to be lifted . . ."

"*TRY HARDER, DAUGHTER. LET LOOSE FROM CONTROL,*" Mara belled out from behind me. Like an entire chorus of carillons, ringing together across a city of belfries. Her voice braided with mine, twining through my song. Strengthening and cementing it. "*YOUR GLEAM IS YOURS, TO MOLD INTO SOMETHING GREATER.*"

Oriell spread her wings wide and arched her back, rib cage and sternum straining against her skin like a corset from the inside. She began beating her wings slowly, and then fully flapping them. I nearly lost my song when a feather molted loose from one and floated by my face—I could *feel* it brush my skin in passing. I could smell the trace of her perfume it carried, frangipani and cloved orange over ambergris.

She had made the feather real, transmuted it from dream to matter with her gleam.

And if she strove that much harder, I could sense that she would lift.

"*MORE, ORIELL, AND THEN MORE STILL,*" Mara boomed beside me. She could feel the power building too. "*LISTEN TO YOUR KIN, LET HER HELP YOU RISE!*"

Whatever Oriell's tears had initially been, now she was clearly crying from the strain. Her wings were beating so hard they buffeted the room with whooshing air, all our hair and clothes billowing up. With a very unladylike grunt of grueling effort, she crouched and then launched up—

And stayed there, lifted, arms flung out, delight blazing in her face.

Her wings gusted us with every beat, one leg bent at the knee and the other pointed like a gymnast's to the floor, the untied green ribbons of her pointe shoes swaying beneath.

Striving for beauty even now.

Seeing her up there, so exactly like an angel—if angels had tattoos and piercings, and tattered leotards—shocked me so hard it snatched the song from me. And as soon as the song broke off, so did her flight.

The wings vanished in an instant. Feathers wisped into curls of blue, black, and white smoke that died midair. And Oriell tumbled to the ground with a clipped shriek of pain, as her ankle twisted under the collapse of her full weight.

FOURTEEN

IT WAS NOT QUITE TIME TO MOUNT THE HUNT.

Before the moment struck, he needed to summon soldiers.

After some sifting through her ingested memories, he had led Vera back to her dwelling place, in a simple cinder-block building outside the blackened walls of a stone settlement. This city they called Cattaro had the savor of the ages to it, the smoky sense of a place well-cured by the passage of the centuries.

And he recognized the craggy mountains well, the ones that reared like the rocky limbs of half-buried titans against the city's back.

He had climbed them all once to reach her, and soon he would scale them once again.

No one had troubled them on their way, not that it would have slowed them unduly if anyone had. Still, he had preferred finding seclusion undisturbed. Though Vera's light had momentarily appeased the Lightless's unslakable hunger, Herron had found that without the sharper edges of its need spurring him on, he was troublingly far from full strength. Some corded weight wrapped around him, invisible. A rope of something clear and cold, like rattling blocks of ghostly ice strung on an equally ghostly chain.

As if the pillar that had once pinned him still partially remained, haunting him like a specter of its former form. It would take at least a week to gain enough strength to make more pet soldiers like Vera, even if he started now on summoning his bannermen.

Now he sat on Vera's carpeted floor, garbed in clothing she had found for him—things of her time that fit him well enough, belonging to a lover or one of her kin—with a very reluctant calico kitten squirming on his lap. It was the only one young enough not to have vanished into some nook or cranny as soon as he crossed the threshold.

"No need for so much concern yet, tiny sweetling," he purred at it, fondling a neck barely thicker than his thumb. The cat wasn't inclined to do any purring of its own; its bright yellow eyes were round as an owl's, the pupil drowning out the iris. Every once in a while it let out a frantic little mewl, and its heart thrummed so fast inside its tiny chest he could hear it, like the whirring of crickets. "For the moment I am content to simply enjoy the feel of you."

In response, it hissed and drove its claws into the webbing of his hand.

"Oh, *very* rude of you, brash creature," he said, clucking his tongue at it. "And perhaps not so useful in preserving your little life."

Where the claws had pierced his skin, scarlet welled up, rimmed with pearling, inky black. The tendrils of Lightless strained toward the kitten's velvet nose, and before he could call them back they had already plunged. The cat went rigid in his cupped hands, back bowed as far as it would go.

Its soul was much less dense than Vera's had been, light and porous as dandelion fluff, and in moments he had consumed the totality of what it had known and loved. Its delight in madcap, dashing runs and the thrill of the hunt; its predilection for ladybugs and beetles. Its aloof but devoted attachment to its former mistress; the lazy sweetness it had felt in finding slants of light in which to sprawl.

Then all its muscles relaxed at once, little body going slack even as the amber eyes turned to clots of black.

With a shrug, he slung its featherweight over one shoulder like a stole. It was still warm and soft against him, and he liked the tickle of its fishing-wire whiskers and its breath.

"A good deal less spirit in this one than in you, pet," he noted to Vera. "Though that is as it should be."

From her perch high in a corner of the ceiling, where two walls met, she quirked her head at him in mute acknowledgment of his voice, arms and legs splayed backward and out like a clinging bat's. Her hair was still damp and tangled, hanging like lichen on either side of her face, shading the empty glitter of her eyes.

Those eaten by the Lightless not only lost the light they had, but they also changed in other intriguing ways. Vera's body had already been youthful and toned, and with the influx of black flooding its veins and muscle, bones and ligaments, she had become both strong and much more pliable than before. Her joints were no longer locked into the angles they had once been forced to bend, and gravity had become more of a strong suggestion than an ironclad command.

"Come down, pet," he said to her. "Come sit with me. You will serve well, and I could do with a few more like you. But for my bannermen, I require something with a bit more venom and fang."

She sprang down into an easy, silent crouch, then scuttled toward him on all fours with a discordant sort of grace, joints popping back and forth as she crawled. It always made him so happy how readily the consumed obeyed. Even better than riding a properly broken horse.

Once she settled next to him, he rested a hand on her peach-fuzzed nape. He could feel the taint of the Lightless inside her writhe up to meet his grip, and with it, the power flared up like logs tossed onto an already lively flame.

As in any other summoning, there was strength in numbers.

When the rings of ink around his arms began to flicker and revolve, he knew that it was time.

THOUGH THEY MIGHT not know precisely what it meant, even mortals knew—or felt—that there were places where the veil between the worlds thinned all the way down to sheer.

A church had once been built on such a place. Perhaps as a

battlement to stave off the curling dark beneath. Or perhaps from the mistaken perception that the closeness of something so otherworldly meant that this other something must be good.

Or perhaps it was simply to pay respect to what had been there first, which was a tower built from stone and skulls.

The skulls belonged to nearly a thousand fearless men, who had lost their heads there well over two hundred years before. When Ottomans first claimed those lands, pockets of rebels rose to harry them in the hills, nipping at their underbellies and gnawing at their flanks. But during that first uprising on a place called Čegar Hill, once it had become clear that the battle would be lost—and his men impaled in warning to others, as was their opponents' custom—the rebel Serb commander ordered a retreat. He sealed himself and his men deep within their entrenchment and ignited its powder magazine.

To deliver himself and his people to heaven, and ferry their foes to hell.

Once the last of the dust had cleared, and the last of the bodies settled, an Ottoman general surveyed the battlefield. While there might be nothing to display on stakes, he decreed, a monument of warning would be erected just the same. What remained of the rebels would be beheaded, and their skulls embedded into a tower built to mark where they had fallen. When his men had finished, the tower stood fifteen feet tall. Studded with more than nine hundred rotting heads in fourteen rows.

Building such a testament to blood thirst, on ground abutted by the world of straining Lightless, further sheered the veil.

Their world beneath, or beside, or above—even to Herron, who had once plunged into its depths like a diver for black pearls, how it aligned with this one had never been made clear—was a dense, coiled, cohesive thing. No light nor air, water nor earth. Just a tangled mass that was entirely animate, with no space in between. Like a nest of snakes dipped in both slick and sticky tar, squirming and hissing around each other, restless and always prepared to spring through even the shortest-lived opening.

Though they were legion, they were also only one. A very single-minded mind driven by a single dream.

The dream of freedom in some elsewhere rich with luscious light on which to sup, and filled with spacious room in which to *move*.

Though in this place, at the base of Čegar Hill, the veil was near-translucent, that alone was not enough to grant them passage through. They needed a call, a full-fledged invitation. Someone on the other side to slice a welcoming slit, wielding the blade of their own will.

When they heard Herron calling to them, they swarmed as one to this tatter-place both thinnest and closest to him. Only three hundred miles or so inland from where he knelt with his hand on Vera's nape.

And the veil dusted apart like cobwebs, just for a moment, to let the onslaught in.

Had anyone been in the chapel, they would have seen something seep between the creaking floorboards, something that couldn't seem to decide between liquid and smoke. Some malleable matter infused with intent and mind.

The sinuous black formed a wispy runnel along the well-swept floor and poured its way beneath the cage of glass that shielded what was left of the Skull Tower. It wasn't life, or light, but those bones had seen a suitably gory death. A thing like that left scraps of soul behind, meaty echoes on which to feed.

The black rushed steadily up the tower like the creeping thorns that once grew into a sleeping beauty's vicious bower. Of the nearly thousand skulls that had adorned its sides, only a few remained, pocked here and there. Into these remaining ones the Lightless surged, curling into the skulls' cavities and expanding to fill the empty space. As the skulls grew masks of viscous, iridescent black flesh, mimicking the faces that their owners had once worn in life, each popped free from its crumbling stone pocket when it rounded out too large, and landed on the floor with a moist but solid *thwump*.

Once they were free, the full resurrection took hold, though the bodies spawned were transformed rather than restored. As warriors, the Lightless needed sturdy spines and limbs and skin, at least for the chassis. Then wings like black sails on pirate ships, and whipping tails, depending on what suited best.

And there was always room for talons and stingers.

Once all of them reared up to full height, the glass box could no longer contain them. They burst out of it, moving as one, and vanished long before the rain of shattered glass fell to the floor behind them.

FIFTEEN

Iris

THAT LAST TRIP HAD COST ME.

I'd clung with all my will to the balcony above the candlelit atrium. This time, it had been early morning, and Lina had been wearing the same ragged sundress I'd left her in, still looking battered from the battle on the mountaintop. My visits to our world were snipped loose from her time, apparently, and dictated instead by my urgency. Sweeping me to the moment that I most needed to see.

It had been a tremendous effort to maintain the infinite bloom for long enough to hear everything Mara said. But I'd learned what I needed to know, while Mara spoke and then danced the history of our line, the final truth behind our curse.

Her great sacrifice.

Fjolar had been right; it had been nothing like what I thought I'd known.

Nothing was what I thought.

I'd been so cold when the wisteria snapped me back, my teeth chattering so hard I thought my molars might split. Beneath the limestone overhang, Fjolar had sat me on his lap and wrapped us both in the fur cape, curling around me to kindle some warmth. I couldn't find it in me to protest. I was too depleted to endure the Quiet so he could take me somewhere warmer, and I needed his heat.

And my fury toward him had subsided, awash in too much shock and the revelation of how wrong I'd been.

"Well, *that* wasn't from any poison, flower," he said, once my teeth stopped chattering enough to let me talk. "What happened that time? Where did you go? I couldn't rouse you, no matter what I did. Your body was asleep, but the rest of you . . ."

"I can fractal to my world, for a little while," I said hoarsely, shifting around to rest my head against his chest. I couldn't see any point in lying about it to him. Exhausted as I was, my heart pounded so hard it felt like it might rattle itself loose inside me, as if it were made of rusted clockwork. "Through the infinite bloom. Not all of me. Just . . . a piece of me, I think. My body stays here, the way the daughters' did in my world when they traveled here with you, I guess. Like I'm doing the opposite of what they did."

He paused, digesting it. I could hear his own heart speed up against my cheek. "And what did you see this time? Your sister again? The . . . that man who scared you so badly last time?"

"You can stop pretending you don't know who he is." I leaned back to lock eyes with him. "I know what's hidden here now. Mara told the whole coven the truth, and I saw it, heard everything. This kingdom isn't a stage at all. It's a prison, for the soul you and Mara ripped from Herron. The soul you couldn't kill."

"It's even more complicated than that, flower," he said, those stark Valhalla features collapsing into more exhaustion than I had ever seen in him. I might not have gone through with leaping off one of his cliffs, but I could see how much being unable to wake me had worried him. "That generative energy I told you about, that comes from the performance and the courtship—it's what keeps this kingdom spinning, and pins down his soul with its force. But even the unchosen daughters served a purpose. The syllables of the names Mara gave each daughter to capture her essence, and the scents of the soul-perfumes—they're living components of her spell." He picked up one of my chilled hands, bringing my wrist to his nose. "You still smell of yours, you know. And you still sound like Lisarah."

I thought of when I had first heard the names that Mara had given me and Malina: Lisarah and Azareen. The way those three syllables had seemed to float in the air, echoing; the way they evoked our internal multitudes. That was also when Mara had explained the significance of names, the power in phonemes. I hadn't considered it before, but every coven name I knew held three syllables—Faisali, Anais, Naisha, all the rest of them—and all of them had that same lingering portentousness, a nearly tangible weight. Like harbingers or sigils.

The perfumes were a similar thing, though not the same. Those seemed to encompass the physicality of what we were.

"Your scents and names were like interlocking gears in the clockwork spell she set in motion," Fjolar went on. "Every new generation of daughters left behind strengthened Mara's working, bearing down on that pillar of winter. Keeping Herron's soulless body trapped on earth, while my companion and I kept his soul trapped here. All of us doing our parts to contain him."

Until Mama and Dunja—and Lina and I, in turn—had burned everything down. I couldn't quite feel guilty about it; I hadn't known the truth. But I could still feel responsible.

"Why didn't you just tell me?" I murmured, pinching the bridge of my nose. "About Herron loose? And his soul here?"

"And what would you have done if I had told you about him?" he countered. "Don't tell me you wouldn't have battered yourself to pieces against me, trying to get out of here to protect your sister. If you'd known, you wouldn't even have bothered pretending for me."

It shouldn't have mattered, but my cheeks burned anyway. "You knew what I was doing? The entire time?"

He cast me a distinctly fond, indulgent look. "Flower girl. Come on. What do you take me for? Of course I knew your game."

"So why did you let me keep doing it?"

"Because I liked it, of course. I liked seeing you try to win me over. It was . . ." He tilted his head back and forth, considering. "Cute to watch."

"It was *cute*?" I demanded. "Is that why you stole me in the first place?"

"I took you because I wanted you with me," he replied bluntly. "You know I did. But it wasn't only that. I could feel that the kingdom hadn't yet fallen to pieces, and I'm sworn to Mara for however long the spell holds. Your performance itself, and the growing bond between us, were needed to keep the kingdom intact. I wouldn't forswear the pact unless I was sure it no longer did any good." His voice darkened. "Especially not if it means letting that interloper have his soul back, so he can steal even more life. Life that should be only *mine* to take."

Maybe I shouldn't have been so taken aback by the idea of his loyalty to Mara, or the notion that Death had some sort of honor code. But I'd mostly seen only the rampant hedonism, the sullenness when he didn't get his way, the readiness to whittle us down to the quick while we performed for him. Yet there was more to him than that. The flashes of tenderness, the new willingness to be gentle with me when I needed it.

And I understood even the worst of him more than I cared to admit—how powerful and complicated any desire could be. All those years I'd spent dreaming of my escape from Cattaro, yearning for Japan; it hadn't only been that I'd wanted to travel, to see another world that might belong to me. It had also been the venal wish to shake myself loose of Mama, and of the burden of always protecting Lina.

It was possible to want a thing badly for many more reasons than just one.

"So," I began, drumming my free hand on my knee. The back of it was mottled pink and ghostly white, aching with the cold.

Desperation lodged, beating, in my throat like a hummingbird. "How is she going to capture him this time? I saw him, Fjolar. He's—he's monstrous. And he's gathering some kind of hideous army, I saw that, too. I think he might even have someone on the inside; he mentioned a spy-witch, and what else could that mean? We have to help them. I know I have to find his soul and bring it back to them—Lina said so—but once we do, then what? I still won't know how to get out of here."

"I wish I knew, flower girl," he said with a broad-shouldered shrug. "I would help you—and her—however I could. Tell me you finally believe at least that much."

I huffed out a breath, driving my nails into my palm as another veil of desperation settled over me. "Do you even know where it is? If you remake the kingdom to suit your companion every single time, based on things you've drawn from her mind . . ."

This time the regret was written plainly on his face. "Exactly. I don't know what shape the soul would have taken, in this version of our kingdom. And I have no idea where it would be, in this patchwork that I sewed for you."

I yearned for a hair band around my wrist to snap, like I would have done back home to stifle rising panic. In the absence of one, I buried my hand into my own nape and gave my hair a solid tug at the roots, sharp enough until the panic crept down a notch or two. "But he's coming for them, Fjolar. We have to *do* something. We have to go find it, *now*. He's in the mountains already, he—"

"We'll find it together, flower," he soothed, giving my hand a squeeze. A deep, dull ache rumbled through me, like the shifting of tectonic plates. If it had been Luka holding my hand, he would have known I craved the comfort of a much harder grip. But Luka wasn't here, and Fjolar was. "And I know it feels like the clock is ticking madly, but for us, it isn't. This kingdom is a space outside of time. We have as much of it as we need to search."

That bit made some sort of sense, at least. None of my visits with Lina had been synced with my own experience of time in this kingdom.

"In the meantime, you need to rest." He pulled me more tightly against the warm granite of his torso, settling my head into the crook of his shoulder. "You've spent yourself too hard, flower. Sleep a little, and then we'll go hunting ourselves."

"Why are you being so nice to me now?" My eyelids really were terribly heavy. "The things I said to you . . . everything I accused you of . . ."

"Wasn't entirely wrong," he finished, stroking my hair. "Just not what you thought, and not the whole truth. Either way, I loved seeing you fight. I always do. All that fierceness, the principles, that burning loyalty. You're a fearsome thing to watch, flower, even when you're trapped in cold. A firestorm all on your own."

That was the last I heard before I succumbed to sleep. Him calling me a firestorm.

It sounded truer than anything else he'd ever said to me.

SIXTEEN

Malina

"I'M FINE, I'LL BE FINE, IT'S NOT AS THOUGH I'VE NEVER taken a tumble before during practice," Oriell murmured to the two who rushed to her side as soon as she hit the floor. Rubbing her ankle, she looked up at me with stricken eyes. "I'm so sorry, Malina. I *had* it, I really had it while you were singing. All I could think of was that I would reach the sky. It was just when you stopped . . ."

"It's not your fault," I gasped out between big gulps of breath. I hadn't realized how hard I'd been working to channel all that feeling, inscribe it onto Oriell with the quill of the song. It wasn't what I usually did. My songs were invitations to feel the spectrum of emotions, or an echoed depiction of what someone else felt. They weren't meant to be such a forceful command. "I shouldn't have just cut off like that."

"You would have had to stop soon, anyway, pie," Niko said. She had appeared by my side, snaking a slim, strong arm around my waist. I leaned gratefully into her, resting my cheek against the top of her head. Over the years I'd learned that she could more than take my weight. "You were turning a really unfortunate kind of green. Like a little purply? I didn't know faces went that way."

Mara watched me with grave eyes, and for once she couldn't quite keep her face impassive. I could both see and hear the roiling distress beneath the smooth facade.

"Nikoleta is correct, I think," she murmured. "We will try again tomorrow."

We did try again the next day. And the day after that.

But no matter how I struggled, I couldn't make it last.

To make matters worse, it didn't even work on all of them. We found that out when I tried singing to a few of the others, thinking the problem might have been with Oriell. But no matter how much of my gleam I forced into the song, some of them couldn't even do what she had done. The leap from beauty into strength was too much for them.

Mara had molded them into courtesans so well that in some cases it couldn't be undone.

And the effects only lasted as long as my voice. If something hit me on the battlefield—or if I woke up with a sore throat—they wouldn't be able to stir themselves into action. The song didn't linger once my voice died, had no staying power.

Worst of all, I just couldn't sustain a prolonged gleam without Mara boosting it for me with her own song. If I tried to push through without her, I promptly passed out no matter how much strength I funneled into the effort.

Three days later, we weren't any closer to an army, and we'd lost half the remaining winter in our eyes. The looming dread obstructed my own gleam, made me that much less able to inspire others with what song I could muster.

After breakfast that morning, overwhelmed with frustration, I went to find Mara in her chambers, Niko by my side. "Is there anyone else who could help teach me?" I asked her. "I need to get stronger, and I just . . . I don't know how. Not by myself. You won't be able to help me when the time comes, and I need *someone.*"

Or else we're lost, I added silently.

I didn't have to say it out loud. She knew it as well as I did.

Her face turned pensive, then taut. "There *is* someone," she said. "I had hoped to avoid entangling her in my own mare's nest. But now . . ."

We all knew what she meant. If he blew through us, Herron would be everyone's menace soon.

"Who is she?" I asked.

"An old family friend, I suppose you could call her."

"Though *I* wouldn't," Izkara interjected from the corner where she lurked, watching over Mara. She mock-shuddered, then cast me what passed for a sympathetic look from her, which meant she looked like she only half wanted to slap me.

"Still, there is the matter of the favor to collect," Mara mused. "Unpleasant though the asking will surely be. Jasna will want to keep you for a spell, fledgling, if she agrees to help. And we have a few days to spare for it—*he* would not dare strike out while any of my winter still holds him in its grip and renders him weak. I can feel how far away from us he is, still; he has barely moved inland since he dragged himself ashore." She still avoided saying his name, I'd noticed, whenever she could. As if she was still loath to lend him power by calling him out. "He would not gamble and risk losing to me again, not after these many years."

She turned her ponderous gaze to me. "Go and prepare some things to bring with you, fledgling. And you, too, Nikoleta, if you wish to chaperone your lover."

Niko scrambled toward the door in a flash of fine sleek hair and tan limbs. "I'll go get Luka," she tossed over her shoulder to me. "He won't want to miss an excuse to ditch this place."

"SO YOU'VE BROUGHT a war of the worlds to my doorstep, have you?" Jasna said dryly, dropping a rough-turned clay mug of lemonade into Mara's waiting hands. Dunja, Izkara, Niko, Luka, and I already had ours—Dunja had insisted on coming too, to watch over me. Jasna had very deliberately served Mara last. "Blown it in like an ill wind. What a fine guest-gift to offer me, after all these years. Though I would have been happy with something more modest. Just so you know, so as not to overspend for next time."

Jasna's home was in one of the little villages clustered in the Zeta Valley, in a cradle of emerald mountains. A vineyard bursting with ripening grapes surrounded her sprawling stone cottage, and an evergreen forest marched up the mountain slope at its back. It all looked like it had been transported here from centuries ago.

We all sat barefoot around her stone hearth, a brushy hand-made broom laid out along the mantel. From the inside, the cottage seemed much more spacious than it should have been. All rough stone and exposed, worn wooden rafters, as if it had been built around a gallows. Little wicker men and dried wheat dollies hung above every window. Everything smelled like herbs, sliced lemons, and the savor of roasting sausages.

"I would not be here if I could avoid it, *baba*," Mara said through tight lips. "And you know it. But by your honor and your family's word, you owe me and mine what I am come to claim."

"I doubt my great-grandmother foresaw a repayment like this, when she asked your help with the paltry thing *she* needed," Jasna retorted. "But you're right that I'm honor-bound by her word, and the favor owed. And fortunately for you, I don't take kindly to the notion of demons defiling my lady's soil."

Sipping the tart, herbed lemonade—Niko would know what was in it, but now wasn't the time to ask—my gaze drifted as they spoke. Black cast-iron chandeliers hung from the eaves, burning with beeswax candles that dripped searing blobs. In the open corner of the kitchen, cut lilies floated in water in an age-clouded copper sink. The splintered wooden boards that served as shelves groaned under jars of powders and herbs, and accumulated oddities lay strewn everywhere. Hand-sculpted vases, an antique charcoal iron, incense holders in descending order like nesting dolls. A dried puffer fish with a pooched mouth that I just *knew* Niko would try to kiss when no one was looking.

Jasna herself looked heartily ordinary. Freckled, sweet-faced, and barefoot, with a gray-threaded brown braid slung over her homespun yellow sweater and torn jeans. She seemed too young to me to be a grandmother unless she'd had children early, but when Mara called her *baba*, she didn't object. As if it was a term of respect.

"So, what can I do for you, Black Mara?" she asked, lowering herself into a rocking chair so close to the ground it must have been carved a century ago. "I can offer you my own coven's help, along with the favor of the gods who claim us and this land."

"I come seeking *your* particular aid. Not that of your . . . coven, or your gods." I gritted my teeth at the barely restrained disdain in Mara's voice, especially when Jasna's face darkened in response.

"I see you still think of us as kitchen witches, compared to you. Peasants digging in this world's dirt," she said, low and echoing. As if something much older and bigger stood behind her shoulder, speaking with her voice. "But our roots run deep, and our gods attend us when we call. And where are yours, in your hour of need? So have a care how you speak to me, you upstart girl. And a girl you are in the Great Lady's eyes, no matter how old."

Izkara sprang from her seat and lowered into a ready crouch. "Show sorai respect," she grated in her gravelly half-animal voice. "Or I will make you."

Jasna's gaze shifted to her, and her eyes also seemed like a screen hiding something larger behind them. I could almost hear it, like the beating of tremendous wings. For a moment, I thought I saw a stir of something in the rafters. A cloud of feathers drifting above

Jasna like a distant, diffuse halo. "Heel, you rude mongrel of a watchdog," she rumbled. "You're in *my* house now. Sit down before I make *you* sorry."

Mara bowed her head, running her tongue along the inside of her full lower lip. Humility didn't come easily to her, but it did come. She flicked a warning gaze toward Izkara, who thumped back down and twined her fingers into a single tight fist in her lap, huffing short breaths through her nose.

"Forgive me, *baba*," Mara said stiffly. "We will accept whatever you have to share, gladly and with thanks."

The precarious moment of crackling ozone passed. Jasna settled back into her chair, that secondary presence subsiding. The molt of feathers above her, if they'd even been there, dissolved back to air. I let my shoulders drop from where they'd hunched up to my ears.

"As to what we need, we seek your mortal wisdom. My far-daughter"—she paused, glanced at me—"Malina's will requires strengthening for what lies ahead."

"Hmm." Jasna leaned back pensively, rocking herself with her right foot. Her eyes grazed over me, and I froze under the weight of even their peremptory regard. They were an ephemeral blue, like the sea under a clouded sky. Clear and arresting. "Why even bother with plain, old mortal will? When has all your fabled gleam not been enough for you?"

"I'm sorry," I broke in, speaking for the first time. "But what's the difference, exactly?"

"The little bird speaks!" She clapped her hands together. "And here I thought your old mother might have your tongue tied up in a hex bag." A sly, needling glance at Mara. "Not that she would, of course. She's above doing harm just because she can. As am I, for that matter, and in that we find our common ground. As for will . . ."

She looked at me directly now, unblinking as an owl, her sun-browned, blunt-nailed hands folded in her lap. "While your gleam is part of you—a magic you were born with, running through your blood—your will *is* you. The force of everything you are, brought to bear on bending the world into whatever it is you want. Unlike your sequins and sparkles, with enough work, anyone can learn to wield their will. Though, as with anything, some of us are stronger than others."

She shifted her gaze to Mara. "But I ask again, Black Mara. Why come to my door with this? Has all that lofty beauty truly failed you?"

A muscle twitched in Mara's jaw. "It is not enough. Not anymore. The gleam is not what it once was—not even in my far-daughter, and she is much stronger than many of the others."

"Oh, isn't that sweet to hear!" Jasna gave a charming, hooting laugh. Her smile was gap-toothed, sunshine through clouds, and it brought her close to beautiful. Even for all her taunting, I heard no actual malice in her. Just a pleasant, rhythmic rushing like waves rolling home to a placid beach. A vast yet simple peace that even news of advancing demons somehow hadn't disturbed. "Baba Emilija would've been beside herself with glee if she were here. A strong believer in 'pretty is as pretty does,' she was."

"Yes, she was," Mara agreed mildly. "Yet also in my debt. So will you help?"

"Of course. I live by my word, as a true witch should. How much time do I have with your girl?" Those steady eyes landed on me again, assessing. "And what does she do, in your glitzy way?"

"She sings what she hears," Mara replied shortly, steepling her long fingers and then lacing them beneath her chin. "And you have two days with her, perhaps three on the outside."

Or until the gray in my dark eye ebbed down to a quarter at the most, to leave us with a buffer. More than enough time for me to head back to Mara's stronghold if she sensed Herron coming.

A sudden flicker caught my eye, on the widow's walk above. Like a pixelation, a wavering in the shadows beneath the eaves. I thought I saw something, like I'd almost seen on the chalet's balcony. Almost heard the rush of rain.

Bubbling hope rose up my throat. *Riss*. What if it was somehow Riss?

But then it vanished, and I deflated. There was nothing there but the swaying strings of wrinkled peppers and garlic dangling from the decorative railing.

I turned back to Jasna, who was scoffing from deep in her throat. "Two *days*? Do you care to set any other impossible tasks for me, like from the old tales? Maybe you want a dress sewn from the fabric of the dawn? Or snowdrops to fill ten baskets? I'm no storybook witch, girl, no more than you are. Working with will properly is like using any other tool. Learning to touch it, know it, wield its heft—it all takes time."

Mara lifted her slim shoulders once and spread her hands. "Then teach her what you can, *baba*, in the time we have. This world will thank you for it."

"'This world,'" Jasna echoed mockingly. "Arrogant as ever. What do you know of this world?"

"More than I once did. Or I would not have come to you."

"And what do *you* say, little bird?" She quirked her head at me.

"I'll teach you what I can. But only if it's what you want."

"I do," I said, so firmly the conviction felt almost uncomfortable in my mouth. "I was the one who asked for this."

"Then perhaps you're not a lost cause after all." Her gaze slid to Niko, then to Luka. "And you two? No tourists allowed. If you stay too, you'll help. You certainly have the raw materials; I can smell it." She sniffed playfully at the air. "The potential on you both."

Niko lit like a paper lantern at the prospect of being involved, and even Luka's somber look slipped a little with his nod.

Jasna beamed, and rubbed her hands briskly together. "Good enough for me! Now let's see what mischief Granny Witch can teach you."

AFTER MARA AND Izkara left, leaving Dunja outside to keep guard, we ate at Jasna's long trestle table. She fed us beefsteak tomatoes and diced cucumbers from her garden, and fresh-baked rolls spread with young, mild cheese and filled with spicy sausage. The lemonade had been replaced with sweet red wine from Jasna's own vineyard, differently herbed.

I'd gotten so used to fancy coven food, everything sliced into transparent curls or annoyingly deconstructed, that I thought I'd die of these simple joys. Luka apparently felt the same, barely surfacing from his plate.

Jasna watched us in consternation. "Did they not feed you children at that ridiculous palace of a house?"

"I prefer food I can't see through," Luka mumbled through a wolfish bite. It was so close to what I'd been thinking that I nearly laughed through my own full mouth. "And the wine . . . is that woodruff, and meadowsweet? What were you going for with those? Gentle victory? Triumphant peace? Kind of optimistic for our circumstances."

"Something like that, yes," Jasna replied in a faintly surprised, approving tone. "I thought they'd do you good, all the same. The three of you could do with a glass half full. Who taught you herbs, boy? They did a fine job of it."

Luka chewed once more, then swallowed hard. "My mother. She used them like you do."

"I didn't think you remembered any of that, beast," Niko said, soft.

"Of course I remember, gnat," he said, just as tender. "I always told you I wouldn't forget."

I glanced over at Niko, watched her bite her lip with well-worn sadness. Even after three years, they both still missed Koštana badly, I knew. *I* still missed her, and she hadn't even been my mother.

But the melancholy didn't last. There was a lightness here, I realized, an undercurrent of deep-rooted joy that I'd never heard at the chalet. The entire cottage felt like Jasna, just like Mara's stronghold felt like her. But unlike in my own kin's home, there was nothing baleful here, no oppressive taint. No rancid guilt, no ancient curse. No Mama breathing her doleful cold down my neck.

Just books, gardening and sewing tools, and the grassy, meadow scent of fresh and drying herbs. Pragmatic magic, and common contentment.

It made me feel so safe. It reminded me of hope, and the magic Riss and I had once weaved with Mama in our garden just for the sake of happiness.

Once we were done eating, Jasna took all three of us over to the sink filled with leaves and lilies. She sprinkled coarse salt into it, then picked up a double-sided blade with a gleaming ebony hilt. I didn't recognize any of the intricate little sigils engraved into it. Murmuring under her breath, she dipped the point into the water, breathing slow and steady through her nose.

"What are you doing?" I asked, just above a whisper.

She gave me a half smile, her eyes still closed. "Cleansing. Consecrating the water by my own hand, and in the Lady's name."

I remembered she'd called on this lady before. "Who is she? Your lady, I mean."

"The maiden and the mother, and also the wizened crone," Jasna replied, pitched low with reverence. "The lady of the moon, the stars, and especially of the earth. Devoted steward of all that walks and crawls and flies over her beloved face. She's our cradle and grave, our home and hearth. The wellspring of our rebirth."

This lady sounded beautiful, I thought, somehow familiar. And Jasna *loved* her, I could hear its clarion pitch. Exalted, freely given adoration. "Does she have a name?"

"Oh yes, many, many names. She's simply the Lady to those unsworn to her. And though she's everywhere, around these parts we call her Zorica, sometimes. Dawn Star, mother of the sun."

One by one, she dipped our hands into the water before dabbing it with her roughened fingers onto our ankles, throats, and foreheads. "Have a little of this, too," she murmured, offering oil that smelled like eucalyptus, mint, and cinnamon. "In the same places the cleansed water touched. And anywhere else you'd like to smell nice."

I dabbed it everywhere, like perfume. It made me feel an earthy, refreshed kind of clean, like I'd waded naked through a mountain spring. I lingered with her at the sink once Luka and Niko moved back to the table, breathing in the smell of water and the lilies.

Jasna watched my pleasure, smiling. When I caught her eye, she tipped me a wink. "You're one of hers too, just so you know. You might be born to Mara's line, but you belong to the grove no less than I do, as one of the Lady's hidden children. You can feel it, can't you, the pull when you're near me? That's why you've fallen in with these two." She inclined her head toward Niko and Luka in turn. "They're hers too, especially the girl."

I thought of how Niko sounded like wings, like flight—like the feathers that had seemed to rain down over Jasna. Maybe that was somehow part of this goddess's mark. Maybe just a few months ago I would have questioned if I even believed in goddesses or gods. But there wasn't much room left in me for that kind of doubt, not anymore. I'd left that simple, easy world behind.

"Through their mother, I'd guess," she went on. "Dedication to the Lady often runs down maternal lines. Though yours likely wouldn't have."

I turned the idea over gingerly in my head, the thought of belonging to something other than a legacy of forced beauty and servitude. Such a precious, unexpected gift—maybe even one from our faceless father.

I caught her arm grazingly as she turned away. "Why do you hate her? Mara, I mean? She can't help what she is."

Her eyes went soft as morning mist. "Oh, I don't hate her, bird, don't think that of me. I hate very few things. It's a wasteful, violent way to spend one's will. But I don't like her, you're right. She's not fully of this place—you know that much—and of course that's not her fault. But she chooses to act like a queen, nose upturned, with scant regard for our world's sacred things. It isn't right."

I remembered Mara's story, the casual way she had dismissed her own tribe's gods. Her snarling, spitting hatred for the icons of Christianity. "Stars and gods," she always said, but even that was more of a curse than an oath. I'd thought it was all the sacrifice that had made her that way, but maybe it was how she'd started out.

"Always so haughty," Jasna continued dourly, gaining steam. "It rubs me all wrong. As if being the by-blow of some shiny, wayward godling passing by from elsewhere—or whatever it was that made her—exempts her from owing respect to the gods that hail from here. I'd wager changing that outlook would have saved her some trouble in the past."

"But she did do your great-grandmother a favor, didn't she?" I pointed out.

"Yes, *that.*" Jasna rolled her eyes. "My great-grandmother had too many overeager suitors, and no interest in being some village lumpkin's put-upon wife. Most of them she got rid of herself, but one just wouldn't take the boot. So she asked Mara and her sirens for her help in 'stealing' him from her, in exchange for a future favor. Don't know what happened to that oaf. Do know he never bothered her again."

I nearly burst out laughing at that. The first fiction Mara had told us, about our family's curse, was that it had been cast by a jealous witch whose lover had been stolen by one of Mara's tribe. She'd clearly used Jasna's great-grandmother for inspiration. And I couldn't imagine anyone more unlikely than Jasna to curse someone over a man.

Something else occurred to me. "I saw a church, in the village," I said carefully. "What do . . ." I trailed off, unsure how to finish the thought without offending her.

She raised a merry, unruly eyebrow. "What do the priests think of me? My family's been here since before this thought to be a village, patching wounds and catching babies. The priests and I know enough to leave each other well alone. Now, come."

She led me back to the cleared table, her arms full of jars and vials she'd gathered from the shelves. "Let's see, let's see," she muttered to herself. "Something traditional, I think, but with a twist." She dropped pinches of herbs and resins from the jars into a simple granite mortar, before grinding it all together briskly with the pestle, her cheeks turning ruddy with the effort. There was nothing studied about the efficient motions of her hands and the strength she put into the grind, nothing pretty, but I could still feel the buzz of magic building. "Can one of you clever kits tell me what all went in here?"

"Frankincense, obviously," Niko said, sounding like such a know-it-all I smirked beside her. "And myrrh and benzoin. Mmm, and sandalwood. Gum acacia, too, I think. Would a little sage help too?"

"And sweet orange oil, maybe," Luka added. "Mama always liked to add a dash. She said it made things *friendly*. Not an exact science to it, but it somehow sounded right." He shrugged a shoulder. "Even to me."

"Good on you both," Jasna said, nodding. She'd brought a little electric pot to the table, half filled with water, and set it to bubbling. "There's a lot of fire and air in this particular mix. Lovely for sparking the will, but maybe a little bright and flighty—and our little bird brings much of her own light already, doesn't she? Some sage could ground her, lend a little earth." She smiled at Luka. "You're right, as well. A little orange oil won't hurt."

Niko wrinkled her nose. "Is that . . . a fondue pot?"

"It is, and why shouldn't it be?" Jasna retorted. "Do you demand a cauldron for authenticity?" She scraped the mixture deftly into the burbling water, sliding a lid over it to capture the fragrant steam. "Now lean close and breathe the goodness in."

I closed my eyes and parted my lips, feeling the heat of steam against their soft inner flesh. It smelled sharp, sweet, and dizzying, herbal yet old as sacrament. With it I could feel the balance shift from levity to sanctity.

"Go on, breathe deep," Jasna instructed, her voice even and smooth, a steady meter. "Fill your lungs with all the latent power in these herbs. The smell of magic born of this earth, and worked since time itself was barely weaned. Burned in cauldrons and censers and"—amusement touched her voice—"fondue pots, for love and strength and healing, banishment and summoning, reverence and wrath."

I could feel the gleam straining inside me, responding to the scent and the rhythm of her words as my mind unfurled. I nearly started humming out of habit.

"No, bird," Jasna cautioned gently, as if she could feel it. "That's the easy path. You were born knowing how to walk it; to you, it's like breath. Dive deeper now, look harder. The Lady brooks no shortcuts, no crutches, no laziness. Find the *other* strength."

I frowned, my eyes still shut. I didn't know what she meant.

"Oh yes you do, bird," she chided. "Don't pull that ornery face with me. You know where to go already; I've even seen you do it. Think of what you search for when you make your shield. That pretty birdcage you build for yourself, to keep things out when they get too loud."

I drew a sharp breath. "How do you—you can *see* the bubble?"

"Of course I can see it," she said, a smile coloring her voice. "What do you take me for, a witchling wet behind the ears? And it's not a 'bubble' like a child blows through a loop, but a witch's shield.

If you can shape your will into a shield, you can shape it into anything. Just look for the place in you that echoes with intent. The certainty that you can mold the world—that if you lead steadily and well, reality will leap to follow. Do you know it yet, little bird? Can you feel it's true?"

My hands had heated with the sound of her voice, and my whole spine seemed to glow. I felt so whole, connected to the earth where I touched the floor with my bare soles. Grounded like a wire.

There *was* a place inside me, like a cavern. Sparkling with stalactites of potential.

"Yes," I said slowly, edged with wonder. "I think I do know where it is."

SEVENTEEN

Iris

TOGETHER, FJOLAR AND I SLOGGED THROUGH THE KINGdom, delving into each piece for whatever shape a caged demon soul might take.

The Quiet had stopped being such a torment. Now I instinctively wound my wisteria nest around me whenever we hopped a seam, to seal myself safe, and I'd discovered that being in that nowhere-place even made it a little easier to fractal myself toward Lina and search for any sign of a traitor in her midst. Maybe it was the nature of the fabric, its purpose as both a boundary and connective tissue. When I was in it, I swam that much closer to the shores of my own world.

Every time I tried it, I caught brief glimpses of my sister by extending myself through the buds and branches of my own bloom.

I saw Lina wandering the chalet grounds, sitting in a stone cottage with Luka and Niko, singing to a Great Hall filled with coven daughters wielding their gleams. But I was so faint, barely there and then gone like a breath. My presence was too wan without the catalyst of a great, propulsive need. She didn't see me, and I only ever stayed enough to catch sight of her beloved face.

And feel the roiling darkness lapping toward her, trembling with eagerness to close in.

Because I never saw her without whiplashing to wherever Herron was. Sitting cross-legged with a limp kitten in his lap, exhaling darkness down some poor boy's throat, and once, stalking through the West Gate in Old Town Cattaro, his handsome, savage face tilted to the sky.

A stone's throw from where Čiča Jovan lived.

He was trespassing on *my* turf, and there was nothing I could do about it—no way to help Lina, Jovan, *anyone*—until I found that goddamned soul. Knowing that I was working on a different timeline than they were did nothing to still the underlying clamor of panic and rage, the dragging sense that somehow I was still being much too slow. I couldn't find the soul; I couldn't find any spies.

And I couldn't shed the creeping, nasty feeling that every time I saw Herron, he somehow saw me back.

It all took its toll on my body; even holding Fjolar's hand, I often went woozy and watery in the knees. It didn't help that I wasn't eating enough. We found most of my food in the kingdom's wooded regions, nuts, fruit, and edible flowers that Fjolar foraged for me—all of them beautiful, luckily, or else they wouldn't have been there for the picking.

And in one of these, the crooked wood, I first saw the owl.

The crooked wood was a pine forest swathed in deep summer, with all its trees growing uncannily twisted, swooping ninety degrees from the ground at their base before sweeping up into a smooth, curved silhouette like half a cello. Cottages sat tucked between them, painted candy colors and decorated with flowers like exquisite Easter-egg decals.

"It's a little bit of Poland, for my mistress's pleasure," Fjolar told me when I asked, sweeping into a courtier's bow to make me laugh, his pale hair dappled with leaf shadows. He'd been trying so hard to keep me from getting bogged down in despair, but there was only so much he could do for me. Still, I found the effort sweet, heartening when I needed it.

It was becoming hard to remember what it had even been like, not spending all my time by his side.

"The parts of it I thought you'd like," he added. "The trees are from the Crooked Forest in West Pomerania, and the houses from the village of Zalipie. They like their flowers there, almost as much as you do."

I thought of my bedroom ceiling at home in Cattaro, its hanging parasols painted with a wisteria tunnel, and knew exactly where he had gleaned this from.

"I know all about wagers with you," I tossed back feebly, too worn out for real banter. "Can we look inside the cottages? The soul might be in one."

We searched each from root cellar to attic. And though all their inside walls were also charmingly painted with flowers, I found with a plummeting heart that not a single one held anything like what we were looking for.

But outside, a flash of sunlight on wings, caught from the corner of my eye, momentarily startled me out of despondency. I whipped around, shading my eyes, trying to see where it had gone. "Fjolar!" I called out breathlessly. "There's a *bird* here!"

He froze. "A bird? I don't think so, flower. There aren't any animals here, and I would know. The things that mimic life here are for decoration only."

"But I saw—" Another tawny flicker, and this time I turned quickly enough to follow it. A neat brown owl, small for its kind, took flight from a cottage roof to the nearest branch of a crooked tree. There it settled, staring straight at me with impassive, dark-rimmed jade-and-golden eyes.

I crept up to the tree, holding my breath, afraid any sudden movement would chase her off. Hand still laced with mine, Fjolar trailed me reluctantly. "Hello," I whispered, so happy to see a living thing besides the two of us—if Fjolar even counted as a living thing—that I almost wanted to cry. "How did you get here?"

"Don't quote me on this, but I don't think she's going to answer you, flower," Fjolar said dryly. The owl turned her round gaze on him and issued a very deliberate screech in his direction.

"I don't think she likes you." I bit back laughter, standing on tiptoes and reaching a hand high up, thinking she wouldn't let me touch her. She did; awed, I stroked her feathers, velveteen with a waxen finish, with my fingertip. "But she and I are clearly meant to be friends."

"Once you're done petting, we should go," Fjolar said, and I drew back to look at him, startled by the brusque tone of his voice. Ever since the frosty savanna, he'd been so much gentler with me, solicitous and careful with my brittleness. But now his blue eyes were narrowed in a feline, predatory way—unnervingly familiar from all the times he'd leveled that challenging gaze at me. "I don't know how this uninvited guest snuck in here, but there are many, many other places left for us to search. Do you really want to linger?"

"You're right," I murmured, lowering my hand. "Let's keep moving."

But I was inordinately sorry to leave her behind as Fjolar led us to a threshold—a natural arch formed by the overhang of the branches above—and we stepped into the void of the Quiet together, and on to the next piece.

PLACE AFTER PLACE after place. All blurring together like an artist's muddied palette. Each was shatteringly beautiful in its own way, but I was getting so tired of being wonderstruck without a purpose.

In a tiny boat, Fjolar poled me like a gondolier through a series of linked caverns lit by dangling glowworms, like a stone sky studded with twinkling, pale-blue constellations. We visited rivers with submerged balls of flame that catapulted out of them like falling stars in reverse, and a field that flickered with an endless, electric symphony of lightning. He led me through a Spanish castle like an Aztec temple, half submerged in its own overflowing pool and fountains, the building itself drowning in creeping moss and foliage. It looked exactly like a mausoleum for a demon's soul, but its musty, dank rooms were empty and reeked of stagnant water.

And everywhere we went, I caught flashes of owl. Sometimes just the slant of her shadow, and other times an actual glimpse of talon, tail, or feathers from the corner of my eye. It wasn't always brown, as far as I could tell. Occasionally I saw streaks of gray or russet or even snowy white at the very edges of my vision, vanishing with the next blink. But the oddest thing was that the feel of her stayed the same.

As if it were always a single owl simply wearing different feathers.

And the longer we wandered, the stranger I felt, even holding tightly to Fjolar's hand.

By the time he brought me to a thundering waterfall, backed by basalt columns formed from lava and hardened into a scored sheet of rock, I realized I could barely stand on my own any longer. "What's *wrong* with me?" I drawled, sagging boneless against him. "My brain feels like it wants to slither sideways. Does that even make sense?"

He hitched me up against his side with an arm around my waist. "I think you're very tired, flower. Maybe even past exhausted. We might be outside of your world's time, but time here *does* pass in its way—and you're still a human girl who hasn't slept in a very long while. Why don't we rest here for a bit?"

"No," I protested. "There's nothing here; we've already searched. We have to move on, we have to keep looking—"

He didn't try to contradict me. Instead, he simply withdrew his arm and took a single step away from me. Without his support, my knees gave way like melting rubber, and I tumbled hard to the ground. It wasn't that I could barely stand. I actually couldn't stand at all, without him to bear me up.

And that was all it took. I burst into loud, messy tears like a stupid little girl, until I was sobbing so hard I choked on each breath.

"I'm so *tired*," I wept, smearing a shaking hand across my face. "So tired, and so fucking useless. I can't do anything to help them, I—"

Silently, he dropped down next to me and tugged me onto his lap. I clung to him and cried shamelessly into his chest, my shoulders heaving so hard they hurt, salt clogging my throat. He rocked me, murmuring soothing nothings into my hair, until the storm of tears passed over me.

"Come on, flower," he said quietly, between my hitching gasps. "There's something spectacular at the top of this waterfall, and I think you need it. You're no good to Lina like this, are you? You *have* to let yourself rest."

I shook my head once, and even that slight effort made me want to curl up and die in the root ball of some welcoming tree. "But I can't even climb up there."

"You don't have to climb anything, flower girl," he said. "Not when you have me."

With Fjolar carrying me half slung over his shoulder, we made our way up the hiking trail that wound to the top. I nearly gasped when he set me back down on my feet. A hot spring like a natural infinity pool crested over the waterfall's crown, the cascade blurring the edges where the basin dropped off into nothing.

Fjolar gave me a lazy half smile, pleased with my pleasure. "The original Svartifoss waterfall doesn't have this added feature, but I thought you'd like it. Why don't we get you in, for a hot soak? It'll melt away some of that fatigue."

I couldn't think of anything I wanted more.

"Just for a bit, though," I said weakly. "And then we start again."

"Of course, flower. Just for a bit."

Sitting near the pool's edge, I peeled my clothes off, awkwardly listing from one side to the other. Once I'd shed everything except my bra and panties, I stole a glance at Fjolar over my shoulder. He'd already stripped down to his tapered waist, his flower-tattooed arms bunching with muscle and his chest absurdly sculpted. His platinum hair was scraped back into a knot, revealing the shorn undersides and the helices of those gauged earrings he always wore.

I felt a familiar tightening at my center, directly linked with how much I wanted to run my palms over that known softness. Apparently not even debilitating fatigue could dispel that want.

"No need for modesty, flower. Nothing I haven't seen before." He began unbuttoning his black slacks, and I looked away. "But keep them on, if it makes you comfortable."

Throwing caution to the winds, I stripped down to the skin. What did it matter, anyway? It was just the two of us here, like it always was. Like, it seemed to me, it had always been.

I scooted myself gingerly to the pool's lip. The ground was strewn with sharp, glittering chips of the same basalt that formed the fractaling columns dripping behind the water's plummet. Fjolar already sat half submerged, his arms draped over the pool's non-existent rim and curls of steam coiling up around his face, pinking up the fair Viking's skin along his throat and slanting cheekbones. A cloudless, twilit sky stretched out like a peachy pennant to the horizon behind him, farther than the eye could follow.

He smiled at me, and I pretended not to notice the rake of his gaze from my temples to my toes. "Come join me, flower girl. The water's fine, I swear."

"Well, you would say that either way, wouldn't you?" I countered, but I was already one foot in. The pool fell perfectly short of scalding, seeping through fatigued muscle all the way down to weary bone. Instead of easing the rest of the way in, I sank into a crouch, until the steaming water touched the underside of my chin. The heat swirled around me in natural currents, lapping at knots and snarled, sore muscles I hadn't even known I carried.

An inlaid ledge circled the pool's circumference, and I scooted up onto it, next to him, with my leg pressed against the length of his. A breeze lifted a wisp of hair at my temple, leaving goose bumps in its wake, and for a moment I let myself savor how incomparably delicious this world made for me could be. Sitting beside him felt so right it almost ached.

The usual guilt reared up. I wasn't supposed to ever *like* being stolen away, being secluded here with him. Not when I had so much responsibility to everyone left behind. So what was I meant to do with these rare gems, the times I liked it more than anything? The times that I liked *him*?

"How real is this lovely little wading pool?" I asked, clearing the sadness from my throat. "I know it must be, at least in part."

He rearranged the arm behind my shoulders so his hand rested behind my neck. "There's a rock pool at the top of the Victoria Falls, in Zambia. Called the Angel's Armchair by some, and the Devil's Punchbowl by others. I'll let you guess which I prefer."

"Real puzzler there," I murmured, tipping my head back to dip the full length of my hair in the water. It didn't smell like sulfur, though I knew it should. More like the clean scent of running rivers on the hottest summer day.

Something twinged painfully in my neck. Wincing, I tilted my head from side to side, trying to release the tightened tendons.

"If you move a little, and slide in front of me, I could help with that," he offered, all innocence. But I knew he knew I heard it, the undertow of invitation in his voice. No less beguiling now than the first time, and maybe even more given how alone we were. There was no one here but me and him. No sister to demand explanations, no would-be lover lurking on the periphery, making me feel like I had to justify myself.

Without speaking, I pushed off the ledge and landed lightly on my knees. As I shuffled my way in front of him, he sank down behind me. I swept my wet hair to one side as his knees closed tight around me, my back pressed against his muscled front.

I heard the soft release of his sigh. He circled his fingers around my throat, running them lightly along its line, then bore down hard onto the burled mass of my shoulders. His thumbs dug into the tender points where my shoulders met my neck, and I couldn't bite back a moan.

"It's all right, flower," he whispered into my ear. "I know you hurt. Let me help you mend, just for a while."

"Just for a while," I agreed, hazily, my head lolling. "A little while."

He chuckled, low, into my ear, and continued with his work. His hands were staggeringly strong, and he didn't treat me like a doll. He drove his thumbs down the length of my shoulders, then moved up my neck with a lighter touch, until he found the twin spots beneath the base of my skull and pressed hard into them.

A dusting of stars filled my vision like a sparkling rain. I arched back against him involuntarily, tipping my head against his shoulder.

His hands stilled. "Flower girl," he said huskily, and I recognized that rasp. "Are you sure you want to move like that?"

I rolled my hips back against him in answer. One of his hands drifted across my chest, tracing my collarbone. His other hand tangled my wet hair into a knot that he could grip, and he turned my face toward his for a kiss.

There was nothing delicate about it. Both of us had waited for so long, and I was done with fighting. Whether it was the world itself nudging me toward wanting him, or simply something I wanted for myself to salve all this hurt, I was so tired of denying how I felt.

He kissed me deep, my head pinned back with the force of his grip. I remembered that first time, when he'd let me take the lead, made me perform for him. Now his breath tangled with my breath, and everything I felt was open mouths and questing tongues. I twisted around in his arms and twined my own around his neck. He lifted me until I straddled his lap—then his hands tightened on my waist.

Frowning, I met his eyes. They were glazed with desire, and something deeper than that. "What's wrong?" I whispered, leaning in for a kiss like a hummingbird sip. "Why are we stopping? Do you not—do you still want me?"

"*Of course* I want you—how could I ever not?" He cupped my face with warm hands, tracing my lower lip with his thumb. "But before we go on, I want you to know. I want you to understand."

"Understand what?" My belly tightened. What else was there that I didn't know? What else hadn't he shared with me?

"That I love you, flower girl," he said, and I nearly quivered at the fervor in his voice. "All of you, so here and real. The strength and fearlessness, the tenderness and sass. And that shining, curious mind. And I want to know . . ."

"What?" I nudged his nose with mine. "What do you want to know?"

"If you think you could love me, too, at least a little." The fine planes of his face glistened with pearled heat, moisture clinging to that soft lower lip. "At least while you're here. I know you miss him, that boy back in your world. But I want to feel like I truly have you, for however long you stay with me."

"Well," I said lightly, "there *is* the tricky part where I can't actually leave."

As soon as I said it, I winced at the glibness, and the pain that arced across his face. "I don't want you to love me like a prisoner, flower. Maybe once that would have been enough. But it's not anymore."

"I don't feel that way." I tilted my forehead against his without closing my eyes. His were open too, unflinching, so close I could see every spoke in his azure irises. "I promise. It's all been so complicated, but it's different now. I feel it too. You're different than you used to be. And whether it's because of this place, or because of me . . ."

It wasn't an easy thing to say—like it hadn't been easy to say to Luka, whom I wouldn't, couldn't, think about right now, even if it made me a traitor. I'd spent my life like a watchdog keeping guard over my own heart. Yet here we were, and I couldn't bring myself to lie.

"I *could* love you, for what that's worth," I finished. "I don't yet, and it doesn't change what I need to do, or how much I want to go back to where I belong. But yes, I could. I could, very much."

"Thank you for that, Iris, my flower girl," he breathed against my lips. "*Could* is enough, for now."

EIGHTEEN

Malina

WE SPENT TWO DAYS WITH JASNA. SHE PUT NIKO AND LUKA to work, harvesting her herb garden and distilling the plants to tinctures, while she tried to teach me to harness my will. But without her lighting the way for me like a torch, I couldn't even find that cavern of potential. I *could* will my bubble—my shield—into being, but only because I'd already done that for years. Otherwise, it was just so much easier to tap directly into the sweet sap of my gleam.

When push came to shove, I defaulted to the gleam every time. I didn't know how to stop myself.

When my frustration finally threatened to crush me, Jasna laid a coarse, work-worn hand over mine. "Let's stop for a while, little bird. Enjoy a change of scenery, get a little food in you. Chat a bit."

Niko looked up from where she sat, grinding herbs into the incense that Jasna used to hone focus. Stray dried leaves dusted her dark hair, and she looked like something that made its home in forests. "I'll come too. I could use the break from grinding my fingers into nubs."

"You won't, you fiery kit," Jasna responded tartly. "You're not attached to this one at the hip, are you? And if you are, that's part of the trouble. You'll stay with your brother, and keep at what you're doing."

"But I—"

"But nothing." Jasna chopped a definitive hand through that air. "Just Malina and me. She'll survive without you for an hour, I promise."

"I'm coming too," Dunja added, dropping down smoothly from above our heads with barely a sound, like some kind of avenging angel. She'd developed the unnerving habit of prowling the rafters high above us, walking them toe-to-heel like a cat. She liked the vantage point of the height, she said. "Baby witch doesn't go anywhere without me. Not when there are demons to consider."

Jasna planted her hands staunchly on her hips. "And if I say no to you, too?"

Dunja returned a gimlet gaze. "Try me, granny. Besides, these are Mara's orders."

Jasna scoffed, rolling her eyes. "As if you follow hers, or anyone's, instead of making up your own. Fine. You too then, ghost. But only because I'm too old for brawls I'm bound to lose."

In a wheezing yellow Fiat possibly older than I was, she drove the three of us to a brick-house tavern in the village. Empty so early in the day, it reeked of years of cigarette smoke sunk into its yellowed, lacy curtains and popcorn ceiling, and of home-brewed beer and stewed lamb. The sole server, a gawky teenage boy with a shock of dark hair, gaped slack-jawed at Dunja and me as he sat us.

For a moment, I couldn't even figure why. I'd been surrounded by unfathomable beauty for so long that I'd almost forgotten a normal world even existed beyond us.

One that would fall to Herron if I failed, I thought, withering into myself. There was so much more at stake here than just people I loved.

"Have whatever you want, bird," Jasna said, sipping a dark, frothy beer. "It may not smell like it in here, but everything is surprisingly good."

I ordered beef, cooked beneath an iron bell dome buried under embers and ash. It was as delicious as she'd said, the stewed meat melting down buttery in my mouth, the crisp potatoes salty with savory grease. But for once, I could barely eat. At least Dunja made no pretense at eating, either, glaring disdainfully at her pork loin. She did eat sometimes, I'd seen her do it. She just didn't like to anymore. The necessities of sustaining her physical body offended her in a general sense.

Jasna paused, a hearty forkful of cheese and prosciutto halfway to her mouth, her ocean eyes shifting between us. "No food for either of you, eh? I know ghost hates deigning to eat, but what's stolen *your* appetite, bird?"

I swallowed hard, biting my lip to keep it from trembling. "I just . . . I can't do anything more than what I've already done. Not by myself. I don't know how. I'm not strong enough, obviously, and there's not enough time to learn. I'm going to fail everyone, and I—"

"I don't, I can't, not by myself, pretty please, everybody help me," Jasna mimicked, jabbing the air with her fork at each point. "*That* is your problem, little bird. You're always waiting to be shown the way, to be led neatly by the hand. Of course you are, when you've always had someone to lean on. It's only natural that you've come to rely on help. But I—or anyone else—can only take you so far. The rest is on you, after that."

I dropped my fork and gripped the table's lip. "That's not fair. I'm *trying*. Maybe I'm just no good for this one thing. The thing we just happen to need very badly," I added bitterly.

"You're spoiled, is what you are," Jasna replied, without rancor. "You're not used to magic being the toil and trouble that it is for the rest of us mortals. And you might not recognize it, but you're in a snit over having to really work at something, for once."

I gaped at her, my insides churning with hurt. "Are you calling me *lazy*? I've worked so hard for you, and for Mara—"

"Then work harder," she interrupted briskly. "Work differently. If you don't even trust yourself to lead, why would reality follow the likes of you anywhere? Master yourself, little bird. Learn to stand on your own feet."

"You've no idea what hell she's already walked through on her own feet, granny," Dunja broke in, her voice low and dangerous. Her delicate profile looked like a coin cameo, minted from steel.

I could hear the threat of her, a metallic swish like a knife drawn from its scabbard. "So why don't you take it a little easy on the guilt? And if you can't restrain yourself from dealing out more wisdom, why not share some with me instead? I, for one, would relish hearing what you think of a thing like me."

Jasna smiled at that, wide and genuine, crow's-feet wrinkling into a crosshatch around her mutable eyes. "Pick on someone my own size, you mean, ghost? And why would I do that, when you're making my own point for me? Though it's sweet to see you so ready to protect your niece however she needs. As for wise words, you don't need any. You'll know your purpose just fine when you see it, I think. And though you didn't hear it from me . . ."

She leaned forward conspiratorially, but I could hear the sincerity sluicing off her like clear water. "You're still a person, ghost, *not* a thing. No matter what anyone did to make you so convinced otherwise."

HOURS LATER, I was back in the Great Hall where I'd let Oriell fall, intent on trying again. Jasna had hugged me before we left, pressed a fragrant, parchment-wrapped parcel of incense to my chest. "You can do it, I know. The Lady doesn't choose the weak-willed for her own."

To ease the pressure on me, Mara had gathered only a fraction of the daughters who'd been here last time. I would start with four—Ylessia and Naisha, along with a honey-blonde I called Bee Girl and a brunette with a blunt bob and bangs. Her name might have been Seleni, but I couldn't remember her gleam.

"Maybe let's try it differently this time?" I started slowly, breathing the fragrant smoke lingering in the air. I'd lit censers in every corner of the room to help me find my way back to that sparkling cavern. "Not one by one, but all of you at once. Release— summon—whatever you do with your gleam, and then we'll start."

I'd thought out various approaches during the long drive back, Jasna's chiding echoing in my head. I couldn't sing a separate song for every single witch on a battlefield at the same time. Instead, I'd have to sing something that stirred all of them at once—a single point on which to focus my will, if I could find it.

A wordless ripple of glances ran among the four, and they spread out to give each other extra room. As if they were preparing to synchronize.

Which was exactly what it turned out to be.

The air around Ylessia flowered into celestial fireworks. Little nebulas whirled into life around her, pinwheels of orange and magenta and vermilion. Comets like lit match heads zipped by her, trailing the smallest tails. Tiny, fiery suns whipped into orbit high above her head, a mimicry of marbled planets and pockmarked moons slingshotting around them.

As if she had become gravity herself, the dense center of her own orrery.

At the same time, Naisha began to change, into a kind of snake I'd never seen. Trails of scales shuffled down her body like falling dominoes, into a central line of scarlet rimmed with black, with robin's-egg blue lighting the edges of her silhouette. Even her hair changed to matching colors, swatches of it shifting like a chameleon. Her narrow nose melted back into her face, leaving only slits, and her eyes elongated into almonds of glossy black.

To her right, Bee Girl called down a gorgeous plague of insects. Everything at her beck and call had wings. Bees, hornets, and wasps swarmed around her in perfect silence, and a cloud of midges, moths, and butterflies churned so thick it nearly hid her from sight.

She must have been the one who filled the dangling bell jars in the atrium each night. Now they flitted around her, crawled up and down her skin and through her hair. Green-backed beetles and bright ladybugs, and a circle of dragonflies like a coronet above her head. They followed the flowing gestures of her arms, each flick of her head and torso curve. Like calligraphy painted by flight.

In concert, Seleni threw herself into her floor gymnast's routine, and I wondered how I could possibly have forgotten her gleam. As soon as she moved, a phalanx of shadows darkened into life. The simulacra fell into step behind her and flanked her on both sides. All of them were dark silhouettes, exact replicas of her own shape, mimicking the slightest movement that she made.

What I needed was to unite them, to give them purpose. To inspire them to flesh out the dream behind their gleams. Because this wasn't about taming insects or galaxies or shadows, just like it hadn't been about fostering flight. It was about making them *want* to do it for themselves, and for each other.

Teaching them how to master what gleam they had and turn it from glitter into might.

I closed my eyes and reached for the potential inside me like

Jasna had taught me, strove for the glimmering cavern of stalactites that I'd brushed so briefly. As soon as I fumbled for it, I faltered. Instead, I found myself remembering how it had felt when I myself had gleamed in earnest. When I'd sung to protect Riss by winning against her, because losing to her would have meant that she'd be taken away from me.

Just like she was taken now.

A shortcut, maybe—exactly the kind Jasna wouldn't approve of—but it was the only thing I could think to do. Maybe that was how my will worked.

When I began to sing, this time the song was a banner unrolled in sympathy and challenge, to all of them.

"Rise up, rise up, defend your blood."

Ylessia's creations turned livid, so blistering I could feel their radiant heat from where I stood. Some of them exerted a pull like actual gravity, and much more of it than they should have had given their size. Shock burst into victory on her pert face as she worked to control them, spinning them around like orbs of swelter-ing flame, turning her tiny universe into a floating arsenal.

Along with the heat came a tremendous, high-pitched noise— the aggregate buzzing of Bee Girl's living swarm. They circled her like a tornado of stingers, and I could see her shuddering at its cen-ter. Being blanketed by them must have been much less lovely now that their tiny legs, wings, and bodies were more than just illusion.

But the things that she could do with them if she wanted. So many pincers and stingers at her disposal.

Triumph sparked in me and blazed to life, like one of Ylessia's fiery orbs. I was doing this—I was *making* this happen.

In the meantime, Naisha morphed more fully into animal, rather than hovering in between like she usually did. Her arms stayed scaled but free, while her legs seamed together into a coiling tail, like a lamia coming to life. A forked tongue flicked from between her flattened lips, and her hair fused tightly to her head and neck, rippling into the sheen of scales.

And Seleni's simulacrum army had turned to strapping flesh. She was touching them with gleeful abandon, bubbling over with laughter as they mobbed her. "They're all *real*," she called out, over the room's rising clamor. "They're really here!"

I'd been so swept up in my own effort that I hadn't noticed, but Mara's roses had crept around the room, hovering as I sang. Some of them were hosting ladybugs and bees, while others prodded at Ylessia's miniature gas giants.

I'd thought that it was me, that this was what harnessed will felt like.

But it was Mara standing behind me, funneling into me the full force I needed to fan their gleams to life.

My new-kindled triumph blew out, all at once. She was supporting me as I sang, piercing through my song with her roses. Pinning it in place with her will instead of mine.

She couldn't stop herself from helping me, any more than I could do this on my own.

THE NEXT FEW days blended into a smeared, headachy blur of effort. I woke, ate, sang until I couldn't stand up any longer, then fell straight into bed. With Mara by my side, we trained the daughters hour after hour, but I could still only do it when she backed me. And we only had slightly more than a quarter of winter left—a little over a week before it melted entirely, based on the pace our eyes had been shifting.

Mara never said it out loud, but I could hear the dire tolling of her bell. If I couldn't manage to sing the others into soldiers myself and free her to take on Herron when he came, we were lost. Everything would be lost, and I'd never see Riss again.

I'd work myself down to the bone before I let that happen, no matter what Jasna thought of me.

I was so caught up that it took me a while to even notice that I hadn't seen Luka since we'd returned to the chalet. But then after one of my singing sessions, I nearly rammed into him by the Great Hall's arching doors.

"Lina," he said guardedly, eyes stealing over my shoulder, a plate of sliced fruit and glossy petits fours in his hands. "I thought you'd already left."

"Seleni wanted to keep training a little longer." I eyed him curiously. He sounded even twitchier than he felt, all jumbled trills and discordant twang. "It's nice to see you. You've been like a ghost these days. Where have you been keeping yourself?"

He finally met my eyes, almost defiantly. "Jasna gave me some of her books, magical theory and pantheistic theology. I've been reading about gods who can open doorways, thinking of other ways we might be able to look into for getting Iris back."

I tilted my head, confused. "She'll be free when winter runs out. The kingdom will break apart, then, and we'll get her back. Mara promised. She swore it to me."

If Herron didn't eat us all first, I added to myself.

"She might have promised." He locked grim eyes with me. "But how does she *know* for sure? It's not like any of this has ever happened before. And no one else is doing anything about it. If alternatives exist, someone should at least try to sketch them out."

It hadn't even occurred to me to doubt Mara. I'd been so consumed with building the army, as if that were the only way to help Riss, but still. Still, I should have at least considered that maybe everything wasn't so simple. When had *anything* ever been simple for us here?

I might have guilted myself into a cinder if Oriell hadn't slipped between us just then, setting a dainty, green-tipped hand on Luka's arm. A collection of unusual rings graced nearly all her fingers, and she'd swapped out the threadbare leotard for an emerald-green sequined corset. A choker set with a dragonfly made from watch parts laced around her throat.

She tipped her head to the side in a teal cascade, and practically *twinkled* at Luka. "Oh, you brought me something sweet this time! Thank you, you gem of a man," she cooed at him, in a throaty purr I'd never heard from her in practice. "I thought we could go outside for my snack today, what do you think? It might be nice to stretch my legs a bit, after all that stretching of the wings."

She lifted a bare foot and easily caught her ankle behind her to demonstrate, extending it back into a sinuous line that defined every muscle in her leg. Even I couldn't help tracing them with my gaze. A glance at Luka confirmed the purpose of the display. He looked about half past enraptured.

"Oriell," I said, struggling to even out my tone. This wasn't her fault, I repeated stolidly to myself. This was *not* her fault, not really. She'd been bred and trained to seduce, and now she finally had the chance to perform. "Luka and I were just chatting. Maybe he can"—I narrowly restrained myself from grinding my teeth—"meet you outside when we're done?"

She dipped into an adorable half curtsy, followed by a low-pitched chuckle. "Of course, Malina, I'm sorry to interrupt. Luka, I'll be waiting at our lea."

Once she'd sashayed off, her skirt swinging around full hips with every stride, I rounded on Luka. "Your *lea*?" I hissed at him, trying to keep my voice low. "Now you have a *lea* with her? We have demons massing against us, Riss is gone, and you're flirting with one of our grandmothers? Weren't you just telling me about all your research? Would that be in your spare time, when you're not hand-feeding Oriell?"

He worked his jaw from side to side, exactly like Niko did as a prelude to an explosion. That resemblance between them, the fine lines of her face translated into his masculine features, only made me madder. As if she were the one cheating.

"I don't have to explain myself to you," he grated out. "You and my sister have each other—or you would, if you weren't half killing yourself from dawn to dusk to convince yourself you're actually helping get Riss back. I don't have that luxury, Malina. I think about her every. Single. Day. Where she is, who she's with. So if

Oriell wants to keep me company while I wait to see if I'll ever get her back . . ." He gave an aggressive, full-body shrug, clenching his fists. Despite myself, I took a step away from him. "Then I'll take a little comfort, and you can keep your judgment."

He stalked off without a backward glance, leaving me trembling with a nauseous mix of empathy and rage.

NIKO STARTED WHEN I banged into our room, slamming the door behind me. She was sprawled out on her belly on our bed, picking through vials fanned out over the pillows. Dusk had gathered already—I hadn't noticed how late it had gotten, and so quick. The room was bathed in the plummy light that fell before the heavy curtain of mountain night.

"Everything okay, pie?" She flipped over onto her back. "I asked Shimora for some of Mara's oils, the ones she uses for crafting soulscent. To see if I can refine Jasna's herbs into something you can wear. I thought it might work better than incense to help you focus, if it was on your skin. And I think I've got—"

Before she could finish, I crawled up on the bed next to her and buried my head under the downy pillows. The vials rolled around me, clinking against each other like chimes. "I think he's sleeping with Oriell," I mumbled into the mattress.

Niko snatched the pillow off my head. "I'm sorry, what?"

"Luka. Your brother. Known for his scruples." My cheeks wouldn't quit burning, and I couldn't pin down which part of it made me the most furious. "He and Oriell, can you believe it? Apparently she's just the right antidote for missing Riss."

She sat up and drew her knees tightly to her chest, her face turning pensive. "Is it so terrible, do you think? That he would need someone while she's gone?"

I turned over to my side to face her, trying to contain my astonishment. "How can you even ask that? I'd think you of all people would be the first to hold it against him. She's trapped somewhere, who knows how far away from us, and he's gallivanting with one of our *relatives?*"

"I don't know what to think," she continued in that careful tone. Like she didn't want to hurt my feelings, but couldn't hold back from having her say. "He loved her for years, you know that much. And she always kept him at a distance. They'd barely had one night together before she left, and—"

"She didn't leave on purpose," I broke in. "Death *took* her."

"Right. Death. Also known as Fjolar, who she'd been meeting for secret-rendezvous date nights right before everything else happened. If it were me in Luka's place, I would be losing my mind every which way. Doing whatever I had to do to make it through until you came back."

"What exactly are you saying? That it's okay, given the circumstances, for Luka to stray like that?"

"I'm saying that just because Riss's gone, it doesn't mean her feelings matter more than the rest of ours," Niko said gently, reaching out to tuck a curl behind my ear. "As much as you're always ready to let her take first place, in anything."

"I'm not—"

"Yes. You are. Look at what you're doing to yourself, just to get through the day without her. You've done the best you can. Even Mara would let it go by now, if she couldn't see how much you need something to occupy every last drop of your time before he descends on us. And for what it's worth . . ."

She lifted that dark, beautiful, tear-slicked gaze, and I realized with a shock that I couldn't remember the last time I'd really looked her in the eye. I spent most of my hours miles away from her in my mind.

"I'm still here," she went on, her voice wavering. "You still have me. I'm still me, and I *miss* you, Lina. We have no idea how this is going to end—and I'm starting to think it's going to be very, very bad—but it feels like I've lost you already. I don't even . . . you don't have to touch me, if you don't want to. But it would be so good if you would just look at me, remember that I'm here. And that we might not have all that much longer together."

She'd called me selfish back in Cattaro when I wouldn't be with her openly, while I argued that not all of us could be so blithe. That self-preservation sometimes relied on lies. But maybe there had never really been two sides of that story. Maybe that was just another thing I liked to tell myself in the dark.

Maybe I'd always been selfish beneath the sweetness everyone saw, and was still being selfish now.

So I looked at her, really looked. Her fine hair fell in smooth, brown waves, parted far from the right and swept across one finely lined eye. The dress she wore must have been borrowed, but it fit as if it had been cut for her. A Grecian violet drape that left both slender shoulders bare and brought her tan skin to gleaming life.

I reached out and traced the slope of her little aquiline nose, the delicate lines of her lips. The beloved heart shape of her face, that tiny, stubborn chin. She closed her eyes at my touch, letting out a deep, shuddering sigh.

"Lie back, princess," I said, placing my fingers over her sternum and giving her a gentle push. "And which of the oils did you like best?"

"You choose." She lay back against the pillow and let her arms fall above her head, watching me with half-lidded eyes. "I want to see what you pick."

I gathered the vials in cupped palms and sorted through them, my breath quickening. Fruits, florals, and musks, various accords. Plenty for me to work with.

"If it's my choice, I don't see why a princess should be limited to just one, do you?" On hands and knees, I moved back until I knelt between her feet. Picking them up one by one, I dabbed a touch of freesia on the insides of her ankles. Followed by a kiss pressed to each silky instep. She jerked a little, swallowing a gasp. She had always been very ticklish just there, in the place I traced with the tip of my tongue.

"Oh, strong start," she said breathlessly, arching her back a little. "Curious to see where you go next."

"That makes two of us," I murmured, trailing kisses up her calves to her tender inner knees, before applying dabs of burnt cherry. Followed by more kisses leading up her thighs, laughing a little against her skin as she squirmed under my touch. Gently I sank my teeth into the delicate skin around her hip bone. "If you take this dress off, that might affect my choices too, you know?"

She caught me by the hair and pulled me up to her, until our breath mingled and our lips almost met. "You don't have to ask me twice."

NINETEEN

NOW IT WAS *NEARLY* TIME, SO *CLOSE* TO TIME.

Vera had already reaped five more soldiers to add to his ranks, while the embodied Lightless from Čegar Hill made their way toward Mara in the mountains.

But that maddening feeling of being shackled by ice had still not left him, and more galling yet, he could sense traces of the gleam still lingering in this city. Like the ripe, sweet smell of mead when there wasn't a pitcher within reach. It wasn't any of her daughters; he knew all of them were with her. If he cast his mind out far enough, he could nearly *see* them clustered in the distance, like a swarm of fireflies iridescing past the thicket of miles that grew between them.

Lovely Mara all alight, surrounded by the constellation of her own living stars.

No, this particular glowing linger betokened something else—traces of the gleam still wound around mortals that someone of Mara's blood had loved. He recognized it as an echo of the protection she'd cast over her clan, like a fluid sheath of light. Her people had all bathed in its reflected glow, the way the moon basked in borrowed sun.

As far as he could tell, there were only two of them, and not so far away. Somewhere close to his grasp, sheltered by Cattaro's blackened walls.

And he wanted them both, for his own. It was only fair that she see familiar faces turned against her, as he had. The treacherous eyes of someone that her blood had once trusted and loved.

He called Vera over to him, gripped her by the shoulders, and met her clotted gaze. "I have one last thing left for you to do, pet," he told her. "Let me use your eyes again. I'll show you the way to them, and you'll show me what you find. And then after that, perhaps we'll have our very first taste of something sweet."

NEV STILL VISITED the café every other night, missing the cocoon of its kitchen. Maybe it was macabre of her, given the brutal way Jasmina had died here, but it somehow still felt like the safest place she knew. And the only place where she still felt close to them, even now when baking too many macarons barely made a dent in her pain. If that wasn't the very fucking definition of rock bottom, Nev didn't know what was.

It had been weeks, and Riss and Lina were still nowhere to be found. Then to make matters worse, Niko and Luka had up and vanished too. That they had gone without bothering to tell her where—or at least Jovan, for fuck's sake, and he was practically the girls' grandfather—had left her permanently stranded between helpless fury and devastation. She couldn't even imagine how their father felt.

How *dare* they, she fumed to herself, whipping batter into a lacy froth. How dare they pretend that Riss and Lina had been theirs to save alone? As if Nev hadn't spent years with them and Jasmina, laughing and arguing and fighting over scraps of sweetened dough.

They had been hers, too, damn it. They had been like family, and she missed all three of them so much.

Not even tugging her father's network of strings had yielded a single useful lead. Every morning, she visited Jovan for news, but there was none. Watching him flounder so badly, lose himself to grief, broke her heart over and over. He had been so stalwart before he lost his girls, craggy as a mountain. And now more of him crumbled away each day.

Damn it, why couldn't they just fucking *call*?

Cursing, she flung the wooden spoon against the counter so hard the handle snapped in two. Immediately chagrined to have marred Jasmina's perfect kitchen, she bent to pick up the chips that had splintered off.

And all the hairs on her neck stood up in unison.

Someone was behind her, she was sure. Someone standing very still.

She straightened slowly, heart leaping to her throat. Her mind flashed to the image of Jasmina left bloodless on the floor, the tiles around her violently scarlet. What kind of reckless idiot was she, to keep coming back here alone? What had possessed her to come here at all?

But that wasn't how she was going out, she decided in the next instant. Absolutely *fuck* that noise.

Instead she lunged for the stand of butcher knives, sliding one out and brandishing it as she whirled around.

It was just a girl, and the pounding fear left her like a receding flood. Just a girl about her age, looking more than a little ragged around the edges. Her eyes were cast down, her hair lank and loose, and her yellow spaghetti-strap top was torn and smeared with dirt. Concern crept in to replace the fear. Maybe something bad had happened to her. Maybe someone had hurt this girl. It wouldn't have surprised Nev a bit.

It was so hard to be safe in this world.

"Hey," Nev said, lowering the knife and tucking the hand that held it behind her. "Sorry about—this—you just startled me. How did you get in here? Are you okay? I can call—"

The girl lifted her head and looked at her with eyes that swam with oil. And as she lashed out at Nev, the knife clattered behind her to the floor.

JOVAN HAD FAILED all three of his girls. And each night he plumbed the depths of the failure, until it ate away at him like an acid no amount of fine brandy could dilute.

Perhaps if he hadn't spent so many years chasing Jasmina's love, it might have turned out differently. He could have kept the three of them close, sheltered them from all their daily storms. But she had been so singular, such an artwork of a woman. Irresistible to even the untrained eye. And he had been a man long unaccustomed to accepting *no*.

Even once they had settled into being friends—to the extent that a man could be true friends with a woman he had never learned how not to love—he could feel that she held back. Some days he could barely stand to see the toll that life took on her, and the one she exacted in turn on both her daughters. Especially his deft and darling Iris, so much more like her mother than she knew.

And now one of them was dead, and the other two—who knew? He couldn't imagine that they would abandon him like this, without even a farewell word. Not his devoted Iris, not Malina in all her sweetness. If they hadn't reached out by now, he didn't think they ever would.

Another slug of brandy, more liquid fire down the gullet. On the better nights, it did burn away the roughest of the edges, and fill his mind with too much smoke to think.

If only he could see them just one more time. He had thought he'd have what was left of his life to teach Iris, to pass on both the gallery and the studio to her if she wanted them. That much would have been enough.

And instead he hadn't even had the chance to say good-bye.

His hand curled around the cut-glass tumbler, arthritis spearing through his knuckles. *Please, Lord*, he prayed, *I know we don't speak all that often, nor do these old feet carry me to your house as often as they should. But if you'd spare me just one more moment with them, I swear I'll make it up to you. Some fine new glass, whatever needs repairs. Whichever of your monasteries that could use these old man's hands can have me.*

And when a hand landed on his shoulder, his last thought was of awestruck wonder that his prayer had been answered.

TWENTY

Malina

NIKO WAS STILL CURLED DAMP AROUND ME WHEN I SCRAM-bled awake, heart shuddering in my chest. For a moment, I couldn't even pinpoint what was wrong. While she slept on, I propped myself up on my elbows, eyes narrowing as I listened hard.

And there it was. A rasping, slithering hiss. The hungry prowl of something just beyond our windows—that same sound I'd heard through Mama, beneath her winter gale. The sound that meant Herron, faint and distant, as if carried on the wind from miles and miles away.

But it wasn't distant now. It was nearly here, slouching over our threshold.

I leaped out of bed so gracelessly and hard that my soles stung when they met the parquet. The *thunk* of my landing startled Niko awake too. "Lina?" she mumbled, grimacing. "What is it?"

Instead of answering, I flicked on the ornate stained-glass lamp on the vanity table and nearly tumbled into the mirror, terrified I'd find both eyes suddenly brown. Leached of winter.

But the gray in my hourglass eye was exactly as it had been when I went to sleep.

"Lina," Niko said again, and now she sounded properly afraid, wings ruffled in readiness for panicked flight. "What's going on?"

"I'm not sure," I said, tugging on the clothes Niko had tugged off me and tossed to the floor. "But something's outside, I can hear it. I have to go wake Mara."

Niko scrambled off the bed, winding the sheets around her. "I'm coming with you."

"No, princess." I crossed over to her and caught her little face, pressed a fierce kiss onto her forehead. "If something's out there, I can't be worried about you next to me. You stay here, and bolt the door. I'll come get you as soon as I'm sure it's safe. Okay? Please?"

Whatever she saw in my face convinced her, for once. She gave me a shaky nod and let me go. I heard the bolt slide into place once I shut the door behind me, and I allowed myself a moment of deep, low-pitched relief that whatever happened, at least she'd be secure.

Outside, I nearly ran into someone, stifling a scream. But it was only Izkara, prowling the chalet in her nighttime rounds, partly shifted to brown bear.

"What are you doing out here?" she barked at me. "It's late. I could have clawed—"

"I think something's out there," I began, frantic. "I think—"

As if on cue, the screams began.

WE'D THOUGHT WE had so much more time. Mara had been so sure Herron wouldn't strike while still vulnerable, before the last of the winter in Mama thawed.

But even she couldn't know everything, just like Luka had suspected. She hadn't sensed Herron coming because he *hadn't* come.

But his soldiers had, and they were what I'd heard.

Now they swarmed in through the Great Hall's windows and skylights, shattering them all. Opening us up from every side. The screaming blotted out any other sound. Blood-curdling as it was, it was almost a mercy. It left room for nothing but survival, and even before I started singing it'd whipped everyone into frenzy. With Izkara and Amaya on either side, I roamed the balconies circling the atrium, my heart knocking against my chest like a battering ram as I belted out the fighting song.

"Rise up, rise up, defend your blood!

Rise up, rise up, defend your blood!

Rise up, rise up, rise up!"

Even with Mara's help—I couldn't see her, but I could feel her bolstering me—the chanting quality of it didn't seem loud enough, or *anything* enough.

Nowhere near enough to stave off the chaos raging around us.

There weren't so many of them, from what I could tell, not compared to two hundred of us. Maybe eight or nine. But they were strong, and so wrong, beyond hideous. All of them looked like they'd started out human, but they moved like they'd been spliced from grafts of hell. In stutters and spurts, here and then there, black streamers trailing behind them.

Clinging to balustrades and flinging themselves from the balconies, landing like they had no weight.

Joints bending at angles that should have snapped both tendon and bone.

The jellied, smoky black of their eyes flitting from one target to another.

By the time I reached the Great Hall, the fixture that had hung from the eaves lay in a sparkling glass ruin at the center. The stink of the room was worse than terrible. Blood, sweet rot, and a reek both sharp and feral. Some of the daughters had already fallen, lying crumpled like bloodied, broken dolls.

The others were even worse—they had black eyes themselves now, and they trailed behind the invaders like lost shadows.

I couldn't see Mara, but her roses crept everywhere. An airborne tangle of thorn, flower, and branching roots, carefully cradling the taken daughters so they couldn't do any harm, and seeking out the invaders to strangle. But where they touched the creatures, her will burst into flame on the vine. It hurt them, too—they let out monstrous, bellowing shrieks at decibels that would have shredded still-human throats—but it didn't kill them.

Like a force dashing up against an equal and opposite force.

One of the creatures had Naisha pinned to the wall, a bulge-veined hand around her neck. She was shuddering against its grip like a strobe light, snatching desperately at my song. I could see her straining to grasp the serpent form, but she couldn't sustain it. Not with something oil-eyed and ravenous bearing down on her.

I almost turned away, couldn't bear to look, sure we had lost her. But then a snarling Izkara materialized behind them in her panther shape and sank massive yellow jaws into the creature's neck. Ripping its head nearly halfway off in a spray of blood and black smoke. I was so close I felt the spatter of its blood, its strange, wrong smell. Acetone, mold, and burning rubber.

"Lina!"

I wheeled away from the carnage, terror ripping through me. Niko was racing down the left wing of the spiraled stairs, something clutched in her hand.

Vials, I realized. She was bringing me those oils she'd made, to try to help me sing.

She was trying to help me, like everyone always did. And now she'd die for it.

Because one of the creatures was a half step behind her. Something that had once been a strong, pretty, tan-skinned girl, now demon-eyed and webbed with black veins bulging across its face. It caught Niko, whipped her around, let its jaw unhinge horribly wide. Oily black poured from its mouth, reaching for her with snaking tendrils.

My entire world flared impossibly wide and then narrowed, in a single moment, needling to a focal point.

Funneling into "no."

No, there was no one to help me. Not Mara, not Riss, not Niko.

Especially not Niko, who needed me most.

No, I wouldn't let this happen. This wasn't the world I wanted. And so I wouldn't allow it to exist.

NO.

I didn't realize I was shrieking "NO" at the very top of my lungs until I heard the hall reverberating with the sound of my own voice. I abruptly, thoroughly understood why the full-gleamed could do what they did, why they left an imprint on the world. Why Mara could weave a spell into the fabric of the universe with her infinite bloom, knot it into reality with her black roses. And why Iris could undo it, tear it down with the force of her wisteria.

Their gift was the gleam made flesh, by the shattering, torrential cascades of their powerful will.

That cavern inside me suddenly loomed so large I couldn't believe I'd ever failed to find it. I was in it, just like it was in me. All those stalactites, all that sharp—it was mine to use, to inflict on the world. To chisel it to the shape of my will.

My far-mother and my sister might have had flowers for will, but I had sharpened stone.

This time when I let loose the song, it echoed inhumanly loud, as if we all stood inside a cave. *My* cave. And it swept up Kisuna—Bee Girl, who stood nearest to Niko and the demon—in its colossal, thundering wave of sound. Her swarms took vivid shape, burst into winged, buzzing life. They surrounded both the monster and Niko, lifting them up like a levitating chain.

Then some parted from the swarm and flew free, to gently set Niko down in one of the atrium's empty balconies, hovering around her like a living shield.

The rest ravaged the demon, stung it as close to death as it could get.

Once it finally dropped, I could see from its misshapen, bloated face how badly they'd devastated it.

Kisuna wasn't the only one fighting back, spurred by my stony song. Oriell guarded Luka in the eastern corner of the Great Hall, with strikes of a chitinous scorpion tail that had fleshed out behind her. A drop glistened at its barbed end, and even in the middle of the wreckage and the gore, I felt a burst of fierce pride for her.

She'd managed to turn her gleam into venom.

And Ylessia was glorious. Her fiery firmament had turned to blistering weapons whipping in orbit around her. There was a strange distortion near her, like an absence of light in midair, as if that specific place was crushing into itself, wadding up into a ball. It wasn't until one of the creatures lost an arm, a leg, and then simply *disappeared* into it that I realized she'd somehow conjured a tiny black hole.

But the things were either fearless or too inhuman to bother much with fear. From what I could tell, their own fallen meant nothing to them. One of them stutter-stepped under Ylessia's defenses, and before any of us could react, gripped her head and wrenched it sideways.

Snapping her neck.

I watched the defiant light ebb from her eyes, and remembered how she'd come to me to offer her friendship what felt like years ago. How hard she'd worked to teach herself to gleam. How much

I'd liked the deep dimples in her cheeks when she smiled freely and not just prettily.

How she'd started to feel like actual family.

One of the creatures leaped from an upper balcony and landed on top of the pile of shattered glass—almost right on top of us. Even with the blood smeared all over her and the hanks of sweaty, marigold hair plastered across her face, I would have recognized Nev anywhere.

She angled her head at me, and for a helplessly hopeful moment, I thought some part of her recognized me, too.

Then she hissed at me through blood-smeared teeth, narrowing those oily eyes that had been so blue and bright with mischief. She *did* recognize me—enough to see that I was the source of the daughters' newfound power.

And that I should be the next to die.

Nev, my Nev, was coming to kill me.

My song faltered, sputtered, and then dissolved, even as Amaya stepped in front of us and spooled out her sapphire flame to drive Nev back.

Izkara caught me before I could collapse. "You have to keep singing," she hissed into my ear. "We won't be enough, not without you. Azareen—Malina—fight for your kin and *sing!*"

I couldn't. I just couldn't. There was nothing left in me.

I sank down, barely feeling my legs fold under me. If it had still been up to me then, we would all have died. There were only three of the creatures left, including what-was-once-Nev, but we'd lost so many.

But they didn't have their king with them. While we still had our queen, with her knights by her side.

Mara stalked down the length of the hall, all in billowing black. Her hair looked longer than it had been—but maybe that was just the corona it made, borne up by her briar. Dunja and Mama walked on either side of her. Dunja in her snowy white, Mama tangled black with roses.

All three of them drew to a stop, and Mara began to sing herself.

It was nothing like my own song—it had no nuance, no emotional range. Instead it was a simple, indomitable demand, like a gushing geyser. It sounded like an essential summoning, the very pinnacle of a command.

To love her, to come to her, and to obey.

Mama wasn't singing, but I could see her hand bruising under Mara's grip, though her face didn't even flicker with a hint of pain. Whatever they were doing, they were doing it together. Maybe all that sheared-off will keeping Mama alive still belonged to Mara somehow, as a reservoir that she could tap into and use to strengthen her own gleam.

The three remaining creatures lifted their heads, twitching. Along with the daughters who'd fallen and risen again, they dropped what they were doing and began a slow skulk toward Mara, irresistibly drawn by the bugling of that goddess-song.

Once they reached the trio, they froze in their tracks, heads tilted to the side like curious dogs.

That was when Dunja sprang to life.

I had forgotten my aunt's ferocity. Her gleam so finely honed by Death, like a freshly whetted blade, that it didn't need any sharpening.

I'd also forgotten what she had done the last time this hall had been a battlefield. The hypnotic dance that had held the daughters captive while she attacked Mara. The fierce stomp of her little foot and the shock wave it sent out, tumbling them down.

While the creatures and the fallen daughters stood enthralled, Dunja flung herself into motion like a whirling dervish. She cut her way through them like a scythe, landing blows that cleaved them limb from limb.

It must have been such a heartbreak for her, even with so little heart left to break. The creatures were just things, but the fallen daughters were her family—the upline of mothers and sisters she had known and loved.

She couldn't afford to spare any of them.

Not even Nev.

THERE WERE SO few of us left. Of Mara's two hundred daughters, only about forty were still alive. Amrisa had made her rounds, doing what she could for the wounded. But some of them had been beyond even her help.

It was impossible to imagine how we'd ever mourn them all, and we were far from being safe enough to even consider sinking fully into grief.

I should have felt at least an inkling of victory, now that I'd finally found my will. It meant we had hope, that Mara would be free to fight Herron when winter finally broke.

But we'd lost so much, too much for me to feel like we'd won anything at all.

We couldn't stay at the chalet. It was all upended from the inside, as if a hurricane had blown through it. Every time I found the strength to lift my head from where I sat bundled up with Niko—Luka in between, with his arms around both of us—I kept having near-hysterical thoughts of Tasmanian Devil cartoons. Everything that could be broken had been mangled, and all the windows gaped like mouths with shards of glass for teeth. Tatters of the Turkish rugs that had lined the mahogany floors were spooled around the splintered furniture. All the wall hangings had been torn, hanging askew on shattered frames or in pieces on the floor.

And anywhere you stood, you could feel the mountain air gusting through the house. The most bereft feeling, being so open to the elements with a roof still above your head.

That was how we all felt too, I could hear it. The unique desolation of a home stripped bare of doors and windows, so empty it whistled with the wind.

We couldn't stay.

"Why would Jasna agree to take us in?" I asked Naisha as I piled into the last of the caravan of cars that had begun trundling up the road from Žabljak this morning. Driven by silent, stone-faced locals who'd clearly been paid enough not to ask questions. "We're dangerous. He'll follow us there, come after her. We could go somewhere else, one of the other coven strongholds. Shimora said . . ."

Shimora, our grandmother.

Who was one of the dead.

"Because Jasna wants to protect you," Naisha said gently, running her fingers through my hair as I bit back burning tears. A score of welts ran down one side of her narrow face, where one of the creatures had raked her with its nails. They looked inflamed, but nowhere near enough to bother Amrisa for healing. Not today. "And besides, if we fall, nothing will be safe from him."

Before we pulled away, I twisted in my seat to watch the chalet disappear from view. Amaya had stayed behind, and I could see her burst into flame like a phoenix. That near-sentient flame she commanded looped around her body, raced up the auburn wick of her hair. She walked toward the chalet, dripping with amber-and-sapphire fire. Sparks fell from her, little licks like molten gems. But none of them caught on grass or pine needles like they should have. They burned only where she willed them, reined in by her gleam.

"What is she doing?" Niko whispered beside me. She was on her knees on the supple leather seat, like a little girl. Her cold hand nestled in mine—she hadn't let go of me since the battle's aftermath. Both of us knew how horribly close we'd come to losing each other. She still sounded like aftershocks of panic, a maddened thrash of flapping wings.

"Burning everything down," Luka replied from the front seat. His voice was hoarse from the steady patter of comfort he'd rained down on us both. And from tears, I thought. Oriell had fallen toward the end, protecting him. I'd seen him on his knees beside her, baring his teeth at the sky. Now I could hear his guilt and the devastation, like a fault line cracking thunderously open.

Another lover he hadn't been able to protect.

"Why?" I choked back tears. "It's just broken things. It could all be fixed."

"Because of the bodies, Linka," he said gently. "There's too many to bury, and there's no time for it anyway. They can't leave them for someone else to find. So they're letting Amaya light their pyre."

TWENTY-ONE

Iris

FJOLAR AND I NAPPED TOGETHER AFTER, IN THE NEST OF our discarded clothes. It was so warm that our skin dried quickly, moisture wicking off into the air. Once we left the water, the languor settled over me like a weight; tucked into the curve of Fjolar's body, I was asleep before I even registered my head settling into the pillowed crook of his arm.

The sleep was dark and dreamless, a satin black I wound around myself like a tangle of bedsheets. I might not have woken for hours or even days—or whatever passed for that amount of time in this place—had something sharp not scratched insistently at my face.

I woke blearily, and slow, squinting into a sky that hadn't shifted even a shade away from its gilded twilight streamers. It gave me a lurching sense of lost balance that I'd only felt once before, in the bone desert. We were usually on the move long before I felt any visceral wrongness at the sky's unchanging state, the absence of markers for the passage of time.

The owl sat on my chest, blinking at me. She was raven black this time, with a star of white blazing on the down of her throat and belly, her eyes still a striated golden and jade. One of her talons hovered in midair, as if she had been preparing to poke me again.

She struck me as a very authoritative kind of owl.

"Hello again," I said to her, giving in to a jaw-popping yawn. I was still so tired, steeped in fatigue. Yet I felt an urgent pull to stay awake—especially when I saw Fjolar still asleep next to me with a fist curled under his chin, eyelids twitching as if he were held fast by a dream. He'd never seemed anything other than vibrantly awake to me before. Even when I stole naps next to him, I always drifted off alone beneath his wakeful gaze.

"Does Death sleep?" I asked the owl. She cocked her head to the side and gave a startlingly emphatic *hoot*. "Right, I didn't think so, either. So what's this about? Does it have something to do with you?"

She ruffled up her feathers, then picked her way daintily to the ground. I'd never seen an owl walk before, but her waddle was neater than I'd have expected, more elegant. And the perky flare of her tail feathers waggling back and forth was actually kind of cute. At the very edge of the path that led down from the Devil's Punch-bowl, where it dipped to the trail that wended around the cliff, she turned and waited, exuding an air of politely restrained impatience.

"You want me to come with you, *really*?" Shaking off my stupor,

I worked my way sluggishly up to my feet. I'd had to lift Fjolar's arm from where it draped over me, and he hadn't even twitched when I set it back down, heavy as a log. Something beyond the pale was definitely happening here. Death, captive to sleep. "This is like every childhood fantasy I ever had, I hope you know that."

Three slow, skeptical blinks.

"I get it, I'm coming." I pulled my black tank top over my head and tugged on my jeans, worked my feet into my sneakers. "All right, ready when you are."

She spread her wings and led.

I followed her down the path in cautious fits and starts as she wheeled above me, afraid to stumble and twist my ankle or snap a bone. Aside from the sound of water dashing itself into the pool at the falls' base, the silence was absolute, like a domed bell jar had been lowered over the two of us. I hadn't been by myself since Fjolar brought me here, and the absence of his presence and his voice was unsettling. As much as I wanted to relish being alone, I'd grown so used to him by my side, his hand always in mine.

Now, I missed both those things. I missed *him*.

The dismay of being away from him was distracting enough that I nearly didn't notice our descent into a grove that definitely hadn't been there before.

When Fjolar and I had first crossed over into this piece of the kingdom, there had been nothing to see but the loom and crash of the waterfall, like a natural citadel surrounded by green plains. That meant this thicket had to be something new, something recently grafted onto his domain. Even the grass inside it was a different shade of green, and the trees within were deciduous and dense, the kind of tall that came with ancient.

As soon as she crossed into the grove, the owl became a woman. There was no wavering of physical boundaries, no obvious transformation. It was more as if she'd been a woman all along, just as she now continued to be an owl.

Once I stepped over the threshold of this haven that manifestly belonged to her, she turned to face me, smiling in the most affectionate, benevolent way. Like I imagined an aunt might look at a favorite niece, one who'd spent a long time away but was no less loved for it. She wore crimson robes loosely belted at the waist, with nothing beneath them, the fabric a few shades brighter than the auburn waves of hair that cascaded nearly past her wide, round hips.

Her face was bold and pleasant without being beautiful: freckled cheeks, squared jaw, and a no-nonsense sort of nose. The kind of face Mama would have dismissed as "handsome"—though there was nothing about this woman that would brook dismissal.

Her eyes hadn't changed from the owl's gold-and-green, and her pupils had remained huge, black, and deep.

She held out both hands to me. Bracelets of braided metal circled both wrists, along with corsages of what looked like sprigs of holly and mistletoe, though the leaves weren't quite the right shape for either.

I laid my palms on hers—dry and warm, a little rough from work—and she gave them a firm squeeze, wrinkling her nose in greeting like a mischievous schoolgirl. She smelled like sage and sandalwood, along with the sharp sweetness of mint. I could recognize the hum of power by now, from Dunja's crackling ozone and Mara's clustered bells, and this woman had it in heaps and spades. Yet there was nothing aggressive about whatever she wielded, nothing that suggested violence or a demand.

"Well met, love," she said, still smiling. Her voice was rich and low, bright with the brink of laughter. Her brow was tattooed in dark blue, a full moon bracketed by waxing and waning phases on either side. The top of her head flickered every now and then, like a heat mirage. I kept thinking I saw a pair of massive, branching antlers draped with moss, but every time I focused on them I found nothing there. "You've led me on quite the chase in this swirling little maze. But I'm glad to have this time with you now, without *him* in tow. And look at you, so shining and lovely. Certainly one of hers, no two ways about it."

"Thank you?" I hazarded. "One of Mara's, do you mean?"

"I do," she confirmed. "Though of course, you're one of mine, too."

"And who are you?"

"I'm known by many names, some freely shared and others oath-bound," she replied serenely. "If you need some way to think of me, the Lady of the Dawn will do. Now, why are you still here?"

"Still here?" I couldn't keep the indignation from my voice; she made it sound like I had a choice in it. "Because he brought me here, and doesn't know how to let me out. So I'm not 'still here' so much as stuck, I'd say."

The Lady arched an eyebrow, her gaze turning sharp beneath it. "I wouldn't call it 'stuck,' love, and nor should you, if you abide by truth at all. What's a prison like this to a might like yours, one who shares her far-mother's infinite bloom? This world might be a lockbox, yes. But what is that, other than a thing held together by glue, and nails, and clasps? It may have been built with you in mind, but it was never built to hold *you* back."

"You're saying I could get out of here?" My heart began to pound painfully. "That it's up to me somehow?"

"Of course it is. It's always been. The only one telling you otherwise is *him*." She made a little moue of distaste. "While I understand that her need was great, I will say I don't approve of what she made of him. Things of his nature aren't meant to dwell in flesh."

"But he says he doesn't know any way out, not for someone here in body as well as soul," I protested.

"And he's always been so straight with you, has he?" she replied tartly, tossing back her copper hair. The sometimes-antlers on her head appeared just long enough to catch the light before they winked out. "Nary a lie out of that one, I'm sure. A paragon of honesty."

"You're saying he's lying to me even now? Even still?" The pain that bloomed at that prospect climbed up my throat like a creeper rose, lined with thorns. "So what else are you saying? I assume you know there's a soul hidden here, that I need to find. I can't leave before I do that, anyway, and we—I—still have no idea where it is."

Her nostrils flared with frustration. "You already know more than enough about this world to find what you need, if only you'd seek higher ground, observe the greater scale of things. I can't tell you more than that—this is his domain, and I overstep merely by being here—but *goodness*, girl. Think on it. Even he's given you enough to work with, and now I've done what I can."

I racked my brain for any hint of understanding, and still came up short. "I just don't see any greater scale . . . ," I began, balling my hands in frustration and smacking one against my thigh.

Her face softened into sympathy. "Maybe it *is* a lot to ask," she conceded. "You may be of her rarefied golden blood, but you're also a very human, very tired girl. Why don't you come and rest with me a bit? I've been known to make some burdens lighter. Would you like to stay a spell, here with me?"

I found that I would, that I craved her continued presence. She felt like lingering summer in September, like the satisfaction of full larders before the fall of winter. "Yes, please, if you don't mind . . . ," I said, nearly finishing the sentence with a name that balanced like a sugar cube at the tip of my tongue before melting away, leaving only a faint sweetness behind.

A different name; her real name, not the placeholder she'd given me.

The Lady turned with a swirl of crimson robes, and strode deeper into the leafy enclave of the grove. Each step of her bare feet was both balanced and precise, and I noticed that her soles were caked with rich, red soil.

She crossed from tree to tree, as if considering, before stopping in front of one with a slim, dark trunk and full canopy, its branches heavy with a crop of bloodred berries—just like the ones around her wrists. She trailed her palms fondly over the bark, then slid down its length to sit cross-legged where the roots snaked into the soil.

"Rowan, one of my very favorites," she said, patting the trunk behind her as if it were a pet. "Sometimes also called mountain ash, or quicken tree. Powerfully protective, but also good for inspiration. Sitting beneath its crown with me might be exactly what you need. Perhaps something will strike you."

She drew her robes across her thighs and patted her lap in invitation, the slant of sunlight through the leaves casting lacy shadows across her face. I knelt down next to her, leaning against the rowan for support. The bark scraped rough against my palm like any other tree, but beneath that it did feel a little like what she'd said.

A buzz of something ferociously protective, and a sense of something both gentle and fortifying.

She patted her lap again, and, like a little girl, I scooted down and rested my head along her soft, robed thigh. For a blessed moment, the knot of constant tension I carried with me, threaded through the fretwork of my being, loosened to nearly nothing. I released breath after peaceful breath, letting myself relax.

"That's it," she soothed, laying a light, warm hand down on my hair. "You're already halfway there, love, you just don't quite know it yet."

I made a noncommittal little sound, burrowing against her thigh. Wherever I was or wasn't yet, all I wanted was for her to keep stroking my hair. And she did, in steady, even circles, like a mother at a bedside rubbing her baby's back—exactly like my mother had done for me, when Lina and I were still little and Mama was still sweet.

The motion and the memory altered my perspective just slightly, like the shadow from a sundial shifting.

Mothers.

Circles.

Spirals.

Gifts.

And just like that, I understood what she had wanted me to know.

I WAS SO furious with Fjolar that I lingered at the waterfall's base long after the grove behind me had vanished, melting away into nothing like an oasis in a desert mirage. It had been here only while the Lady was here, and once she was gone, no trace of it stayed behind.

She was right about one thing: I didn't need to know who she was to understand what she'd come to tell me. Had my thinking been unmuddied by the meddlesome magic of this place, and the beginnings of a more genuine love, I should have been able to piece it together from what he'd told me himself.

This kingdom was made in my image, he kept saying, from the likeness of my mind. Every story he had told me linked it to things I loved. Everything in it carried relevance, a glimmering line of connection winding back to me.

That being the case, I should long since have guessed its shape.

But before I brought this to him, I had to be sure I was right. I needed to find higher ground, she'd said. I needed the perspective of height.

Now that I was clear of the Lady's bower and outside of the sphere of Fjolar's stilling influence, the kingdom resumed its tumult around me—or my senses resumed their suspended revolt. The pounding of the waterfall grew horribly loud, a violent, compounded crash like the falling water might thunder apart the basin. The temperate air turned too warm, and the ruddy gold of the sky became searingly bright. Summoning the bloom would be easier in the Quiet, so I shaded my eyes against the glare and searched for a seam, a boundary that marked a passage point to another piece of the kingdom.

But I couldn't find one, and I didn't feel strong enough to go looking. I had the feeling that I'd be needing all my strength soon; best to start conserving it. And with nowhere to hide from so much light and sound, right where I stood would be as good as anywhere.

I half sat, half collapsed onto the ground, wincing at the stab of prickly grass. Closing my eyes and reaching inside, I found the gathered coil of the wisteria, waiting like a rope ladder for me to fling it out.

Up, I demanded. *Take me higher, lift me up.*

At my urging, the blossoms emerged easily, almost eagerly. I'd been getting a lot of practice out of spinning them into a cradle in the Quiet. Like every time, I knit them with my mind, blooming branch over branch into a pink-and-purple lattice, plaiting their twigs and flowers into sturdy rungs. It shot upward under my guidance, like Jack's beanstalk twisting toward the giants.

With a crackling snap, the ladder solidified. It hung above me, suspended from nothing, swaying with the weight of its own branches and the spiraling corkscrews of its blossoms. I didn't need to climb it with my body; even here, the shell of me could stay behind. All I needed to traverse the framework that I'd built was the nimble scurry of my mind.

Launching, I scaled up and up, high enough that I left the waterfall far below me and behind. Glancing down without fear—even if I let go, the receptacle of my body waited to catch me and break my fall—I could see the speck of Fjolar still curled beside the steaming water of the Devil's Punchbowl. How fitting that he would choose a place with a name like that; he'd even admitted it himself.

He spent so much time telling me what he was, and I spent just as much choosing not to hear it.

This high up, the fabric of this cobbled-together world began to fray. I wasn't climbing closer to an outer level of the atmosphere, because this wasn't my earth and there wasn't one here. No clouds wisped around me, nothing but a trailing gray haze. The kingdom fanned out below me like a twisted chessboard, every square a different color, size, and shape. And the board itself wasn't a board, but a spiral swirling to a central point—from up here it looked both surpassingly strange and achingly familiar. The separate pieces were poured into this mold like pearls, each encased in a filmy, white layer that must have been the seam of Quiet threaded all around and between, stitching them together and keeping them separate.

All together, it took the shape of a coiled-up snake, a nautilus shell, or a furled flower bud.

A natural fractal.

And exactly like my birthday cake—the Sacher torte roulade Mama had once baked me, to echo the flavors of the bougainvillea I had blown for her.

I could almost recognize the pieces that we had visited, based on the shades and contours I saw from here. The ones on the very outside of the kingdom could only lead to the neighboring three pieces: whichever lay behind, in front, and toward the inside. With every tier closer to the center, the more pieces each one abutted. From any single one, we could have reached at least four others.

Fjolar could have waltzed me back and forth between them for months or years, maybe for decades, hopscotching through the kingdom at his whim. I would never have known if he was leading me toward the center.

A center that I could see, even from up here, pulsing with a distinctive, silvery light. That was where the soul would be.

Where he could have taken me from the beginning.

TWENTY-TWO

Iris

HE WAS JUST STIRRING AWAKE AS I CRESTED THE WATER-fall's peak, jittery and out of breath from both the mercury swell of rising fury and the speed of the climb. I'd half jogged up here in my eagerness to confront him, but now that I could see him—bare-chested and beautiful, pale hair still rumpled from where I'd tangled my fingers in it—the maelstrom collapsed into a single point of pain.

You told me you wouldn't lie to me. And then you did it again.

I'd thought I was beginning to know him, but he'd never stopped betraying me.

He smiled lazily at me as I stood over him, blinking sleep away, still too languid to notice the studied blankness of my face. "I napped with you, flower! I've never done that before. I think I even *dreamed*—"

"You've been lying to me again," I broke in. "I know you have. And finally, I think I even understand."

Slowly, he propped himself up onto his elbows. His expression shifted by degrees, to that implacability I recognized from when I had tried to refuse him on the Cattaro beach. A sulk between sullenness and stone. "And what, exactly, do you think you understand?"

"You know where the center of the kingdom is, and you've known this whole time," I accused. "You could have led me there straightaway—because it's a spiral, isn't it? Instead of following it around and around, we could have bisected it. Taken a direct route to the kingdom's core."

He shook his head, eyes steely, still clinging to denial. "Being here with you bolstered the last of the spell. I wouldn't have wanted to take any shortcuts, not while we were doing our part."

"That's not how it really works, though, is it?" I demanded, my voice breaking. "All you needed to do to keep the spell from breaking fully was bring me here right before it broke—and you did that just by stealing me. Once I got here, it didn't matter how long I stayed, did it? You said so yourself; this is a place outside of time. And the kingdom would only need sustaining if Mara was still trying to keep Herron's soul imprisoned—and I *know* she's not, otherwise why would Lina have told me to find it and bring it back? You've been keeping me here just because you could. Even though you *knew* how much I wanted to go back."

His face was still impassive. "Why would I ever do that to you, flower?"

The pain peaked, overwhelmed me, the immensity of the betrayal. Especially given that I should have expected no less from him. I knew better, and still I hadn't learned.

"Because you wanted the kingdom's magic to keep chiseling at me. So you could pry me open, steal my time and love. I know how to get out, once I find the soul—you've practically told me how to unravel this world. I could already have been back where I belong!"

He came to his feet in one explosive motion, a storm raging across his face. His eyes burned with an intensity I didn't recognize, and he clasped both hands behind his neck, gaze boring into the ground.

"You're right, flower," he lashed out hoarsely. "Is that what you want to hear? Well, there you have it—you're absolutely right. I forged this world for you; of course I know where I lodged Herron's soul for safekeeping. But can you blame me? Why shouldn't I have allowed myself the luxury of a little time with you, since it makes no difference to them when you leave here?"

He met my eyes then, heavy with devastation. "You're the *last*, Iris. The final companion I'll ever have, the last love I'll ever know. There's nothing after you, no more fire or beauty or light. Just infinite quiet and dark. The endless cull." He reached out to me, running both hands down the length of my hair.

I shook him off, hating how much I still wanted to lean into that familiar touch, and turned my back to him. "You don't have the first fucking idea of what loving means," I tossed over my shoulder. "Maybe I'm not the best at it myself, but at least I've got the basics down. If you wanted time with me, you could have asked me for it. Not taken it from me like something that belongs to you."

The bitterest pill was that I'd thought that I'd found a little freedom, for once, here with him. And instead I'd been doing what I always did. Fulfilling someone else's desires, bending myself to their demands.

"I was just afraid . . ." Tears turned his voice hoarse. "I was so afraid that you'd say no."

"Then you'd have lived with it, like the rest of us do. You've already had more love than most, stolen as it was." I refused to turn back and look at him, give sympathy a route back in. "I'm going to the center; I know which way to go now. It'll be fresh hell getting there without you, but I'll do it if I have to. So I suppose this is when you decide. If you really believe you love me, then help me get there, and keep me strong until I find it."

He watched me for a long moment, with so much raw tenderness in his eyes that my stupid heart stirred a little. Maybe he'd do it, this one thing I needed so much. The one sacrifice I wanted from him.

Then he shook his head once, and turned away.

HEAVY WITH ANGUISH, I set off on the straight line that would slice like a knife through the patchwork pieces and lead me to the spiral kingdom's center. I had no sense of how long I walked, and without Fjolar's presence to moor me, it was a nauseating, dizzy slog. One miserable, leaden foot after another. Eventually, I even found myself looking forward to passing through the seams of Quiet, where at least I could use my wisteria to protect myself and steal some comfort.

Because as much as the kingdom itself tormented me, the pain of his refusal was infinitely worse. It shouldn't have hurt so much, but it did, because I hadn't been lying when I told him I could have loved him. I'd come to understand parts of him so well, and despite everything, I simply ached to be without him. It had been so long since I was truly alone, and in this world—his world—I was more alone than I'd ever been.

And then I found it.

I knew it for what it was as soon as I stumbled shakily through the final seam. The central piece, the core pearl of the kingdom, felt nothing like the rest.

I could sense the cloy of it as soon as I stepped out of the Quiet. The welt of sky above hovered on the brink of storm, all grays, blacks, and purples streaked across the swollen bellies of the clouds. Every once in a while, a cool spatter of rain blew across my face.

Below the incipient storm stretched an endless field of flowers. Not wildflowers, but cultivated, decorative blossoms. Plump orchids, gladiolus spears, cups of tulips. Pale, slim lilies, bright bursts of carnations and chrysanthemums. Red, yellow, and blush roses, the lush profusion of hydrangea.

Maybe they should have been beautiful, but they all seemed like funeral flowers to me.

A simple medieval abbey sat in their midst. A Gothic basilica with one rose window, three portals, and a single, splendid tall tower.

The wooden portal door swung open for me, creaking heavily on its bronze clasps, before I even reached out. "Oh, nice touch," I muttered to myself.

The inside of the cathedral wasn't truly a church. I stood under what should have been the nave, with pews on either side. But though there was an altar at the farthest end, floodlit by the bruised light spilling through a stained-glass window cast with a single iris, the rest of the room was a gallery. A simple one, all its walls lined with portraits in the same style and size.

I wandered to the first one on my left, trailing my fingers over the gold leaf of the frame. A black-haired, black-eyed woman met my eyes with a ferocious, regal gaze. She looked so much like a younger Mara that at first I thought that might be who she was, but the plaque beneath the painting read "Amrana." In the portrait she held both hands upraised, palms up, a fountain of water twisted into lacy shapes arcing from one hand to the other.

A taper candle inlaid with petals and herbs burned beneath the portrait, and when I bent over the flame, I smelled the curling, complex scent of a soul-perfume. She'd been a brave woman with a savagely tender heart, quick to anger and just as quick to laugh.

Amrana, Mara's daughter. The first of Death's brides.

I made my way from one to the next, inhaling the candles' scents, tracing the lovely lines of their faces. All beautiful, to the last, and each posed with the most incandescent depiction of her gleam, the smell of her soul wreathing her likeness from below.

"It's us," I whispered, wondering if it was appropriate to feel so much reverence. My predecessors had been sacrificed and so badly used, but they *had* performed for Death somewhere beautiful and drenched with love—and they'd been offered up for a greater good. Maybe they deserved my respect, along with the well of sympathy and grief.

But why a simple church for this gallery, I wondered, when a gallery could have been tucked somewhere more extravagant?

Maybe because churches had altars.

My heart began to pound as the pieces fell in place, and I picked up my pace toward the altar. A crystal bell jar etched with complex designs—concentric circles and jagged bolts like lightning—rested on a white marble plinth.

The air grew so cold near the plinth that I could see my own breath. The thing inside the jar was fleshy and silvery, and it still *beat*, though not the way a human heart would have—something more like the ripple of serpentine muscles. It had too many chambers, a honeycomb of them, and was too muscular and veined to even mimic a real heart.

It felt familiar, that pulsing, ravenous dark, from all the times I'd seen him through the infinite bloom.

Herron's soul, shaped like a captive heart.

I went to pick the jar up and hissed at the touch—it was icy cold, clustered with snowy crystals at its base. I turned it around in my hands, looking for an opening, some kind of keyhole, but all I could see were the bas-relief etchings that decorated it, the stipples and holes. The jar was of a single piece, as if it had been blown with the heart already inside it, like a ship inside a bottle.

It was as magical and unlikely as anything else here; it belonged to this world. Unless I pried the heart out of it, I wouldn't be able to take it with me when I left.

So I lifted it over my head—it was heavy, desperately heavy, almost impossible for me to lift that high—and threw it down on the marble floor with as much force as I could muster.

The glass didn't even crack, though the slab beneath it did, spidering all the way through.

Instead, the snow crystals that had rimed the base scattered loose, and the air around the plinth went moist and very warm. As if the cold had somehow contained it, a dark miasma thickened and clotted around the jar—and the thing inside it began to *shriek*.

Wordless as it was, the hissing scream carried a note of victorious gratitude. It almost sounded like it was *thanking* me.

Then I realized, with an awful, creeping chill, that the light inside the chapel had shifted. I walked to the window, craning my head up to the sky. The storm outside was gaining strength, the cloud banks drawing closed. Rain shattered in sheets against the glass.

Which meant the clouds were *moving*. For the first time, a piece of the kingdom had proper weather, a changing sky.

Breaking the jar's icy seal must have somehow spurred the kingdom's time back into motion, like winding a stilled cuckoo clock—linking it back to time in my own world.

Words floated unbidden to the surface of my mind, where they were still scored from the first time I'd seen Herron—in the mountain forest, surrounded by his monstrous menagerie. *The little spy-witch has broken our last shackles*, he'd said.

All this time I'd spent agonizing about who his helper might be, which of Mara's daughters might be the treacherous one, torturing myself over how little I could see of any of them besides Lina.

But it had been me all along. The little spy-witch—he'd meant me. It dawned on me that I'd done a terrible thing.

A thing that was happening to Lina, and to everyone else in my world, right now.

TWENTY-THREE

Malina

JASNA HAD WELCOMED US BACK WITH UNRUFFLED GRACE, given that we really were bringing a war to her doorstep this time around. How all of us even fit in her cottage, I couldn't understand—fifty people shouldn't have been able to pack into it, but there was room. It made me feel almost hopeful, like she might really be able to help protect us.

We were just settling down to try to eat when I felt it.

The last of winter snapping, like the cracking of the frozen surface of a pond.

The melting had been gradual until then, and we were meant to have more time. It was too soon for this. But there it was, a violent, final crack, a splintering shard of pain in my hourglass eye. Surrounded by gasps of fear and surprise, the other daughters clutching at their faces, I stood and stumbled to the nearest mirror.

The pale, terrified girl who peered back at me had two warm, fully brown eyes.

Somehow, Herron had managed to shed winter's shackles early, before we had even a night to recover.

All I had to do to make sure was elbow my way to the others, find Mama, and touch her. When I gripped her shoulders, for the first time, her rose-animated flesh was warm as the air around it.

"What's happening, my cherry girl?" she whispered to me. "There's no more cold."

"It's gone, I think," I whispered back, my throat tight. "The winter. We've lost it."

Everyone else must have been as horrified as I was by the sudden snap, but I'd blown my bubble around me twice as thick as it'd ever been, infused with more will than ever before. I couldn't hear anything through it. My kin's shock and fear was more than I could take, when I had so much of my own.

Except for Mara. Her tolling was so momentous that I couldn't block it out. I turned to look for her, in time to see her slip out the cottage door. Without thinking, I followed her out into the long rows of the vineyard and into the gathering dusk. The sky burned with the last of the sunset, as if some fiery hand had raked it. Maybe it wouldn't have looked that way to me some other day. But all I could think of was the chalet burning, burning, burning behind us with Amaya's unnatural flame.

With the bodies of the fallen smoldering inside. Catching fire like tallow candles, roasting for hours, melting down into runny fat.

So many of my grandmothers, dead. All their gleams reduced to ash.

And Nev. That, I couldn't even stand to think about just yet.

Mara stopped so abruptly that I nearly ran into her back. I skidded to a stop myself, then glanced over her shoulder. There wasn't anything special there, nothing to warrant pause. But when I walked around to face her, I saw that she'd stopped because she just couldn't make herself take another step.

The glacial planes of her face were stricken, splotchy with tears. There was no golden goddess here, not anymore. Just a woman wallowing in grief and yet more guilt.

"I know. I know, and I am so sorry, fledgling," she whispered. Her voice wasn't even tripled, and her fine lips trembled like a little girl's. She'd wrapped herself tight inside her arms, hunching over them. "Stars and gods, I am sorry for everything. I have never been so wholly wrong. Winter has broken much earlier than it should have, and now he comes, with a yet more fearsome horde. This time, I can feel him. Come full, ripe dark, he will be upon us. Sometime past midnight."

That should have been the most important thing, but of course it wasn't. "Why isn't Riss back?" I asked her quietly. The plan had been to rage at her, but then there was her face. She hurt as much as I did, maybe even more. Those had been *her* daughters that we lost, children she'd loved for centuries. "You said when winter fled, the kingdom would collapse and that you'd catch Riss when it did. Why hasn't it happened? Why isn't she here?"

"I do not know why," she replied, low and hoarse. "That is what *should* have happened. But the kingdom belongs solely to Death and his bride. For all that I can feel it too, it has never been under my control. And now it continues to revolve just as it did before. Perhaps it is his doing, some sustaining magic he spins there with your sister. The preservation of the lockbox was ever his domain."

"Of course," I said bitterly. "If there's a way to keep Riss trapped with him, I bet that tricky bastard found it. So what now? How do we get her back?"

"I do not know, daughter." Her voice shook with the admission. She was so unused to helplessness that it almost made me sorry for her. "And it is worse than that. If the kingdom continues to exist, Herron's soul remains trapped within it. Now that winter no longer holds him, without his soul he will be even less human, and more demon. If we cannot destroy it, we cannot destroy him, either, and we are lost before he even arrives—unless Jasna draws her bedamned goddess down in the very flesh to fight him."

The Lady. The way she put it reminded me what Luka had read.

Some gods can open doorways.

I wondered if the Dawn Star might be one of them.

"Forgive me, Malina," she whispered again. "I tried, for all of you. Truly, I tried, as a mother should."

I could have been selfish like I so badly wanted—it would have been easy. She'd tried but failed. The grief and guilt rolled off her, like the mournful bugling of some huge horn. She was ready for a flaying, steeled for it.

Instead, I reached for Mara's hand. She was so astonished she tensed at the gesture, like I might hit her.

Then her face lapsed into lines of abject gratitude. Her cool hand relaxed and curled in mine.

"There might still be something we can do." I squeezed tight, shifting my grip until our hands clasped like warriors'. "It's not over yet, sorai. You fought alone for all these years. Tonight, we'll stand with you."

I WANDERED JASNA'S garden barefoot, looking for the right place. My wrists, throat, and ankles tingled in the evening cool. Before I went out back, Jasna had led me to the lily sink again. She'd sprinkled me with consecrated water and anointed me with the same cinnamon and mint.

Marking me as the Lady's child.

"Does your Lady answer her children even if they aren't sworn to her?" I'd asked her. "Will calling on her even do any good?"

She'd drawn back, her hands still glistening with fragrant oil, and given me a solemn, clear-eyed look. "The Lady does what needs doing, bird. As you've learned to do. And her hand is already over your heart."

The night sky was so clear above me, a cloudless expanse around the shining sickle of the moon. Despite everything, I felt so safe within the circle of the valley's mountains. As if the valley itself were a pair of clasped hands that held me gently in open palms. Jasna's vineyard sprawled over so many acres, the rest of the village far enough away that all I saw were the distant firefly flickers of house lights and the pearly strings of the cars trailing each other over the mountain roads high above.

Out here, we were very much alone.

In half a haze, I began kneeling here and there. Taking careful clippings without damaging the plants. Jasna had told me what would be best. Rosemary, hyssop, holly, and rue. Mugwort, mistletoe, and thistle. Elderflower and betony. And a cluster of rowan-berries from the little tree that grew in the corner of the speared wrought-iron fence.

Then I knelt in front of a birdbath, its water like silk. There was barely any breeze, the night like a held breath. I'd left candles lit and a chalice there, full of Jasna's victorious wine. To offer to the Lady, and then to drink. Once I'd poured some out onto the soil and taken a long sip, I clasped the trimmings in my hands until I felt them heat with will. My spine tingled like it had the first time Jasna taught me, and it felt like a root, reaching down into the earth.

The Lady's earth.

Then I spread my hands and prayed.

I wasn't very good at it at first. I'd never really prayed to any-thing before. But maybe the Lady's hand really was on my heart. Once I began, the words poured out like a remembered psalm. Like something I'd said before.

"Attend me, Lady of the Rowan," I whispered. "Dawn Star, Sun Mother, keeper of the fertile soil. Harken to your seeking daughter even before she gives her oath."

Grape leaves rustled around me, expectant. Even though I still didn't feel any stirring of a breeze.

After the greeting I spoke to her silently, informally. Like she was my mother. I begged her to find Riss, to pry her out of Death's prison for me. To show my sister Herron's soul and tell her how to bring it to us.

If she did it for me—all of it, or any of it—I promised to give her myself.

Even if she did nothing, she had me anyway.

I was so intent I almost didn't hear it at first. But the night was bated with quiet, and I'd heard that warbling thrum before.

When I opened my eyes, for one wild, ecstatic moment I thought I might see the Lady. Instead, there was Riss—her face consumed with terror, tortured as a ghost's.

There was a filmy not-quite-thereness to her, but it was really *her*.

Shock poured over me like hail, and then without warning, she shattered into *everywhere*. Like she had turned herself into a fractal. The night air thickened into a pond broken by a stone, and in every facet I saw a slice of her face.

I couldn't reach her or touch her. And though I could see her speaking, I had no idea what she said. The wind wouldn't carry even a wisp of her voice.

But if she could hear me at all, I had to tell her what we needed her to do.

TWENTY-FOUR

Iris

I COULDN'T DO IT. NO MATTER WHAT I DID, THE JAR remained in one obstinate, uncracked piece.

So I was sitting with my back against the altar, splay-legged like an exhausted child, when Fjolar appeared silently in front of me, his presence displacing a rush of air.

I glared up at him through the hair plastered across my face, sticky with sweat. I'd bashed the jar into the wooden pews, kicked it, stomped on it. I was so tired I could barely move. The jar was now in my lap, wedged between my knees, where I'd been turning it around to examine it. I thought I knew the catch to it now, what that series of deceptively decorative holes was really for.

The jar needed a tiny, sharp-pointed key, and would only open if unlocked.

"So that's your final trick," I said bitterly, picking damp hair from between my lips. "I can't even open it without you."

He dropped into an easy crouch in front of me, rocking onto the balls of his feet. His hair was up, the way I liked it best, and his eyes were unusually bright, that blazing azure slick as stained glass.

It took me a moment to recognize the gloss as tears.

"You can't," he agreed, lifting a hand. His bracelet swung from his strong, veined wrist, the arrowhead like a pendulum. "The key to it is mine."

I lifted both hands to hide my face, unable to quell the rising tide of tears. Everything was lost. Everything. "And you won't give it to me, will you? You wouldn't even *come* here with me. Why would you help me now?"

So gently, he pried my hands away from my face, then held them curled tightly between his own, resisting easily when I tried to pull them back. "I didn't say that, flower. The key is yours if you want it. Just say the word."

Astonished, my eyes flew up to his. "Please, Fjolar. I have to take the soul back. When I tried to open the jar by breaking the glass, I—I don't know. I did *something*, made things worse for Lina. I know I did."

"You did," he confirmed. "You set Herron free, and realigned this kingdom's clock with yours. The battle will begin soon, in your world. But it hasn't yet. We still have a bit more time—if you'll let me have it, as a final gift. A parting present."

"Why would I let you have anything?" I snarled at him. "Why

would I give *you* gifts? You let me come here alone. You let me try to break the jar. You—"

"Because giving you the key means the end of me," he interrupted. "Keeping that soul trapped is the only reason I exist in this form. Once you have the soul—and once you leave—I die, flower girl." He huffed out a little laugh. "The only death that Death itself will know. And if you want to go now, I understand. But if you'll stay a little longer—just a little while—I'd like to tell you about this last place. So you understand. I won't take long, I swear."

I wavered, torn between my pounding urgency and the open plea in his face. Even after everything, the notion that after this he'd stop existing made me quake in a way I wouldn't have expected. It struck the part of my own heart that could—and almost did—love him.

"I know it's a courtesy I wouldn't have shown you if our roles were reversed, flower," he said quietly. "But you *aren't* me. You love to give, live for it. It's one of the thousand reasons I love you."

I watched him for another moment, gauging him for tricks. I'd been fooled so many times before—how could I know this wasn't just another sleight of his hand? More of his endless smoke and mirrors?

But I believed him, yet again. And I couldn't help letting him have this one last chance to prove he deserved all the trust I'd wasted on him.

So I reached for his hand, let him pull me up with the jar cradled under my arm.

"Show me, then." I said. "But be quick about it."

"A GERMAN KING had a gallery once," he murmured, moving to stand behind me as I rested the jar back on the plinth. "An entire pavilion dedicated to thirty-six beautiful women, in the Nymphenburg Palace in Munich. Some were singers and actresses, not just ornaments. And others were close to him—his daughters, wives, mistresses."

"Well, that makes sense, then," I said acerbically. "All performers, one way or another. But why make this a church?"

He tilted his head up to the ceiling. "Well, for one, I thought you might like this."

I followed his gaze. Two chandeliers hung above us, flickering with candles and dripping with crystals; I hadn't even seen them when I came in alone. But their framework was exceptional, elegant with violence: clusters of bullets fused together into bristling flowers, bayonets and blades thinned out to form curlicues and arcs.

"It's from the Ružica Church in Belgrade," he told me. "It doesn't look quite like this—you'll know that by now—but there really are two chandeliers there, made by soldiers from shell casings and weapons abandoned on the battlefield. I thought it might remind you of the one you liked so much, at Our Lady of the Rocks. The one made from glass flowers, between lintels hung with gifts from sailors' brides."

I did remember it, that hushed, sweet church afloat on its artificial island like a miniature Avalon near Perast.

"And the outside is a replica of the Basilica of Saint Denis in France. The one that holds the mummified heart of a dauphin.

So I gave it to you as Herron's 'heart.' I thought it might seem . . . familiar to you this way."

With a pang, I realized it did. It brought back years of fighting tooth and nail with my mother. Sometimes in Lina's defense, sometimes in my own, and sometimes just because that was what we did. And all the many times I'd imagined the shape of my own poor, battered heart, the boxes of glass I'd built in my mind to keep it cool and safe.

For a moment it nearly overwhelmed me, how much of me he knew. No one else I'd ever be with would understand me so thoroughly, from the inside out.

No matter what else he had done, there was something to be said for being so known.

He must have sensed the slight softening, his eyes flicking up to mine. "And look where it is," he murmured, with a ghost of his rakish smile. "Technically it's been right under your nose this entire time."

I looked up to see what he meant. Below the stained-glass iris in the window, there was another one, like a little wink to fractals, and I couldn't help but smile a little at the gesture.

The final portrait in the gallery's collection.

The last of Death's beloveds.

My portrait wasn't surrounded by the same gold-leaf frame the others shared. Instead, mine had a border of blown glass, a fractaled profusion of petals and stems that radiated out and away. I was half smiling in the painting, my long face, domed cheekbones, and angular features unusually soft. My hair spilled over one shoulder in a slick of black so glossy it looked almost wet. And my eyes were a light, warm hazel I didn't recognize, their edges darkened with smudged liner beneath neat black dashes of brows.

In cupped palms, I held a handful of wisteria rising into a fractal like a whirlwind and drifting over my shoulders. Above me it streaked up into the night sky, to burst into pink and purple falling stars.

"Do you remember all of them?" I asked him quietly. "The ones who came before me? *Really* remember them for who they were?"

"Every one of them," he replied, just as hushed. "I know you think it's been nothing but caprice with me, but it was always more than that. I didn't know them like I know you, because they weren't really here, not fully. But what I knew while I loved them, I've never forgotten."

"It's not enough for me to forgive you, you know," I told him, unable to peel my gaze from my own portrait. "Not even close. But I will say that I love my painting just a little."

He pressed a kiss into my hair from behind, light as a breath. "Then that's enough for me, flower girl. More than enough."

I turned to face him one last time. He opened his mouth, then closed it again, fisting a knuckle against his forehead. "I'm actually *afraid*, flower," he said, with a brittle, breathless half laugh. "What an awful feeling. Who would have thought?"

I tugged his hand away from his face and held it in mine. So broad and coarse and strong, with all its many rings. Marked with whorls like a real human hand, one that had been shaped with me in mind. One I'd never touch again, or feel sliding over my skin.

The loss wouldn't be only his. I didn't forgive him—I hated him, even—but it still cut deep to be not just leaving, but also destroying him.

"It has to be now," I said softly. "Even if there was another way, you don't deserve it. Not after everything you've done."

"I know my penance is part of it." He met my eyes with that dazzling cornflower blue and pressed my hand up to his cheek. "I'll just miss you so much, flower. Whatever happens to me, I'll miss you."

"I know," I said. "And I hope—I hope you find something that can pass for peace."

Before he had a chance to say anything else, I rose up on my toes and gave him a warm, full kiss.

"Good-bye," I whispered against his warm lips, so soft against his stubble.

Then the cool, sharp point of the arrowhead landed in my palm.

I closed my fingers around it as empty air settled into the space where his lips had been, with the echoing whisper of a sigh.

TWENTY-FIVE

Malina

I HAD NO IDEA IF RISS HAD HEARD ME. IF THE LADY HAD gotten through to her.

Even if she hadn't, we couldn't do nothing. Herron was still coming, and now both Mara's coven and Jasna's were preparing for battle.

I'd fight with them—without my sister. Like Mara, I had to set aside all that grief for now.

In the middle of her vineyard, Jasna kept a wide circle clear of grapevines, its boundary defined by inlaid stones. Another flat-topped stone stood at the center as an altar, covered with a red linen cloth and the tools of Jasna's craft.

Red and white taper candles flickered on either side of a bouquet, bloodflowers and carnations bound with scarlet thread next to a polished antler rack. A dish of water and one of salt sat in front of them, a glazed clay chalice of red wine to the left. In the center, a smoking censer wafted dragon's blood and myrrh. Eleven blades with handles hewn from different kinds of wood were arranged around the altar.

It was strange to see magic that relied on tools for purpose instead of beauty, and for a moment I wished everything wasn't so dire. The idea that I might never learn their use filled me with yet another, more wistful harmony of sadness.

If we lost tonight, we'd lose so much.

Ten men and women had come at Jasna's call to stand with us. They wore crimson robes belted at the waist, while those of us who belonged to Mara were in flowing white.

Niko and Luka both stood with Jasna's coven, Niko shooting anxious glances at me over her shoulder. She hadn't wanted to be away from me—what if I needed her? But she would be safer there, and for once I refused to rely on her like I always did.

Jasna stepped into the clearing first, carrying the bristly broom from above her fireplace. The besom, I'd heard her call it. Her graying hair was loose, undone from its braid and rippling down her back. A bronze circlet sat on her brow, two crescent moons pressed back-to-back. She walked slowly around the circle, sweeping the broom back and forth, humming something wordless and lilting.

A song that pulled at my marrow, one to which I almost knew the words.

Once she made a full turn and knelt to face the altar, her coven formed a circle around her, each of them drawing the knives. Led by Mara, we followed like Jasna had asked us to do—ringing them in until we formed three concentric circles.

Jasna lowered her blade into the salt and then the water, murmuring an invocation under her breath. She sprinkled some of the crystals into the water bowl, stirring it with the point of her blade. Two of the others came up beside her, and she passed them the salted water and the smoking censer. Together the three walked around the circle, stopping at each cardinal direction.

Greeting them with elements.

We all turned like compass needles toward a magnetic lode, following their progression. But even if we were just visitors compared to them, I could hear the churning swell of power rise around us like some ancient song. It sounded loamy and dark, redolent of earth. It was potent enough that when the sky above us darkened, I actually thought clouds had come, gathering in response.

It wasn't clouds, but the shadows of flying things.

Herron had brought hell with him. And then he broke it loose.

The first screeching devil that descended on us looked like a bat sewn from the jellied skins of snakes. It landed with a rake of talons, trumpeting fury and lashing its whiplike tail. Somehow, it had a human head, and even a stringy, Medusa approximation of hair. Behind the viscous features of its face I could see a suspended skull. As if whatever animated it had engulfed a human skeleton like a massive leech.

I'd known I'd be afraid, but I couldn't have anticipated the breadth of the terror. As its roving, empty eyes settled on me, my voice nearly abandoned me.

Dunja appeared beside me, gripping my hand hard enough to make me gasp. "Come on, baby witch," she whispered fiercely, giving my hand a shake. "Be our warrior songbird one more time, now that you know how. This nasty thing can't even hope to touch you while I'm here. And don't worry for your princess, not this time. She's safe where she is. As safe as she can be, out here."

Throwing a desperate glance behind me, I saw that Jasna and her coven had linked hands, Niko and Luka among them. They whirled around the altar, hair and robes flying. The rest of us faced outward, like their shield.

They'd feed us their own power while we fought, girding us with their will.

If they could do that for us, the least I could do was my part.

And we needed every gout of strength that I could muster for us. More and more of the devils landed in our midst, crashing through the grapes. Their chimera bodies made no sense, beyond equipping them to mutilate. Some had merged into hydras, while others waved crab pincers or gnashed insectile jaws.

And all of them trailed oily streamers of that slick darkness around them, so much deeper than the night.

No wonder he called them the lightless. Our world didn't know this kind of dark.

But this time, I did know how to sing my full will for my kin.

Forcing breath into the bellows of my lungs, I plunged backward into my sharp-toothed cavern and began to sing my stony will. Singing the world toward what I wanted it to be.

"RISE UP, RISE UP, DEFEND YOUR BLOOD!
LET LOOSE YOUR GLEAMS PROTECT YOUR KIN!"

Seleni's shadow army burst into life, like papier-mâché manne-quins growing velvety flesh and blood. I could barely see them as they rushed by me, but under their smooth skin they felt like solid slabs of muscle. They followed her puppet-master lead, scaling one of the beasts and bringing it down in a tangle of wire, vines, and leaves. And Kisuna's winged swarms buzzed all around in a sinister hum.

I couldn't keep track of everything, with my every last cell straining to sustain the song. But I could see Izkara and Nai-sha wreaking havoc in the forms they'd taken on: one a roaring gryphon with a leathery hide, and the other a winged, feathered snake like some Mayan goddess.

Someone else had turned their gleam into a barrage of mag-nified crystals. They fell like lacy snowflakes, but ripped and shredded whatever they touched.

And ribbons of Amaya's gold-and-blue flame streaked all around us, setting the beasts in the vineyard on fierce, bright fire.

Meanwhile, Dunja seemed everywhere at once, a vicious, pale blaze that felled whatever it struck. I saw her snatch one of the devils by its gelatinous head and grind the ballast skull inside to dust with the force of her grip. She didn't stop until she'd torn the rest of it into quivering black gobs, which dissipated into smoke and then vanished. Every now and then the ground quaked under me, and I knew it had to be the aftershock of her stomp as she brought them down around her like axed trees.

I couldn't focus on anything for too long, as I stood with hands clenched and head lifted to the sky. Calling on the choral force of my gleam with everything I had, my veins throbbing from the strain.

And in the middle of the fray, I saw Herron find Mara.

He was just a man, she had said, a man who had swallowed demons. Maybe she had meant that he'd once been a man. But now he was something far past that. He rose above the ground, aloft on writhing black. It held him up like a whirlwind, or a spectral exoskeleton. He flung out almost teasing tendrils of it at Mara—but each of the blows that landed cut so deep I could hear her stifled shrieks.

Her roses thrashed around her, drenched and backlit by the blinding light she was shedding from within. But even brilliantly alight with the gleam, nothing she did seemed enough to fend him off.

"What now, my *sun*?" he taunted her, flinging out a segmented spear of black like a spider leg. It struck her across the face, snapping back her head. The actual spoken words were guttural, coarse pebbles in his throat. But the echoing black around him thundered their meaning clear. "Is it not time for you to set? This world is not yours but mine and theirs, to suck dry of light like an egg. And I would begin by dousing its second sun."

She shrieked something back in that same harsh language, as she lashed out at him with roses flung like javelins. Only to be batted down as if she hadn't even moved. I had the sense of seeing only snippets of their battle, that most of it was happening faster than my eye could follow.

Then Mama appeared from the fray, and I saw that her roses were turning brittle. Petals flaked off her like shelled husks.

"Sorai, it's not enough!" she called out to Mara. "Use me instead. Use all of me!"

Mara glanced back at her, torn—and again, Herron stole the chance to whip her across the face.

"Please, sorai!" Mama dropped to her knees with hands clenched and reaching out. "Let me be of help this time. Let me atone. It's—it's what I want."

Mara nodded once, mouthing something that looked like silent thanks.

Then she began to *grow*.

Her roses coalesced, took on shape around her like battle armor. As she pulled them like a length of coiled rope from where Mama knelt, they wound around her legs and up her arms. Interlocked and webbing, they grew her floral claws and talons, tapering to points.

And buckling tight like a corset around Mara's torso, they knit themselves into a thorned and leafy set of wings.

Somehow, with all the wonders that I'd seen, nothing compared to this. My far-mother launching into the star-scattered sky like a goshawk, her hair whipping around her while she beat petal-feathered wings.

I came from her. I came from *this*. Maybe she wasn't really born of fallen angels, but she looked like she could have been.

Even Herron seemed briefly awestruck. For an instant I saw just a shadow of the old love he must have felt for her flicker across his face, before everything but malice slid away from it.

Then they dashed into each other like colliding storms, black falling into black.

TWENTY-SIX

Iris

I ONLY HAD TO TOUCH THE ARROWHEAD'S POINT TO ONE OF the jar's keyholes, just once. The glass melted away instantly, vanishing like dew, dropping the foul, slick heart right into my waiting hands.

I brought it with me to the nearest seam, beneath the chapel's back entrance. And from there I plunged into the Quiet with the soul clutched to my chest.

Like all the times before, I knit a cocoon for my own protection, sealing myself inside. The branches and blooms curled tight around me, the stamen at the center. *Hold me safe and then deliver me*, I commanded it.

Once I was as secure as I could be, spun up snug, I began snaking offshoots outward and away, following the trail of Quiet. It was the seam that sewed together all the disparate parts of the king-dom, Fjolar had told me so many times. That threaded through it like marbling through a cut of meat.

I should have understood what that meant long before I met the Lady, and maybe I had but couldn't bring myself to face it.

Once the Quiet was gone, the pieces would separate from each other, spilling loose like beads from a snipped necklace thread. What would happen to them, I didn't know. Maybe they would continue existing by themselves, rolling across the fabric of the cosmos like pearls across a hardwood floor. Or maybe they would vanish like wisps when they parted from each other, without the centrifugal spin of Fjolar's and my courtship emanating from within.

What it certainly would do was destroy the kingdom itself, and set me and Herron's soul free as it rattled apart.

A part of me, the part that already mourned Fjolar's loss, was unutterably sad to destroy such a fantasia.

But most of me could hardly wait, pounding with eagerness to be back where I belonged.

I could feel when my wisteria lanced completely through the Quiet, as the branches looped around to meet each other and splice together into an unbroken circle. The connective tissue of the king-dom was now speared through with my will.

And what I willed was for it to break apart.

It was so much easier than I thought it would be, like blowing on a dandelion. At my bidding, it blew away like wisps of thistle-down, and without the kingdom holding me up, my nest and I began to plummet. We plunged into that golden, behemoth world that I'd sunk through like molasses on my way into the kingdom—but this time Fjolar wasn't with me to seal the breach made by my passing.

Like honey dripping from a comb, the gleam of the world followed me through, brilliant as a breaking dawn—as I tumbled into the wreckage of a vineyard half torn down and entirely on fire, with a winged Mara wrestling a giant of a demon in the sky above.

TWENTY-SEVEN

Malina

THE FLOWERS IN MAMA'S SKIN HAD WITHERED AND CURLED, as if they'd been dried and pressed while still attached to her. I knelt by her side, clutching her hand. I could still hear her, but she was so awfully faint.

Just the fading, high echo of chimes stilling in a dying wind.

"I don't . . . I don't have any more to give her," she breathed through cracked lips as Herron and Mara thrashed above us. Her eyes were so bloodshot from strain that the irises blazed bright green against the red, and her lids quivered like dry leaves. "I'm sorry, my cherry girl. I love you so much, and your sister. Please tell her I love her, and say good-bye for me."

I couldn't do this twice. It was too much to ask, of anyone.

"Please don't go," I begged, bent over her with our foreheads pressed together, dripping tears onto her face. "I can find Amrisa, she'll know a way. She can heal you like she healed Mara's burns, and everyone else, she can—"

"I'm not hurt, sweet," she whispered. "I'm finally dying, like the already dead are meant to do. It's all right. I had such sunshine with you girls. Much more than I thought I could have. It was worth it, my cherry girl." She focused her bloodied eyes on me, and I could see the effort that it took. "You were both worth *everything*."

At least this time I was there to see her die.

Iris missed it by moments. She wasn't there, and then she was, tumbling out of a dazzling, light-soaked breach in the night. The split she left behind hovered, leading to somewhere vast and blinding. She rolled onto her knees on the ground, something held curled to her chest.

For a second she just stayed there, her forehead pressed against the soil and shoulders heaving with shuddering breaths. Then she propped herself up, still on her knees, and assessed the burning terrain around her. Her eyes roamed wildly over the flaming ruin of the vineyard, the writhing tangle of demons and Mara's daughters pressing them back.

Then she saw me.

"Lina, I have it!" she called out, standing knock-kneed before stumbling over to me. "The soul, I brought it, and I—"

Her gaze finally landed on Mama, and she clapped her free hand over her mouth, her eyes flicking up to mine.

"She's dead," I said dumbly. "We lost her, again. And I don't know what we do with the soul. Mara can't beat him. She's done everything she can, and he's still winning." I jutted my chin up at the sky. "Look."

In the air, Herron held Mara pinned against him, arms locked across her chest. She sparked in and out like a light-bulb filament, while his snaking tendrils tore her wings apart petal by petal. They fell over us like ashen rain, dissolving before they landed. She'd scratched him across the face with her thorn talons, but even the ragged welts bled black rather than red.

She was still struggling against him with every muscle, but even from down here, her face was tear-slicked with defeat.

"Oh, God," Riss breathed. "It's *him*."

And then, "*Jovan.*"

Then she dropped the soul beside me and took off—straight toward Herron and Mara.

TWENTY-EIGHT

Iris

IT WAS ČIČA JOVAN.

He was *here*, right below the threshing battle between the demon and Mara with her black-rose wings. Swaying, he stood at its brink—and if he lurched any closer to it, he'd be swept up in their whirlwind and destroyed.

I'd been too late to save Mama—again, to hell with everything—but I could still save him.

He didn't even have his battle cane, I thought as I sprinted toward him, stricken with terror. How was he even standing up so straight?

"Jovan," I gasped out as I reached him, my hand landing on his shoulder. "Jovan, it's me—come, get back—"

He wheeled to greet me, and the words turned to sour ash in my mouth.

His eyes were oil in his beloved face. It even dripped from them, in rivulets, across the slack flaps of his cheeks. Blood streaked across it, had dried his white hair into tufts. He looked almost like a carrion bird, with blood and flesh lodged in its beak.

"No," I whispered, bottoming out with dread and devastation. "Not *this*."

He growled low, then shrieked at me, a grotesque, mindless hunger flowing across his face.

"Not that one, pet." A distorted, glottal voice crashed over us, impossibly loud, enough to pierce through the crackle of the burning battlefield. "That little spy is mine."

Black snaked around my waist, tightening like a vise. All the breath whooshed out of me as it swept me up and turned me—leaving me dangling in midair with my face inches from Herron's.

I struggled against the grip, screaming, though even if it let me go the fall would shatter all my bones. We were what felt like a mile above the ground.

The demon peered at my face in slow perusal. His eyes strobed between green and iridescent black, and his face was threaded with pulsing black veins. Dark hair floated around him like ink in water, and he smiled at me, almost sweet, licking full lips.

"I know you, little spy-witch," he growled, in that hellish, velveteen cadence that came from beyond his words. "Peering at me like a fawn from behind a tree, stealing glances at me like a sprite hiding in a mirror. Thank you for breaking loose my bonds."

"*You took Jovan!*" I screamed into his face, enraged and terrified and beyond all reason. I could hear Mara faintly, bellowing something at me, but I didn't know what she said and couldn't bring myself to care. Nothing mattered but me and this *thing*. "You took him, and you killed my mother, and now you're going to die!"

Amusement flared in his eyes. "Ah, so he was *yours*, that old man who smelled of light. I thought that it was not quite her scent lingering on him. And I'd very much like to see you try to kill me for them, pretty fawn. For you, I'll even hold still."

I'd never thought of using the infinite bloom to kill. I didn't know if it even could be used for that. But I needed this perversion to die, by my hand—and the wisteria responded to my need.

It roped out of me thicker and wilder than it ever had before, pulsing with magenta and violet light. It struck at him like a spear, and then coiled around him like a carnivorous vine.

Fierce triumph shook me, and I spooled out more and still more, flinging it at him. It hurt like it never had before. I'd already used so much; I'd destroyed an entire world before I landed here. But I had to be strong, like I always did. And I *would* be strong enough to murder him.

Then he opened his mouth, and more bilious black came surging out. It wrapped around my wisteria like a weedy parasite, its tendrils both sticky and sharp. It clamped down on the braided flowers and branches, so hard I could feel the monumental weight as it bore down—and began sucking my bloom into Herron's mouth.

He was *eating* me.

As he inhaled my wisteria, he paused every now and then to sink his teeth into its slim branches, cracking them beneath his molars and grinding the soft petals between them. The black seeped from his mouth like a hungry mist, eating away at the blooms wherever it touched them. And it *hurt*, oh God, it hurt like infinite agony, agony folded over and around itself into a fractal of endless pain.

With every gnash of his jaw, I could feel parts of me slipping away. The memory of a fingertip swiped lingeringly beneath my chin—Fjolar? Luka? I couldn't *remember*—a low, husky laugh that I recognized as Mama's when she was young and still in love with her twin girls. The intricate network of wrinkles at the corners of Čiča Jovan's eyes when he smiled at me in approval over a new technique I'd cast in glass.

Going, going, going. Everything was going or gone, leaving me like a receding tide. He was still at my edges, nibbling at my periphery, but the pain grew even more intense as he sank into the meat of me—and started eating memories of my sister.

I remembered more of Malina than I'd even known, I realized. Far, far back, I remembered opening my sticky eyes in a warm, dim place filled with opaque light, only to find my sister already looking back at me. We'd held hands in the womb; we'd held them in the cradle. And when we were old enough for our fingers to be deft, we'd braided her curls and my straight hair together, tangling it into such a snarl that Mama had to cut our shared plait out.

Then the memory winked out like a candle flame between licked fingers, and the terror fully overwhelmed me.

I couldn't do this alone. I couldn't save myself.

And if I kept trying, I'd lose everything.

"LINA!" I shrieked hoarsely, with everything I had left. "LINA, HELP ME!"

TWENTY-NINE

Malina

WHY WERE ALL THESE BASTARDS FOREVER TRYING TO steal my sister?

She was mine, goddamn it. She belonged with me.

Riss shrieked out sobs as Herron sucked up her flowers into his maw. And then she called my name, called for my help.

At that, I flooded with raw will, was suddenly made of it. My sister *needed* me. And I'd take care of her, like she'd always taken care of me.

"You can't have her," I whispered to Herron, but it must have been somehow loud. Far above, Herron froze, eyes narrowing. Riss's bucking body stilled. The sickening rush of her wisteria into his mouth stopped too, suspended. "You can't have my sister."

If you lead steadily and well, little bird, reality will leap to follow,

Jasna had said. And I thought I'd already learned how to do it. Except I wasn't a little bird, no one's songbird, nor a fledgling. I was an eagle, and if I spread my wings they could blot out the sky. Reality *would* follow me wherever I led. The cavern inside me was even vaster and deeper than I'd felt yet—and it shimmered with the waiting stalactites of glowing will.

If Mara was made of angels, then so was I. And when I sang this time, I willed it louder than the music of the stars.

My ankle wobbled at my step, sent a shock of pain—it must have twisted during the battle. I ignored it, ignored everything but singing. The ground lurched and rocked under my feet. My hands balled into tight fists by my sides. This was my song, mine and only mine. I didn't borrow anyone else's strength for it.

"MY SISTER IS NOT YOURS BUT MINE AND MINE AND MINE," I sang at him, wrath and ownership molded into melody. *"FIND SOMETHING ELSE TO EAT, YOU BLIGHT, YOU NIGHTMARE SLUG!"*

He strained against my song, spewed out more dark. His hair had merged with the darkness that flooded from him, and both blotted out the stars in the night sky above. Like the corona of a full eclipse. It didn't matter, meant nothing to me. I couldn't destroy him—that wasn't my battle—but I also wouldn't let him budge until he gave me what I wanted.

I was a daughter of both light and earth.

And he would give me back my sister.

"*Have her*, then, you shrill harpy of a brat," he bellowed through the battering of my song. "She's not what I came for, anyway!"

He flung Riss down like a child tossing away a toy. She would have broken herself on the ground, if Mara hadn't thrown out a woven hammock of roses to catch her fall. It was threadbare and faint, woven of seedlings. But it was hers, and it was enough.

She had caught Riss in her net of roses after all, just like she'd promised me. Even if it hadn't been the way she'd planned.

Wound in them, Riss drifted down, and I reached out to catch her as she descended.

"You're with me," I murmured to her, pulling her half onto my lap. Her eyes fluttered—a new hazel I'd never seen before, like sunshine slanting over maple wood, bracketed with burst blood vessels. And she was so pale I could see the faint threads of veins under her eyes. But she was alive, and I was going to keep her that way. "You're going to be fine."

Above us, Mara had taken advantage and regrouped. The roses of her wings filled and darkened back into life, fueled by the last of her will. With a wordless echo of my song that was more a sense than sound, she flung herself back at Herron.

"You will have no more of my daughters," she bellowed in her savage knell, smoldering and near-deafening as a bell fresh from the forge. "NO MORE!"

Something flared, blinding at the periphery of my sight. I turned—and saw Jasna leading Dunja to the golden breach that Riss had made when she arrived. Behind her, the rest of her coven still circled their altar stone. None of the creatures had even brushed them. I could almost see the dome of power they had raised from the ground. A whirling flicker in the air around them, like a school of minnows circling.

"Draw down your gods," Jasna was saying to Dunja, and the peal of her voice carried much louder and clearer than it should have. I could see her shadow cast on the ground by the light spilling from the split in the air. It stretched many feet farther behind than her own height, and it wore trailing robes and an antler rack that weren't really there.

"You're strong enough to hold them, and already a vessel," she went on. "Their world is pure love, just as his is pure nothing, with ours standing between them as the battleground. And love will always, always win. They're here waiting—I see you see them—but they can't cross without your invitation. So *invite* them, girl. Invite them in, as that befouled man invited his filthy hordes. Be a person, rather than a ghost."

Dunja gave her an uncertain look, then glanced back at me cradling Riss. Whatever she saw in us decided her. She shot me one of her brief, savage smiles, like a descendant of the Amazons.

Then she turned back to the breach and fell to her knees in front of it, arms uplifted.

The gold poured into her as if it had been waiting like a dewdrop on a leaf, quivering with eagerness to fall.

Dunja arched her back, mouth opening wide, swallowing the light. It sluiced and pulsed, shimmering waterfalls of it running down her throat.

Watching, Riss stirred against me. "I almost did that," she whispered, awestruck. "I was there, before I made it to his kingdom. I crossed through it too, on the way back. It's beautiful there.

I think—Lina, I think that's home."

"*This* is home," I told her, blindly fumbling for her hand. "But I know what you mean, and I think you're right."

The cascade finally subsided, and Dunja swept up. Both Iris and I shaded our eyes. For the first time that night, a hush fell over the vineyard. Above the sear of fire and the sweet-wine smell of burned, crushed grapes, a heady perfume tide rolled out in waves. I recognized it as Mara's scent, the Garden-of-Eden lushness of ripest, sweetest fruits. The nectar of ambrosia born from a tree of everlasting love.

A kind of love that didn't grow on earth.

Dunja didn't look like she had grown from earth anymore, either.

She towered over the battlefield, swathed in folds of gold. Like light incarnate. Something like wings rippled behind her, if bat wings could be made transparent and cast from a precious-metal mold. She also had more arms than was the norm, I noticed. Definitely more than she'd had before, but they seemed natural as all the rest of it. Her hair ran with honeyed runnels, her features shone, gilded and glittering. Marks scrolled across her forehead and down one cheek, looping letters of some alphabet I'd never seen.

And her eyes had grown so huge, pupils twisted into cloverleafs like crossed infinity signs.

So tremendous.

So beyond beautiful.

Our aunt turned to a goddess of light.

Two steps took her to where Herron tussled with Mara. Next to her, their mortal combat had all the scale of toddlers playing tug-of-war over a toy.

With immense, delicate fingers, she lifted Mara from Herron's grip and gently deposited her next to us. I shifted Riss next to me and lifted Mara's head onto my lap.

"You can rest now, sorai," I murmured to her, combing my fingers through Mara's sweat-drenched curls. "She's got it from here."

Mara let out the deepest, most careworn sigh, then closed her eyes. I would have been afraid we'd lose her, too, but though her chest rose and fell only slightly, breath was breath. And I could still hear the ringing of her bell. Mist-shrouded, dampened, and so far away.

But there.

Our far-mother was made of courage, too much to just die before she saw us safe.

Above us, Dunja reached for Herron. He shied frantically away from her, the dark around him scrabbling away from her gold. But there wasn't anywhere for him to go. She cupped him in her hands and brought him to her chest, then engulfed him in a fiery embrace. Everywhere he touched her, he burst into instant flame. Her face placid above his struggle and shrieks, she pressed and pressed him against herself until he simply burned away.

What was left of the devils followed in his stead. They went up in yowling showers of sparks, burning to cinders wherever they stood.

Watching her and watching them, I could understand.

How humans who'd caught glimpses of these warring worlds

had seen both salvation and damnation in them. It probably wasn't that simple—nothing ever was. Maybe there was something to Herron's dark that none of us would ever know, something that had drawn him to it.

But now, looking at Dunja, who could resist that clarion light?

Sweeping her liquid gaze across us all, Dunja bent and gently held out a giant, glowing palm that could easily have cupped both me and Riss. Her light fell over us, a loving solar flare, cauterizing any lingering shadows.

"Baby witch," she crooned to Riss in a behemoth voice, like whale song played by an infinite number of violins. "Where is the rest?"

Her hand trembling, Riss pointed to the lumpy, glinting thing she'd brought with her and dropped beside us when she ran. I still couldn't tell what it actually was, something silvery and black that glistened like meat. But I knew it had to be Herron's soul.

Dunja smiled in thanks, showing teeth that beamed painfully bright—then lifted the lump and promptly dropped it in her mouth. A little grimace rippled across her serene face as she swallowed, like a baby tasting a lemon.

Then she lifted easily, turning to where Jasna stood haloed by the breach. The older woman hadn't moved, but she dipped her head when Dunja touched two fingers to her heart in a salute.

"Thank you, lady," Dunja said. "They—we—*I* owe you a debt for your help."

"You owe me nothing," Jasna replied. "He trespassed on my soil. Do you know what to do next?"

Dunja tipped back her head and laughed. A rich, rolling sound like a sunrise turned to song. "Oh, I'm going *home*, of course. And after that, who knows, who knows? Perhaps . . ." A platinum tinge of wistfulness crept into her face. "Perhaps after that, I'll find him again, somehow."

She turned back to me and Riss, blew us each a kiss. "Tell sorai good-bye, when she wakes. And my baby witches—don't forget your aunt."

I shook my head furiously, choking on tears. I knew it was right, knew she had to go. But why did they all have to leave?

As she turned her back to us and stepped daintily through the breach, it sealed shut behind her with a blowtorch hiss.

THIRTY

Iris

THE GRIEF DESCENDED WITH THE ASHES.

It took days to fully douse Jasna's burned wreckage of a vine-yard, trampled by Herron's demons and seared by Amaya's flames. The villagers turned up to help, and though they whispered to each other behind their work-worn hands and looked at us with fleeting, fearful eyes, they didn't ask any probing questions.

They'd felt the ground rocking with the battle from miles away, seen the lapping of the fire against the sky—but an earthquake and a careless bonfire that had blazed out of control were answer enough for them. They didn't need to consider monsters darker than the night, glimpsed from the corner of the eye.

I wished I could do the same myself. Sometimes ignorance was the wiser choice, and easier on the heart and mind.

Malina and I helped where we could, but neither of us had much to give. Not to the effort, nor to each other. We'd lost so much that the world felt both new and somehow tainted, raw and rotten like a fresh-peeled fruit plucked too late. It should have been some comfort to bear it together, but for once, it wasn't. We had an overlap of anguish—Mama, Nev, Jovan—but Lina had also lost family that she'd come to know, coven daughters who were strangers to me. Women she'd trained and learned to respect, who meant something more to her than they ever would to me except a list of lovely names.

Niko understood the loss better than I could; she'd been there for it. I rarely saw her drift far from Lina's side. She was always there, petting, gentling, watching over her "pie"—and Lina took care of her in kind. They spent most of their time in Jasna's herb garden, tending to it and cutting plants for healing tinctures and tonics that I refused to drink.

That garden wasn't my place, not the way it was theirs. And even if it had been, I no longer belonged with them.

They hadn't lost Fjolar like I had. They hadn't almost-loved and then killed Death.

I couldn't blame them for their distance like I would have once. I was too tired for blame, and I was different, too. Alien, disjointed, out of step with the whole world around me. The passing of time bothered me, the heartache of losing day to night over and over, instead of seeing a steadfast sky above. The kingdom had marked me like a brand, in some indelible way.

The only one who could have understood my newness, and my

shameful longing for Fjolar—the only one who would have helped me through both without judgment—was Dunja.

Our aunt turned goddess, and then lost to light.

I didn't even have her to turn to, now that my own mother was truly gone.

And then there was Luka.

He haunted me, a ghost hovering around my edges. Gazing at me with those watchful hazel eyes, muscles always tensed under his fine-cut face. Uncertain around me in a way he'd never been before. He'd held me through that first rending, weeping night of loss after Dunja destroyed Herron, but that had been comfort lent in catastrophe. Now, in the absence of tragedy, we couldn't seem to find each other.

I couldn't find my own best friend.

Maybe it was me who was the ghost again. Like I'd been to Lina every time she saw me fractaled.

Maybe I'd never be anything but a stranger again, the prodigal daughter who should never have come home.

THE THIRD NIGHT, I couldn't sleep. I was still so tired, bogged down as if my veins ran with silt instead of blood, and all I wanted was the comfort of oblivion. Which, of course, wouldn't come.

Even sleep wouldn't indulge me here reliably, not anymore.

As far as I could tell, none of the surviving coven daughters were similarly troubled. The cottage was filled with a soft symphony of sleeping breath, the thirty gathered women drowsing away the gathered exhaustion of difficult days. Niko and Lina actually had one of the spare bedrooms to themselves, as if they were Jasna's designated royalty.

At least I wouldn't have to see them curled together in the kind of peace I couldn't seem to find.

I stepped between pallets and bedrolls, picking my way carefully through them until I made it to the kitchen, where I found a storm lantern to light my way. Then I wrapped myself in one of Jasna's hand-knit sweaters to ward off the mountain chill, my nose wrinkling at the fabric's scent; everything she owned was fragrant with wild onion, beeswax, and herbs. I should have loved the earthiness of it, the homespun warmth. But I didn't. Some part of me had delighted in the allure of Mara's exotic haven—the same part that had thrilled to Fjolar's kingdom in all its overwrought glory.

I just didn't *like* it here. It felt like the essence of Cattaro, or Montenegro itself distilled down to an absolute.

And it was still the opposite of what I wanted.

Outside, I sat on Jasna's porch swing, setting myself to swinging with a push of bare toes against the cool cement. The night was pure, with enough of a pine breeze to slice through the lingering reek of char. I could smell honey and night-blooming flowers, even cold running water somewhere far from here.

That was another artifact of the kingdom: my senses had never waned to what they'd been before. Scents were stronger, noises louder. Everything was somehow more. Sometimes I even thought in cadence, in rhyming stanzas, as if I'd never stepped out of that magical, performative groove.

The chair sank beside me, groaning, and I startled. I'd been so caught up in considering my own heightened senses that I hadn't heard Luka step outside. The irony of it made me laugh a little, lightly.

Luka turned to look at me, draping an arm over the back of the chair. So careful where he placed it, not quite close enough that I could feel it behind my neck. Moonlight limned his cleverly chiseled features, ran silvery fingers through his shock of hair.

"Something funny, Missy?" He smiled a little, an echo of the half-dimpled smile he used to give me. "Whatever it is, don't let me ruin it. It's nice to hear you laugh."

I opened my mouth to reply, and just as quickly realized I had nothing to say.

Silence collected around us like sediment, and he looked away.

"Do you still love me?" he asked eventually, blunt and quiet. I could hear the trepidation in his voice.

I let the pause settle in like an exhale between us, thinking.

"I don't know," I finally replied. "I think I do, under everything else. But it feels far away right now. Or very deep down, maybe. Like bedrock. I know it's there, because it's always there. But I can't exactly *feel* it." I glanced over at him, steeling myself for his pain, grateful that I didn't have Malina's ability to hear it. "I'm sorry, Luka. Do you . . . do you still love me?"

A muscle ticked beneath his jaw, but his face stayed placid in profile. He didn't look at me again. "Of course I do, Missy. I always do. But at the same time, I don't know, either. It's—things happened, while you were gone. I missed you, badly. Terribly. There was someone . . ." He trailed off, swallowing.

"It's all right," I murmured, feeling a faint, grazing pain. Like the scrape of a cat's tongue, but not unpleasant. Jealousy too far removed to wound. "You were alone, and whatever you did, it was what you needed to do. Believe me, I understand. I understand so much."

And I did. For all the lies and endless manipulation, I still missed Fjolar like a phantom limb. His smell, the sardonic lilt of his voice, the roughness and tenderness of each caress. His demands, his wonder at the sight of me, the clench and twist of his many betrayals.

It was so near the surface, eclipsing everything else beneath it. I couldn't see past its mass, or through its remembered, distorted light.

It would pass, I knew. I would heal, and become something else, again.

Because everything changed. That was the true beauty of this living world, even if I wasn't quite ready to appreciate it yet.

"Do you think . . . ?" Luka began. "Do you think, some-day . . . ?"

I reached for his hand. It was warm and large, but not like Fjolar's. His palm was less coarse, his fingers longer and slimmer, laced differently with mine. He wrapped his other hand around my wrist and squeezed, hard enough that I nearly gasped. He did remember, then.

So did I.

"Yes," I said, soft as a breath. "I do think, someday. But not now."

He sat with me for a while longer, watching the wheeling of the stars across the sky. They twinkled in the shimmering way they always did in this world; the astronomical term for it was "seeing," I remembered. A strange way to put it, but nice.

As if even while we watched them, the stars saw us back.

I STAYED OUTSIDE for hours, long after Luka left. He squeezed my hand in parting, but didn't try to kiss me or speak. We weren't each other's to kiss—not now, though maybe someday.

And there was nothing left to say.

I was still there when Mara slipped outside, all in black, a satchel slung over her shoulder. She startled when she saw me, exactly like a normal, mortal woman, clapping a hand over her heart.

"Lisarah," she began, then caught herself. "Iris. I did not think to find you out here. You, or anyone."

I shrugged a shoulder. "Inside didn't seem like the place to be. Not that anywhere seems the place to be, at least for me. And you, sorai? Leaving us like a thief in the night?"

The phrase brought back the memory of all the times Mama had said it, nocked it at me like an arrow for sneaking outside. The thought of her prodded pain back to life, the blister of her loss that lived inside me.

Mara wavered for a moment, as if caught between the desire to leave without explaining herself—the woman she'd been before hadn't owed explanations to anyone—and the urge to shrug on the skin of someone new.

Finally she moved to sit beside me. And even now, stripped of her tripled tones, she smelled like love, largesse, and light. I breathed it in, sweet fruit and frankincense, and when she drew me close to her, I didn't resist. My head dropped onto her shoulder of its own accord, my eyes half closing as she stroked my hair with her ember's touch.

"I am leaving," she admitted, resting her cheek on my crown. "You love me still, my far-daughter—even you, who once nearly tore me apart, because you cannot help but love me. And while you all ring yourselves around me, none of you will live so freely as you now can and should. And I . . ." She heaved a long, heavy sigh. "I no longer wish to be this family's sun. There are things I would do, and people I would find. It will be good, for everyone, to make a life without me at its eye."

"I understand," I said simply, marveling at how much change had already befallen us. I'd hated her once, tried to burn her with all the forceful loathing of my heart.

And now I was so close to her I could feel her silken throat clench with held-back tears.

She didn't want to leave us, not really. Because she loved us more than anything, as was her nature to do. But she'd do it, because we needed it, and to give what was needed was in her nature too.

"You do?" she whispered into my hair, and for a moment I heard an echo of Mama in her rich, husky human voice.

"I do." I bit my lip and let myself cry. Just a single tear for now, hot and smarting down my cheek, but there would be more. "Because I'm leaving too."

EPILOGUE

TWO SISTERS STOOD IN THE DOORWAY OF A WITCH'S COT-
tage. One outside, the other in. Their hands entwined across the
threshold, a sprig of sage above them.

"Do you have to go?" one whispered. Tears glistened in her dark
eyes, and her lower lip—cherry-cleft—trembled like a child's.

"I do," the other one replied. Her angled face looked composed,
but her pale hazel eyes were just as glossy full. "Do you have to stay?
You could leave too, and come with me. We could see everything,
all the things we talked about."

"The things *you* talked about, you mean," the first reminded.
"The things *I* want to see are here. How they grow, how I can use
them, the gods they belong to. They're what I want to know."

The other lifted their joined hands to her lips and kissed them.

"Then I'll know where to find you once I'm done. But first, I want to see my tree."

A chill, Montenegrin wind rushed down from where it curled around a jagged mountain peak, blown from the earth that claimed both sisters as its own. It lifted their hair like a mother's gentle hands, and dried the tears on both their cheeks.

And if anyone had asked the sisters if their many mothers loved them, both knew what they would say.

ACKNOWLEDGMENTS

Sequels are tricky beasts. Both my wonderful editors warned me about this before I started writing, and I believed them, because they're brilliant women who tend to be right about pretty much everything. But, I told myself, this would really be more like a third book than a second, since I'd already rewritten *Wicked* so extensively. I would probably be okay.

I was definitely not okay. Shudder.

To my clients whom I blithely patted on the head and assured that the sophomore slump would pass soon and everything would be fine, just fine—I'm really sorry, you guys, and thank you for your love and generous support as I struggled and moaned and generally muddled my way through until I finally fell in love with this book. (By the way, if you're looking for a source of consistent wonder, *Atlas Obscura* by Joshua Foer, Dylan Thuras, and Ella Morton was my reference for many of Iris's forays in Death's kingdom. It's gorgeous, and you should check it out.)

Huge thanks, too, to Claudia, Melissa, and the whole Katherine Tegen team for handholding me throughout. The past year was a rough one for everyone, and still you handled this project—and me—with such grace and generous amounts of TLC. And brainstorming! Thank you for the plot twists, ladies, and here's to many more.

My thanks to Holly/Galadriel and my sweet, hilarious, fiendish Tay—love you, and am so happy to call you my friend even when the leaves are falling and stuff.

And of course, to my friends, family, and Caleb, who got me through this book—especially my mom, Reader of All the Drafts; my BFFs in Boston and elsewhere; and the 'Berries—thank you so much for your love, support, and constancy. I'm so lucky to have you all.